A Home for Old Ladies

Kev Richardson

A Wings ePress, Inc.
Contemporary Romance Novel

Wings ePress, Inc.

Edited by: Joan Powell
Copy Edited by: Elizabeth Struble
Senior Editor: Leslie Hodges
Executive Editor: Marilyn Kapp
Cover Artist: Trisha Fitzgerald

Wings ePress Books
www.wingsepress.com

Published In the United States Of America

Wings ePress Inc.
3000 N. Rock Road
Newton, KS 67114

What They Are Saying About
A Home for Old Ladies

5+ Stars!

Kev Richardson outdoes himself in telling the tale of lasting love that inspired his life. In **A Home for Old Ladies,** Richardson touches your heartstrings recounting Evan and Maggie's tale of inner-fire at first sight, the joy of a lasting relationship as they follow their individual careers, and the cozy evenings spent together by an open hearth. The extensive renovation of the family's estate, Stanford Lodge, is the very power that holds the family unit together until daughter, Leanne and her brother, Paul, grow up to follow their own paths. I fell in love with Evan Robson and his sweet relationship with Maggie. The love scenes are so dear, so tender and so touching I wished I could be she.

Jo Ellen Conger
Conger Book Reviews - USA

A Home For Old Ladies is restored from derelict to what its time-worn patients would have imagined of their hospice in its heyday. They had watched it die. New generation lovers use those old ladies' dreams as inspiration for restoration. Such labours of love exemplify how togetherness, understanding, conjoining—all the essences of sharing can help remould an already shattered family. Every essence of solidarity proves essential in the renaissance of such a home, the bonding of family love that undoubtedly inspired its creation.

Richardson overlays his own experiences on such a backdrop, sharing with his Maggie, an inspiring tale of absorbing all such negatives as doubt, insecurity and fear of rejection. Can externally injected family rifts be overcome with the shared joy of together building a new environment?

Libby Abbott,
Aussie eBook Reviews

A Home for Old Ladies is a charming read from the first to the last page, a story of an Australian family in the 1970's who strove to make each day count. Their love and support of each other made a difference. It also brought them sorrow. For a glimpse of Australia during the 1970's, this is the book to read.

Katherine Pym,
author

Dedication

Maggie
...without whom, the Home for Old Ladies may not
have lived on

* * *

A Home for Old Ladies

BOOK 1

One

Ours wasn't a whirlwind courtship, neither were we green kids lusting for marriage. Sex? Maybe!

I was forty-one, widowed with two littlies and she, a twenty-eight-year-old career girl enjoying life in a lane bordering on fast. I was the Dinkum Aussie and she an immigrant from England, seeking winter sunshine.

Sydney sparkled as a city for finding pleasure, especially for those with good jobs and a hunger for the arts. Careful eyes on the future, of course, were also capital assets. I had been, for the last several minutes, eyeing her up and down, her long blond hair a teasing feature. In a clinging knee-length cocktail dress in a soft peach shade and wearing little jewellery, she stood out in one group, there, while I was in one, here.

Was that a deliberate smile she just flashed?

I excused myself from my circle, edging my way towards her. Near everyone held a glass of wine in one hand and a cigarette in the other. In 1970, smoking was part of social living and few wanted to be the odd-girl-or-guy out.

It was a Point Piper apartment, some fifty singles mingling in the crush.

Is she with any of those guys in her group? Or maybe all are just workmates of Cat's? She certainly has a bemused smile on her face at me moving directly for her.

I knew none of the folk she was with, yet edged into their little circle. I was a six-footer with a still trim body. Competitive swimming in earlier years had helped me keep fit. The guy next to her was more robust.

And shorter than me, I reckon. He stands awfully close to her, the elbow of his 'glass' hand, touching hers.

"Do I know you?" she asked with the most delightful dimpled smile. "Your face is somehow familiar?"

It's a come-on! Had I met her already? Surely I would remember!

"Sorry, but we haven't met. I'd certainly recall at least that delightful accent."

It was British, clearly of one not only well educated but moving in sophisticated circles there.

"Oh, you picked it?"

"Easily. My name is Evan, Evan Robson…a friend of Cat's."

I let her note my eyes roving her every inch.

And is the gormless one now pushing even closer to her? And is she as slightly edging just that inch away?

Her left hand held a cigarette and fingers showed neither ring nor ring mark.

"We are all Cat's workmates," she answered.

Cat had been offered a two-year contract job in London and decided to snap up the opportunity. This was her farewell party.

"You are a book condenser too? At *Reader's Digest*?"

"Yes. And I'm certainly going to miss her. She has taught me so much."

"How long have you been there?"

"Just a year. It was my first job here."

She began introducing me around, leaving the fellow by her elbow until last.

"Evan, this is Max. He is a Copy Editor. And my name is Maggie."

She passed her glass to Max so she could extend a hand to be shaken.

At her touch, a little tremor ran through me. Her eyes seemed to leap out as she gave another dimpled smile. They were a delightful shade of green.

Green leaves atop the peach-tree? The blossom tips?

Mine again roved her body.

She is certainly well-formed, maybe five-eight or nine? And that hair, delightfully blond and pulled into a thick pony-tail forward over a shoulder.

It hung loosely, so thick as to quite hide her ear.

It seems she wears only one earring, that fine beaten silver pendant dangling almost to the naked shoulder. Naturally holding her chin a little high, she knows she looks good; absolutely exudes confidence.

"And what is your line of work, Evan?"

"The printing and packaging industry."

"Packaging for what?"

"A variety. Our major clients are Colgate Palmolive, Wrigley, Nestlé and most of the major cosmetic people. I head the marketing arm."

"Interesting indeed. My father is in packaging. He is with Vauxhall Motors, designs its retail packaging for spare parts."

"Oh, and where is that?"

"Luton. Luton Beds."

"Beds, definitely Beds," I heard from Max, barely half under his breath.

And is that her teeth grinding, I can hear?

Yet she as instantly broke the moment's silence. She held her glass towards me.

"Could you hold this for me, Evan? I must inspect the little girl's room. I shan't be long."

I almost felt the breeze from the cold shoulder she seemed to snub at Max. I watched her nodding to workmates and "hello"ing other faces.

Our little cluster indulged in small-talk until she returned. It was then obvious how, instead of retaking the place between Max and me, she urged herself the other side of me. Now it was me squeezed between her and Max.

My mind smirked. *He better not start nudging my elbow!*

Then, as she retrieved her glass, Cat joined us.

"Ah, Evan, I'm pleased you've found someone to chat with. Hope they haven't been telling you too many secrets about me."

"You're going to miss them, I'd reckon, Cat."

She put on her dainty smile. "Not many," she quipped with a snigger. She topped it with the hint of a curtsy to all, then moved on.

"You've known Cat long?" Maggie asked.

"A year or two. We are neighbours. We sort of use each other for dating when not conveniently finding somebody else—or that's the way we joke about it. It's more a brother-sister relationship than personal."

"You live in the same condo?"

"Yes."

"She told me she had a friend on the top floor. Is that you?"

"I'd reckon so, although many residents are passing friends."

"You must have glorious views of the harbour from up there. And city skyline?"

"I look straight across to the Opera House, so yes, I have the city skyline and all the harbour, east. I just miss the bridge to the west; other buildings get in my way."

We chatted on with such small-talk.

"Was it the work with Cat that brought you from England?"

She could see I was trying to edge Max out of any chance of conversation.

"Oh, not at all. My coming here is a funny story, a long one these folk know. Maybe we can find an opportunity on some other occasion?"

Her eyes had the most glorious glitter.

She seems able to switch their glow on and off. I feel so thrilled the way she turns the glitter on while looking directly into my eyes. And the smile is utterly bewitching.

"But you are happy here?"

"Indeed. I'd had it described as the land that is young, free and where opportunity grows on trees. So far, it hasn't disappointed me. I am quite enjoying it."

She took a sip from her glass, giving me another glorious stare over its rim.

I then noticed the crowd thinning. Cat was at the door farewelling people.

"Many of tonight's guests are in the theatre," Maggie explained. "That is why this little soiree was a five p.m. affair. They are off to work."

"You are in theatre?"

"Yes. I love small theatre. I go into rehearsals shortly; a Brecht play. It will be my second play here. I did a lot of Shakespeare in England."

"I just love your accent, or at least what we Aussies call accent."

She openly laughed. "Stage-work has a lot to do with that and in London I worked in the Diplomatic Corps; secretarial work. That environment influences diction."

As space cleared somewhat, background music became a smidge more audible.

Max was talking to the guy on his left so I whispered... "Would you like to dance now we have space?"

She smiled again, her eyes almost betraying a giggle.

As we moved off, glasses lodged on a table, I could feel Max's eyes burning into my back.

"Max is watching us."

"So?"

We held each other loosely while falling into the rhythm of Benny Goodman jazz.

And her body movements are so fluid!

I loved dancing. Kit and I had won cups in jitterbug and jive in our early days.

But they are not memories for now. Could this begin a new era in my life?

Eight years of widowhood had taught me how to start anew, including that I not again rush into a romance hinting of 'ownership'.

Cat had sort of caught me. Yet being a career type, she didn't want too close a friendship and that suited me fine.

Last thing I was looking for, was another marriage.

Kit and I marrying so young has me now realising how much fun we missed. We simply got bogged down with debts rather than waiting for better-paid jobs. I am now enjoying the freedom missed in youth.

"Don't worry about Max," Maggie's voice drifted through my touch of blues. "In fact, I'm trying to give him the message. He is looking for a wife and that isn't me. I'm a career type, happy to leave mothering to my little sister, Audrey, back in England. She is already married and I'm simply glad it is her and not me in that situation."

"I was worried that I might be intruding on something with Max?"

She gave my hand a strong squeeze.

"No, indeed, Evan. You are like a breath of fresh air. Max is becoming an utter bore. He is simply too possessive."

"I'd say you are succeeding. He looks murderous."

She bubbled into a quiet laugh. "Are you doing anything after this little to-do? It is timed to conclude by eight."

"Is that an invitation?"

"It is if you would like it so. You don't have to worry about Max. We could go eat somewhere?"

I heaved a deliberate sigh. "I brought Cat. I'm to drive her home with all the gifts she anticipated!"

She laughed, looking across at the table piled high with boxed goodies.

"Oh! That is disappointing. Maybe we can find another opportunity?"

I grabbed the chance. "Yes indeed, Maggie. You promised to tell me the story of your emigration."

"Could we meet for dinner one evening? It will need to be soon. End of next week I go into rehearsals."

"I would like that. I'll give you my card when Max switches off his glare."

She gave me her dimpled smile again as we turned in a twirl. I felt all a-tingle again.

"Where do you live, Maggie?"

"Waverton."

I stopped our slow rhythm and stood back, retaining the clasp of hands.

She looked at me with one eyebrow raised.

Ah! An expression to always disconcert me. I've tried and tried in front of mirrors and feel utterly defeated at not being able to do it.

"Where, in Waverton?"

"Do you know Bay Road?"

We resumed dancing.

"Indeed I do, girl. In fact I'm about to leave my apartment in Cat's building. My flatmate is moving out, so I am moving. I am just waiting for its present tenant to quit. I am moving to Waverton's Bay Road."

Now she stopped dancing and stood back. "Where?"

"As you come down the hill, a hundred yards before the station."

"Good heavens. I live in Toongara Rd. I walk to the train every day."

"Bloody hell. They say it's a small world. You must walk past my new place."

I described the building and she knew it.

What a coincidence!

"What time train do you take?"

"None, Maggie. I drive. I work at Rosebery, not near a train line."

"South side? You drive across the bridge every day?"

"Twice. I spend most nights at home."

She twisted her head and deliberately pursed her lips...

"I shan't even ask what keeps you from home the other nights."

Two

Maggie's Muse

Como, Italy, two years prior...
Five minutes and I'm packed!

Jane had written that her flatmate in London was moving out.

Mags, if you were serious in saying you could be reaching the stage of coming home, now is a good time. Janet is going home to Birmingham, so if you want to come back and share again, I can afford to hold the room until you get here. Let me know.

Maggie and Jane had worked together in the Diplomatic Corps. She had sickened of spending three hours a day commuting between Luton and London, saw it a useless waste of both productive time in career work and mingling with social friends. She was a 'people' person, enjoyed the companionship social intercourse gave one in learning to get along with others. Mixing with people proved simply a *penchant* answering so many wants in her life.

For seven of her after-school years she was in the Luton Girls' Choir, a group of girls singing for pleasure, travelling all the British Isles. Once reaching famous stage, it began tours on the Continent but her family couldn't afford her touring Europe. She so relished the travel tales her friends recounted, that she pledged to indeed, some day, go places. Marriage and family were not for her. She would become a business-woman who travelled, would see the wonderful sights of Europe and beyond.

She majored in Short-Hand and Typing. In provincial England in the nineteen sixties, it was the ultimate offering for girls wanting a career. She blitzed her school—first place granting her a position in the Diplomatic Corps in London.

Such opportunities were limited to girls of working-class families, so she grabbed it, finding herself sharing secretarial duties with Jane.

Wow! For the first time in her life she felt 'things from outside' were beginning to steer her life into something worthwhile—an exciting job requiring the French and Italian languages she'd made good grades in, opportunities of meeting eminent gentlemen of the British Diplomatic Corps. She was bound to secrecy, of course, a condition in taking up the award position.

She only sort of missed home, her mum and dad, Audrey, even Martin who simply never turned out the sort of brother she'd wanted. Five years younger seemed too much for him to lean towards her in any way. He never seemed interested in making anything exciting in his life beyond a mundane job, marrying and having a family. Audrey on the other hand, was boy crazy.

How many boys did she fall in love with in her short single life? She spent half of it crying over lost loves. Strange, it was, how the three of us turned out so differently.

Her parents had never had a 'fling'. They'd been school-day sweethearts and married when the war hit Britain. Maggie was the result of their last-chance at loving, it seemed, before her dad was shipped in uniform, to France.

He had been working at the Vauxhall Motor Company, Luton's major industry, which became a popular target for German bombers.

She had grown up during the Battle of Britain, thinking the under-stairs was the normal place for sleeping.

Now, suddenly, her nostalgia trip was blown asunder by a loud knocking on her door. She left her packing...

It was Francesco, her landlord and almost surrogate father.

His hands were in a pleading clasp under his chin.

"Bruno dice che se si vuole prendere l'autobus, si deve lasciare in quindici minuti."

Maggie kissed him on the forehead, her usual greeting for him.

"Tell Bruno I won't need fifteen minutes. I am already packed. We can leave for the bus in five minutes."

Her two year stint in Como, with visits to the magic lures of *Milano, Firenze, Roma* and *Pisa,* was over. And, of course, her schoolgirl abilities in the Italian language had blossomed into instinctive use.

She and Jane had saved enough to take a two-week holiday into Italy. They couldn't afford large tours so settled on the little town of Como in its far north. At one of its night-clubs, thinking they might meet some gorgeous Italian men, they took a table. The owner, Francesco, had been table-hopping, and when he sat with them, it emerged that Maggie was a singer, her Luton Girls' Choir years.

Francesco asked her to do a number. She asked if Edit Piaf's *Non, Je ne Regrette Rien* might be appropriate; she felt akin to Piaf's love of independent life.

"Just sing at your chosen pace and we will fall in with you," the bandleader said.

Her rendition in French went over so well that a tourist asked if she could sing it in English.

"Of course, *Madame,*" Maggie told her in her most cultured English. Francesco gave the nod and she sang it in English.

After considerable conversation with Jane, it was agreed that Jane would return to work and Maggie would stay on, singing in the night-club. It paid good money—enough at least, to live on the continent for a time.

It was just too good an opportunity to pass up. Now here I am, two years on, returning to London and Jane.

She had but few qualms about getting a secretarial position at an executive level.

~ * ~

A year later, it was a bitterly cold London winter.

Yes, she had fallen into another responsible position with the Diplomatic Corps and was making money enough that the girls had booked two weeks of mid-winter, in Majorca.

"And no cheap stuff this time," they had agreed.

Each would pay seventy pounds at a luxury resort.

"Sunshine in winter?" they scoffed, toasting each other on their grand plan.

The very next day Maggie brought home from the office, a copy of an Australian newspaper, the *Sydney Morning Herald*'s International version, just for the fun of reading up whatever might be happening in the opposite corner of the world.

In fact, if visiting it, should one travel just a little too far, you would be on your way home again!

Her eyes were captivated by an advertisement...

Come to Australia for Ten English pounds!

Her eyes bored into the small print.

"Jane!"

Jane had been quietly reading and her body jumped near a foot into the air.

"What on earth!!!"

Maggie composed herself, to slowly inform her...

"We have just booked passage to Majorca, for two weeks at a cost of seventy pounds each?"

"So?"

"It says here, that we can go to Australia, for two years, for ten pounds each."

Maggie passed her the paper and waited.

Australia had realised after the Great War, that whilst it had one of the world's largest countries, its population was but seven million people, some seventy-five percent employed in agriculture and sheep or cattle farming; twenty percent in service industries; and only five percent in mechanical industry. The war had taught it that it could no longer exist as a solely agricultural nation. It needed secondary industry yet had few technological skills. It must build dams for power if it were to become more self-sufficient, but lacked tradesmen. Europe had been devastated by war—millions of people were homeless, people with all the skills Australia lacked. It had opened this immigration scheme to attract people skilled in any capacity, or even to work as labourers, to make enquiries.

To qualify for the ten pound fare, applicants must be prepared to work at a job approved by the Federal Government, for a period of two years. An option, then, would be to apply for Australian citizenship.

"We can apply to Australia House here in London, Jane. You know what Liz has been telling us."

Liz, a friend of old, had already migrated with her parents. She now ran a small boarding house for only two or three girls, on Sydney's 'North Shore', the harbour-side suburb of Waverton.

Both London girls had heads squarely set on their shoulders. Neither was still a teenage kid simply looking for adventure. Australia seemed to have a lot going for it. Hadn't it grown out of a prison settlement to a country still pretty raw, yet with lots of potential? And sunshine? And winters where it didn't snow except, it seemed, in a little corner of the country they kept in mothballs?

They did it.

Only hard thing they had to face was saying goodbye to families.

Who knows what our big decision is to mean in the rest of our lives?

They knew that if after two years they weren't happy, they need only stay long enough to earn their fare home again.

Maggie saw it as an opportunity to learn more of the world, as she had found in Italy.

Go for it, girl! said her sub-conscious.

Three

In Sydney a year later, as their train sped over the longest single span in the world, Jane was reading, Maggie looking through the window at the motor traffic lanes, cars creeping in stops and starts as they did during every peak hour.

Evan will be in that mess of pottage, she thought.

Her mind darted back to last night. *Did he seek me out? Or did I seek him?*

Whichever, it was a wonderful chance meeting. I know little about him but he just somehow touches sensitive nerves at just the right spots at just the right pressures. I really do want to see him again—test out those sensitive touches and sensitive nerves. His door certainly seems open.

Her mind cast to having checked the third finger of his left hand. There had been no tell-tale white band indicating recent removal of a ring.

He is just so well sun-tanned and there was no white mark.

She pondered on having been so foolish as leaving the next contact to him. She had given him her home number. He was to ring her once checking his diary. She looked back to the motor-traffic, trying to imagine the frustration drivers must feel in such situations. She was no driver, had never got around to learning.

Why would a girl need to drive when London is a city with efficient public transport at everyone's elbow?

Sydney was so different—two halves with but a single bridge. Office guys living on the North Shore seemed always complaining that scores of lanes from different directions must eventually merge into five. Then came toll-gates.

They all hate it, yet it seems Evan is one with no option but to submit to it every day. And oh how I regret that dreadful error of suggesting to the guys at work, that if the toll-gates were removed and drivers instead bought windshield stickers, that that would ease the pile-ups!

"No, girl," she was promptly told. "That would only move the pile-ups into the city proper. Toll-gates actually filter the streams into the narrow downtown streets."

So there it was, she the non-driver thinking she could solve the big problem.

So, girl, back to the important things—like Evan. What an amazing coincidence that he is moving into an apartment just ten minutes' walk from home?

Home was a big house with a glimpse of the harbour view, if one stood at the right spot on their veranda. It had a large living-room and three decent-sized bedrooms, certainly decent after the cubbyhole she and Jane shared in London.

It's an old building Evan is moving into, but older buildings in this country all seem to have big rooms and high ceilings, desirable in hot climates.

She wondered if he would live alone there.

He said his 'flatmate' was moving out of his present apartment in Cat's tower, but with a cheaper rent, maybe he will live alone? And Marketing Manager? The clients he mentioned are all worldwide organisations, so he seems pretty well positioned.

As the train reached the south end of the bridge, rocketing into the underground tube, Jane prodded her.

"Tell me more about this friend of Cat. The Clark Gable type? Charles Boyer?"

"More like Louis Jordan, I'd reckon. Or Tony Curtis. Maybe taller. About six feet. Very dark complexion, and with a teasing smile."

"Ooh. When do I get to meet him?"

"He said he'll call after sorting out something in his programme. He has two nights every week permanently booked on family dinners and teaches at a Sales College on Friday nights. So with me beginning rehearsals on Friday, and Liz, dreary woman, wanting me to take her baby-sitting job come Wednesday so she can continue wooing this Stephen freak, doesn't leave much choice. Evan is trying to change one of his family dinner nights."

Jane left the train at Town Hall and Maggie continued on to Central.

I so enjoy how this train always bursts from the underground. Well nearly always. The sudden bursting into bright sunshine and blue skies is so much more enjoyable than emerging from London's tube. There, one had to expect anything. Blue skies and sunshine were comparative rarities.

It was a short walk to the *Readers Digest* works. Having the train almost door to door from home was extremely convenient.

Who wants the inconvenience of driving a car? And working in the city, one must pay for a parking station, with still a walk to your office.

Work would seem strange, however, with no Cat.

Her empty desk will look so forlorn.

Her replacement was already hired but currently in the training school on an upper floor. Maggie expected to be called on to help her settle in. Condensing was an art unto itself, lopping thousands of words out of a text without endangering either the story or its writing style, which many critics called 'cheating' on a story. The Digest's attitude was that it still brought the tale to many who might otherwise never buy so many full books, so the author reached a bigger market anyway and likely still got some sort of royalty.

Maggie had to have a 'bob-each-way' on the matter. If condensers didn't appreciate writing skills and relish in good stories, there would be no such service. She simply chose not to delve too deeply into the morals of what she was doing. It was a discipline needing strong conviction, but it paid good wages.

~ * ~

Back to Evan...

I was indeed in my normal frustration of bumper to bloody bumper, crossing the bridge. Every morning as I inched the car forward in stops and starts, I watched with envy, the trains speeding past.

I was a 'like to get to the office early' type—before the day's telephone calls began—time to do some plotting before interruptions put paid to routine.

My mind then, of course, looking at the trains, turned to the bewitching Maggie.

She came on so strongly, had no qualms speaking her mind on what she thinks of Max. How would a girl like her, who has everything to attract any guy, get tangled up with a bloke like him in the first place? He seemed to feel he bloody owns her, yet she is obviously a free spirit. Loneliness? But how can a girl like her be lonely? I'd reckon guys are queuing up. How many are ahead of me, I wonder? And she's got a busy schedule starting next Friday? And me with my heavy schedule? When can we be together?

My every Tuesday and Thursday night called for dinner with my kids and every Friday night was teaching Salesmanship at a Tech. College, all a great balk to any bloke's social opportunities. And having my kids with me every week-end?

Social time was bloody hard to find.

It is why I prefer having a flatmate. I so often get tied up with mates in a pub after work, talking shop or anything else, and have but two nights in the week for that. They become part of my routine.

To save the situation of arriving home around seven or eight at night, only to then have to turn around and cook, it was easier if one had a flatmate who could cook. A brief phone-call could easily, then, help overcome any change in plans.

Oh why can't any bastard more clever than me, invent an instant sort of oven?

I had to get by with quick-cook foods like grilling chops and boiling up peas and potatoes. At least I had my Tuesday and Thursday night dinners cooked for me, and Friday night dinner before class was invariably a meat-pie and peas at a diner.

At least it being a Friday gives me the weekend to affirm dinner dates with the kids. Tomorrow I shall phone Maggie and see if she can make dinner either Monday or Wednesday.

Mmmm. Where? No, not my favourite for the first occasion; something smarter; yes, French it will be. I know just the place.

~ * ~

Maggie and Jane arrived home from Saturday shopping by taxi. Liz was taking a bath.

"I've finished the vacuuming," they heard from behind her closed door, "and Louis Jordan left a message for you, Mags, on the answer-phone. He wants you to call him. He said you have his card. He sounds gorgeous."

"Don't call him Louis Jordan, dreary woman," Maggie called back. "His name is Evan Robson and he seems to definitely have his own sense of being."

"You said he looks like Louis or Tony Curtis."

"When you asked what he was like, I said he is the Tony Curtis or Louis Jordan type. Evan has his very own looks, not necessarily film-star material. Nothing as crass as your Stephen, however."

They didn't often hold conversations through closed doors, yet when messages were put on mental 'hold', they'd often been forgotten with dire results.

"I'll call him right back, Jane. Can you put the shopping away?"

Her understanding friend simply wriggled her fingers at the phone.

At Evan's end, he was waiting, his kids engrossed in a game of draughts. He let it ring to its third beep-beep.

"Hello, Evan."

"Evan, it's Maggie. Thank you for your call."

He again trembled at her delightful accent. *It's so bloody cultured!*

"Nice that you've called back so soon. Are you still available for dinner?"

"Yes of course. I am wondering what night you can make it before next Friday?"

"It will have to be either Monday or Wednesday. Or both if you like?"

Now she felt a tremble.

"Monday is fine, Evan. Liz, dreary woman, one of my household, has asked me to sub for her on Wednesday as she has a date. We do that for each other here, and I owe her. Do you have anything planned for the weekend?"

"Weekends are not easy for me. I am building a beach-house up at Copacabana and need to keep an eye on what the builders are doing. That cuts Saturday out. And Sunday mornings during the Rugby season, I take my son to matches."

Son? Maggie thought. *I won't enquire now. I'll leave that until we're at dinner. And Rugby? Ugh! I hate football!*

"Where is Copacabana?" she inquired.

"North about two hours. Next beach north from Terrigal Beach."

"I've never travelled up the beaches past Avalon. I've been to Balmoral in the harbour but never to a surf beach. I didn't see an ocean until ten-years-old. I cannot even swim."

Evan let her hear his quiet giggle.

"Life in Australia is different, Maggie. Half the population goes surfing on weekends, for many months every year."

"Not this girl! So we can dine together Monday?"

"Yes, indeed. Would you like to eat in the city? Or I know somewhere local."

"I like to get home and shower. With foreknowledge, I can now reserve the bathroom for first shower. It sometimes comes down to that in this household. Liz and Jane both seem to take hours over a shower. Somewhere local please?"

"Fine. Seven o'clock at Toongara Road."

"Yes. The light over the house number is broken. From Bay Road, take the right hand fork and we are the green house on your right. To pinpoint us, I will switch on the blue light in the veranda ceiling."

"Great. See you then."

"I shall look forward to it."

"Me too."

Four

Monday evening, I was promptly away from the office to shower and don collar and tie, yet for this occasion, with suit-coat unbuttoned.

I sprayed myself with *7-11* and checked the clock. Six forty-six p.m.

It was a two minute drive, so I found myself pacing with frustration.

I checked again that my shoes had a good shine and that my wallet was in my pocket.

The clock said six forty-seven.

I decided to leave anyway. I'd never been able to cope with wasting time.

I shall drive very slowly.

I drove slowly yet on turning into Toongara Road's right-hand fork, it was only three houses along that a green house had a blue light burning in its veranda ceiling.

The dashboard clock showed six fifty-one.

Bloody hell! You're acting like a teenage kid with a hard on.

I drove quickly past in case someone came to the veranda to see a cruising car. I drove until finding somewhere to turn about, then parked. Six fifty-three.

At right on seven o'clock, I cruised north and parked at the green house. One minute late was about right, to have to apologise for.

The path was steep, many steps through rock-gardens of shrubs and lots of gum-trees with large tree-ferns wired to their trunks.

I gave the brass knocker two taps and the door was quickly opened by a buxom woman likely younger than Maggie, yet looking a tad older.

It was a rather dark vestibule so I simply followed into the light.

The buxom one introduced herself as she walked. "I am Liz."

Once into the brightly lit living-room, she turned and stood.

I had to stop or walk right into her. She began circling me, one hand ahip, the other massaging her chin with fingers, eying me up and down.

"Mmmm," she sighed, then raised her voice to call loudly… "More Louis than Tony, I'd reckon, Mags. Certainly a point or three up on Max."

I couldn't help but grin.

"Does that mean I pass muster?"

Just then, a diminutive one walked into the room, smiling.

"I'm Jane," she said. "Maggie will be but a moment."

Before I could utter a word, Liz raised her voice to a boom.

"I'm the one who has to write their parents, Evan, telling them what sort of company their daughters keep. I need to suss out everybody. But so far, yes, you seem up to par."

"Should I say thank you for that?"

"You don't need to," Liz answered. She leaned forward and kissed my cheek.

Maggie arrived then, looking delightful in a dress neither chic nor formal, a simple beige knee-length cling-thing again leaving a shoulder bare, with the sort of matching stole one could loosely toss over a shoulder. Not too high-heeled sandals set it all off nicely. The same long beaten-silver ear-ring dangled from the pierced left ear.

Am I to get a chance to see if she actually has both ears pierced?

Yet my flippant thought quickly turned to things more practical.

This loose pony-tail again simply drawn forward over the right shoulder. Is it a trade-mark thing with her? It certainly is an enchanting style.

Again she wore little make-up. I looked to see if she wore mascara, because she was very fair in every way, yet the eye-lashes seemed creamy rather than blond.

I wasn't sure.

"Absolutely delightful," I told her, which won me a dimpled smile.

"You all are English, then?"

"Yes, we go back a long way. It seemed entirely natural for us to flat together. We understand each others' foibles and know that no matter how we might seem to be sparring, we are in fact bolstering a sister relationship."

"You are each, then, very fortunate."

"Where do you dine?" asked the big Liz who, I reckoned, would weigh in at fifteen or sixteen stone, hands again to hip.

"*La Pistache*, Blues Point Road."

"I know it," Liz answered. "I was taken there once and got left with the bill."

"I assure you Maggie will be luckier," I replied.

"So is his inspection over?" Maggie said with a grin. "Their tongues will wag, however, Evan, after we've gone. Yet it seems they approve."

As we walked to the door, Liz's booming voice called after us...

"Have a nice dinner. And be gentle with her, Evan. If I ever find her in tears over you, you'll be in for a pasting."

We turned to see Jane simply smiling, and Liz giving us both a big wink.

They waited on the veranda to wave us off and from street level we heard a loud wolf-whistle.

"That will be Liz acknowledging this very nice and new Ford Fairmont."

I held the passenger door for her.

"Not mine of course. It's what the company wants me to be seen in."

~ * ~

La Pistache proved, as usual, good service and great food.

Its ceiling mural of drifting cirrus cloud had odd shafts of light from recessed globes, shining on particular tables. Others were lit with single candles. All tables were dressed in starched white linen and were well spaced. We chose a candle-lit table with a single red rose in a mini-vase.

"What wine do you like, Maggie?"

"Moselle. I'm afraid I'm not at all partial to heavy reds. Your choice?"

"Definitely heavy reds. We shall have a bottle each."

"A half for me, please?"

"Are you sure? I'm hoping we can make it a long dinner. I want to know all about you, your home, your work, your theatre life, and you promised a story on how you came to immigrate. If you cannot finish a bottle, we shall keep the cork so you can take it for breakfast."

She laughed and let me choose her wine.

She ordered a prawn cocktail and *Coq au Vin* while I opted for a dozen oysters *naturel* and a 'bloody blue' filet.

"I am a very, very rare-steak man," I explained. "I like my steaks not only thick but the inside red-rare and bloody. Sometimes I order Tartare."

She didn't try to hide a little shudder.

"I enjoy Australian steaks, yet certainly medium.

"Whilst we await appetisers, Maggie, tell me how and why you left home and family to live in Australia?"

"Have you ever experienced a London winter?"

"I've never been to that part of the world."

"Have you ever been so cold that even wearing so many clothes you cannot get your arms into yet another sleeve, and with a duvet as well as two blankets, you still cannot sleep for shivering?"

"I've seen snow only once. My kids wanted to experience it. We have it only two months a year in the country's south-east corner, a six hour drive. We nearly froze despite plenty of clothing. It is agonisingly painful when spending more time on your back, in snow, than upright on skis. I swore never to see snow a second time."

"Kids, you say? So you have more than the boy you take to Rugby?"

She obviously takes aboard every little detail I drop.

"A daughter of eleven. My son is thirteen. They live with a family close by. I dine there Tuesdays and Thursdays and I have them every weekend. Living alone, I cannot father them at home. My career takes many evenings and overnights away."

She cast her eyes down, fingering the base of her wine-glass. Then she took out a cigarette, insisting she smoke her own, yet let me light it for her.

"That sounds a very difficult life for you."

"A restrictive life. I have to toss up between personal inconveniences and practical demands, so one has to find a routine giving the children and me, as well as the inconveniences, advantages that otherwise are impossible. We can still have adventures together as a threesome family, like our visit to the snow."

"I cannot ski either. I'm simply not sports-minded and my mind knows it."

Oh how she quickly avoided getting further into my domestic problems!

Our starters arrived, so we shelved conversation while they were served.

I topped up our glasses.

"So your tale on coming to Australia?"

She again gave me a smile broad enough to betray dimples. I sensed she knew it would enrapture me.

I almost closed my eyes. *It makes me tingle all the way to my crutch!*

"Jane and I flatted in a Shepherd's Bush attic. With windows shuttered, we had no natural light. Twenty-four hours a day one must have electric light and on a top floor, snow packed on your skylight even stops up that little bit of daylight. We seldom stopped shivering."

She paused while I called for a clean ashtray, then recounted her funny story of finding the article on the £10 travel fee.

"We were lucky, however, Evan, that we never had to live in the shelters that families working for the government had to suffer until enough houses could be built. As highly experienced secretaries, we were immediately sent for interviews with firms on waiting lists. And we had accommodation arranged with Liz."

"And the long sea journey?"

She pursed her lips and straightened her shoulders.

"Oh, how much should I tell you of that?"

Oh how easily this might put my foot in things! I'll just watch his eyes, see if he illustrates even the hint of a frown, she thought.

She explained how she had come to live in Italy for two years.

"Then it was such a coincidence, Evan, Jane and I being booked on an Italian liner for the voyage to Sydney. Maybe I should simply ask you to imagine my journey when I explain that I was the only single longhaired blond on this voyage of several weeks, with a bevy of handsome young Italians in the crew, especially when I could speak their language? My time seemed simply so sought after, I had to keep my wits about me. It certainly wasn't a lonely cruise."

And is that smile a gracious one? she mused. *What will be his approach now?*

"My mind hearkens back to your statement on parting at Cat's farewell."

She raised that one eyebrow that so disconcerted me.

"And what was that? I cannot recall."

"That you daren't even ask what keeps me from home on the nights I don't spend with family—or something to that effect."

She smiled sweetly. "*Au touche, M'sieur.*"

She then added, "I felt no undue shame, yet I must admit that on some occasions during the voyage, Jane had to sleep alone."

What I can't see under the table, thought Evan, *is if she has fingers and ankles, crossed!*

I just feel I should be honest with him, she mused.

Yet she was saved by a bell when the waiter arrived to take empty plates away.

He twitched. *I need to give that thought. I should leave any response until then. I want a lot of water flowing under my bridge with this young woman before making too hasty an assessment.*

Let time pass! his alter-ego shrieked.

"And your family, Maggie?"

She let out a great sigh. *Oh, what a relief.*

"I hadn't lived at home in years, Evan, so parting for a distant clime wasn't that great a burden. A younger sister and brother had each married, so my parents at last had their house to themselves. I love theatre, am career minded and wanted to travel. Bearing bawling children is not my ideal in life. I leave that for women who dream of motherhood; my sister, for instance. Rural Bedfordshire lacked meaningful work and spending three hours a day back and forth to London was a big slice out of a girl's life. I moved to London and phoned my parents every week. And once here, having Jane and Liz alongside, keeps missing home easier."

"You also told me you had a yen for travel?"

"I travelled a lot in Britain. Have you heard of the Luton Girls Choir?"

"Oh, indeed. My mother is a fan."

She told him about that part of her life, then on her travels in Italy.

"I didn't particularly like Rome. It is big and crass. Great historically, of course. But *Firenze* and *Venézia* are indeed parts of a dream-world, as was *Como* up in Italy's vagina. We..."

"Italy's what?"

"Vagina. It's as far up Italy's leg as a girl can get!"

I couldn't avoid leaning back, laughing aloud.

She too had the most mischievous of smiles on her face.

I couldn't stop giggling and she even reached her napkin across the table to wipe my tear-filled eyes.

When the main course was served, I sliced a sliver from my steak to show her how the inside was still raw. She shrugged shoulders.

She told me about living there, singing in the night-club.

"One can miss a family, yet staying home, one misses many opportunities."

"Have you always worked in publishing?"

She briefed through her time in the Diplomatic Corps where her languages further developed.

"I have never known someone who has lived abroad, Maggie, other than an aunt who spent years in India on missionary work."

I explained how Australians, whilst many moved much around our own country, few had travelled overseas. "With the nearest English speaking people more than a month's sailing distance on even the biggest liners, very few could afford either the time from work, or the cost of such a journey. Only after World War II did international flights begin."

"But what about you, Evan? I've been doing all the talking. Most unlike me. I like listening to others' experiences."

"I'm well-travelled in my own country, driven all the east coast and into the centre's deserts. For several years I was driving my two kids overnight to Brisbane twice a month. My father died when I was but a boy and now my sister and mother both live in Brisbane."

"You drove overnight? Why?"

"Lulu likes to see her grand-children growing up. She is now on her own after three husbands and..."

"Lulu?"

I laughed. "When mother buried her third husband, my sister Valerie and I nicknamed her Lucretia. It quickly became Lu for short, then Lulu. It stuck. Nor did I want my two young children missing out on her experiences. When the children were small, my wife died and another family took them in. I eat there two nights a week and have them on weekends. About every second week I would take off with them in the car at five or six p.m. on a Friday evening, making

Brisbane in about twelve hours. En-route, we would eat sandwiches and bottled drinks. Only time we stopped was to refuel half way. We would return on Sunday nights."

"Good heavens. For how long were you doing this?"

"Four or five years. We stopped only when they outgrew sleeping on the back seat."

"Well you certainly have a nice car. I read that night driving is dangerous because of wombats and kangaroos. Have you ever hit one?"

"A wombat. Both creatures are night-stalkers and wombats move only slowly. When crossing a road, car headlights mesmerise them, they simply stand and stare into the glare. Swerving at speed is dangerous, so yes, they are easily hit."

"And the one you hit?"

"He was very dead. I could only pull him off the bitumen. Crows pick the bones free of meat next day, so nothing is left to fester. Snakes, of course, we try to kill."

"I'm on your side there. We have a family of blue-tongue lizards under our house. They frighten me no end."

"Ugly but safe. They are more frightened than you. They are harmless."

Conversation flowed until we both had done justice to our bottles of wine.

Profiteroles now had our attention.

"How old were the children when you were widowed?"

"Six and four. I was pretty much in shock and had no local family. We'd bought an old house and were renovating it. It had internal brick walls torn down, etcetera, simply just in a 'helluva' mess. I was doing it all myself because we were strapped for cash. Friends offered to take Leanne, others wanted Paul until I could sort out what to do. Number one on my list was that I didn't want them separated. The other was all each had. I couldn't afford a housekeeper, yet wanted time to decide what would be best for the long term. I sold the house as it stood, so I could pay fees at a boarding school that took both girls and boys, and took to flatting."

I noticed she had tears in her eyes. I leaned across the table and wiped them.

"I'll make the rest quick. A woman Kit had worked with, doing home typing, wanted to take in both children. Their daughter was a year older than my Paul. She could have no more children and they wanted a big family. During that year's school holidays, my children spent it in their house. At year's end, the kids, hating boarding school, were happy to move in with the Stroud family, yet have weekends with me. I wanted to ensure I remained an influence in their lives. I started teaching a College sales course on Friday nights, to help pay a contribution to my children's keep. The Strouds objected, for they were comfortably off, but I insisted."

Maggie pointed to my plate and I took another bite.

"I'll make the rest quicker. Paul was into surf-boarding and Leanne and I both loved body-surfing, so now earning a more comfortable salary, I decided on a beach-house for our weekends. Right now, its foundations are being laid. Paul will join the board club there and Leanne and I will body-surf all weekend. That is a viable pastime here, eight or nine months every year."

"What a dreadful situation to find yourself in. I can imagine your dilemma."

"I at least have a dawning advantage. Against parental advice, Kit and I married too young. We knew best. Only now do I realise how a few more years of experience would have helped."

I waved my spoon at the air and she seemed to understand what it meant.

"*C'est la vie*, eh?"

"Exactly."

"I too, Evan, discovered after leaving home, that learning from independence is the only way of realising how important other things are in life. One cannot learn when experiencing only what parents discovered in their limited world. Mine had their little patch of England, yet knew next to nothing of what went on beyond the family's fence. I don't decry them. I love them. Yet leaving them gave me a wonderful sense of achievement in finding my own way."

We reached forward, holding hands across the table.

Is a bond being established? What might she have in mind for after dinner? Drive down to harbours edge? Watch the lights of the late ferries? Have a fondle or two? In one sense I'd like it, yet I'd rather she come home with me, see the great harbour views from my balcony? Or go home to her place? Or is first night too soon?

We did none of those things.

"It's been a long night," I said over coffee. Our wine bottles were empty.

We were still holding hands across the table and she obviously had a shoe off. Her stockinged toes were massaging my ankles.

"And a most enjoyable night. I still want to hear about your theatre, however, so should we have another dinner before you start rehearsals on Friday? Wednesday night? Any chance of finding someone else to sub the baby-sitting for Liz?"

"I will find someone else. But please let me share the cost of that dinner?"

"I've a better idea. A little husband and wife restaurant in nearby Neutral Bay, serves great Italian food. It's cheap, yet the food is delightful. A short menu, but every dish excellent, by my Italian standards anyway."

"I should love that. Its name?"

"*Café Accogliente.* And my stock might just go up a point with them if I bring along a beautiful young woman who can share talk of Italy in their own language?"

"I will definitely find someone else to sub for Liz's baby-sitting."

"Good. What does *Accogliente* mean?"

"Cozy. It's name means *Cozy Café.*"

"It is well named then. Seven o'clock again?"

"Deal."

I drove her home.

"I'll walk you to the door in case the blue-tongues are foraging."

She reached for my hand and led me up the path and steps.

"Can I kiss you good-night," she asked on reaching the porch.

We kissed long and deeply. I knew she could feel me hardening for I was deliberately pressing against her more and more as the kisses deepened. Her breasts were rubbing against mine and it seemed to be delighting us both.

"Do you rehearse Sunday nights?" I asked as we broke apart.

"I don't yet know what our director will want. Some like private early sessions with lead players. So there could be some nights during the first couple of weeks and visa-verse in other stages. I'll get an idea only come Friday."

"Wednesday night then?"

"Seven o'clock!"

Five

Café Accogliente proved a wonderfully happy occasion.

"I don't even know their names," I had told her, driving down Ben Boyd Road, "but they welcome me like a son. I often bring friends yet more often come alone. It is indeed a cosy atmosphere and I find its food unique."

"I've been told Australians have quite taken to European tastes since that extensive immigration period. It doesn't surprise me. What does, however, is that for all the years up to then, foreign restaurants weren't known."

"Chinese were imported to work the goldfields and sugar-cane fields, so we had Chinese restaurants. Yet restaurants per sé, were unknown to most. Before the war, dinners were eaten at home or in elegant hotels. We ate well, but it was invariably lamb, beef or offal. The sauces and many nuances given pasta flavours nowadays in Italian restaurants are a thousand times more piquant than Lulu could ever even try to achieve with spaghetti."

When she laughed, I added…

"But when you get to meet Lulu, promise me you will never tell her I said that. But you can tell the old lady here at *Café Accogliente*."

Not only did we eat royally, the hosts were thrilled at me bringing an Italian-speaking friend.

"I told the old couple what you said about comparing their spaghetti with your mother's and they were thrilled. They wanted to know your name, Evan. And mine. They've insisted we call them Donato and Gina. I told them I will be sure to bring my flatmates here to discover her wonderful cooking. I asked if we could order wine by the glass."

"By all means. They make their own ice-creams too, Maggie. I love their Prune Smudge."

"The mind boggles, but if it's as satisfying a taste as everything else, bravo!"

And it was.

On the drive home, I considered my stocks high enough to risk an invitation.

"To reach Waverton from here, Maggie, we must drive past my street. Would you like to check out my view before I move?"

She squeezed my thigh. "To use one of your regular expressions, Oh, indeed!"

I passed the Visitor Car Park sign. *Will she notice that if we were stopping only a few minutes, it would have been sensible to park there?*

I rounded the building to the Residents Only area under it and had to back and fill to get into my spot because some ignorant bastard had parked awkwardly.

"That's a concern I won't have at Waverton, Maggie. It has no off-street parking."

The condo was a long, narrow building atop a steep climb from the harbour, every apartment with a balcony and view. Once inside, I switched on only low lights.

"The view is better if we don't have bright lights at our back."

On my living-room's window wall, I drew back the drapes.

She gasped. The night view over Sydney Harbour and city was indeed spectacular. One of the world's most magnificent waterways lay before her. I led her past my rock garden, amass with flourishing greenery and flowers, and we leaned on the concrete wall.

"What you cannot see at night between the skyscrapers, is the far skyline, the sand-hills of Botany Bay, the far southern extremity of Sydney."

"I would indeed love to see all this by daylight."

"Night-time is not all that bad. With the telescope, it's surprising what one sees through windows in Point Piper and Darling Point apartments."

She raised that eyebrow. "You don't. Surely! Do you?"

"Oh, indeed! You want to try?"

"Ooh! Yes please."

We laughed while I adjusted the tripod and angled the scope. Apart from the Naval Depot on the southern shore, on the several points from the Opera House to the east were exclusive suburbs of high-rise condos and private harbour-side homes.

"Everyone expects there are countless perverts like us in an area like this, my dear. Why do you think some deliberately leave their drapes drawn wide?"

I stood back and invited her to look at the particular window I had targeted.

Her instinctive reaction, of course, will be of amazement at how clear is any particular window some two miles distant.

"Ah," she gasped. "It's only two people sitting watching television."

"That is all I wanted you to see, my dear. I am not a pervert—but I will go pour us coffee and Cognacs while you search around that area. That particular building, if you like, about three floors higher? The blinds are always open."

I walked off and left her to it.

"Do you have wine rather than Cognac?"

"Oh how fortunate. Only today did I buy a Moselle. Quite a coincidence."

She ran after me, to quickly kiss me, then rushed back to the telescope.

~ * ~

"Will you come and help me turn down the bed," I asked as we finished our coffees. "We can take our wines with us."

She pursed her lips. "Should we first put the cork back in the bottle?"

"Do you think it will go off before we want a second glass? Even white wine uncorked, will stay fresh for a day or two?"

"Please just top mine up and put the bottle back in the fridge?"

I did so and led her up the little hallway.

"That door is to the second bedroom, now unoccupied."

At the next, because I had a wine in each hand, I reached out an elbow to hit the light switch. "Bathroom."

I walked on to my bedroom and again with elbow, turned on its light.

I wonder if she will notice that I already have the bed turned down?

The smile on her face told me she had.

"And all the Venetian blind blades slanted downwards!"

"Yes, my dear, quite unlike many of the swanky apartments across the harbour."

I was also sure she had noted my wall of wardrobe doors was all mirrors.

But she made no comment.

I slid open a door and drew out two hangers.

"Maybe you want to hang your things?"

"You seem to think of everything," she whispered, reaching up to kiss me.

I squeezed her tightly before turning her around to slowly pull down her zipper. I could sense her trembling.

Like me!

Little was unsaid by the fingers, however. All twenty seemed eager to play at just the right pressures in just the right places, leading to gasping and grasping.

Neither saw reason not to test this, or that tease learned from our pasts. Each knew it was not so much an exercise in loving each other, it was a time to test each other, try this and try that—each quickly letting the other know if it worked. Gasps and sighs and finger-pauses or pressures, all sent clear messages.

I gloried in the way she twisted her body, using toes as well as fingers to launch attacks, obviously careful not to put too much pressure here or there.

She's obviously had good teachers!

And to the best of my ability I let her feel what a man's fingers could do for a woman lusting for orgasm, yet at the same time, trying to stretch the time factor.

It was sweet loving, especially when the plunging stage arrived. Neither was a quiet lover and both were soon to shrieking stage as we came. And seemingly for ages after. We gasped for breath, blood pulsating such that we thought hearts would burst.

When the writhing finished, we cuddled.

Ah, this woman knows how to make a man feel wanting of her love.

Ah, this man has all it takes to give me a happy life, for ever.

Six

Six months later, at breakfast…

Fred's arm was around her shoulders.

I sat opposite, alongside Fred's paramour of last evening.

"Look at his eyes, Maggie. Aren't they the most gorgeous you've ever seen?"

The subject was Arnold. Fred had met Arnold last night at a gay bar. Maggie and I had just been introduced to him.

I could sense that under the table, she had a hand patting Fred's thigh.

"Fred, my darling," she answered, "every instinct tells me Arnold is a delightful fellow. Yes, his eyes are gorgeous but so are yours. And so are Evan's who has told me so are mine. If Arnold's eyes so beguile you, sweetie, you keep looking at them so I can eat my breakfast. I have to get to work."

She gently pulled his arm from around her shoulders and continued on her cereal.

We were used to Fred occasionally having an evening's lover stay for breakfast. It had all been such a laugh the way it started. The owner of my Waverton apartment had phoned to say the tenant had gone and that I could move in once the cleaning was finished. Saturday was agreed.

"However," the owner asked, "the sub-tenant renting the second bedroom has asked if you intend letting out your spare room. He is hoping he might stay on."

I agreed to interview him if he were prepared to come to my condo apartment.

"It was funny, Maggie," I later told her. "When this guy arrived, I sensed he might be gay. He wasn't the queeny type, or he'd have been given the immediate boot, but I needn't have worried. He came straight out with it."

"I am gay," he said even as we shook hands. "The hand-shake was firm."

"I was raised on a sheep station and I simply hated country life." he had said. "I came to the city to study at the Manly Seminary."

"For the Priesthood?"

"Yes, but after six months I couldn't justify such a future, with being gay."

"Can you cook?"

"I'm pretty good with a leg of mutton," he quipped with a grin, but quickly added, "in fact any sort of baking. And I make great omelettes."

He certainly had an outgoing manner about him, and a touch of humour mingled with respect.

"Work?"

"David Jones. Men's shoes."

"Since when?"

"Two years."

David Jones, Sydney's premier Department Store employed only staff responsible enough to successfully serve people of distinction, so all that sounded positive.

"A month's trial?"

"Yes. I understand that."

"Will you want to bring lovers home?"

"Occasionally. I had an arrangement with the last tenant, that that was okay but for only one or two nights. Even then I kicked in something for his breakfast and we always ate out at night. But the tenant was also gay, of course."

I mused on all that for a minute.

"Only thing I'm not happy about there, is you having friends there over weekends. You'll have to realise that I have my two kids, thirteen and eleven, staying with me every weekend—overnight Saturdays. They will sleep in the veranda-room. I want you to use your priestly instincts while they are around. We'll play it for a month and see how things go. But no screaming queens. Okay?"

"I'm not into screaming queens, sir."

Ah! The 'sir' made me feel a million years old.

"I'm Evan, you'll be Fred, and you pay me the same as you paid the previous tenant—payment prompt during the first seven days each month?"

He nodded in agreement.

"I move in on Saturday," I told him. "My hours are pretty erratic and I eat out every Tuesday, Thursday and Friday."

"I have my own TV. I can hibernate in my room all weekend if you like, Evan."

"I hope that won't be necessary. Let's play it by ear for starters, eh?"

When Maggie and I later talked about it, she laughed.

"Oh, I come across so many gay people in the theatre; guys and gals. I've had gay girls coming on to me on occasions but they get a real short shift. But some are great actors. And many a gay actor I have among social friends. Many a time I've had weeping guys crying on my shoulder, young *and* old."

Fred had fitted into my life not only helpfully in respect of domestic cooking and cleaning, but amicably. I was no Catholic, yet he quite understood that the people surrounding his life all had personal problems and Fred was just ever there, not only prepared to listen, but wanting to help where he could. I liked the guy and so did Maggie.

As our friendship developed, she began spending more nights in my bed than in her own. So we had many breakfasts together. She eventually had more of her personal things in my wardrobe and cupboards than at Toongara Road.

After several months it was agreed she would move in. As the sensible girl she was, she wanted to keep up her rent at Toongara Road 'until further notice'. Whilst she didn't pay rent at Bay Road, she insisted we go halves on wine, for we were both strong drinkers. I agreed to that also, 'until further notice'.

Nor did she want me to evict Fred.

"I like the guy," she insisted. I've stayed here on so many occasions when he has a friend overnight, yet never once have I felt anything but sorry for him being so lonely. I have enough gay friends to recognise that he is another I am proud to know. I would feel forever guilty if you threw him out because I am moving in."

"Christian of you too, my dear."

We let that also ride until further notice.

The apartment, apart from the dining-room sited behind the kitchen to take advantage of the little bit of harbour that could be seen, not only was there a large sitting-room but at the front, an enclosed veranda through our bedroom, looking out on to Bay Road. It was large and I had it furnished as a study-come-private sitting-room, so we had privacy from Fred of an evening if we wanted it. Sleeping bags were there for the kids on Saturday nights.

The eclectic mix worked well. I found Fred a most likeable guy, serious yet with a great sense of humour.

"It would have been a great waste to the outside world if he had hidden himself in priestly shrouds," Maggie claimed.

Fred occasionally joined us on dinner-dates and summer visits to Balmoral Beach when we would go with my kids. I continued going to dinner at the Stroud house twice a week. Maggie would only occasionally come there with me, for she disliked Lynn Stroud.

"I simply feel uncomfortable there," she insisted.

I understood about Lynn. I had similar misgivings yet realised all were better off if I didn't let those misgivings influence me. Maggie would have dinner with Jane and Liz if Fred were not coming home those nights, so she was never left alone.

On weekends, when Maggie had things to do at 'home' while I had the kids up at the beach, Fred arranged his own social life to ensure Maggie had company.

"I'm quite happy to wash out my own undies, Fred," she would sometimes tell him, to then literally shove him out the door to do something of his own pursuits.

It was a happy household. Maggie moving in with me was indeed a boost to my self-satisfaction—a further positive move in my life— one with exciting prospects for a happy future.

~ * ~

Another joy I discovered we could share, was her theatre life.

"You cannot realise, my darling, how wonderful is the sense of leaving your own life for hours at a time, to literally become someone else. The stage does that for one. You talk about your surfing being like a 'barbed-wire pull-through', an experiencing casting worry or stress from your mind, an outer force defying all your inner tensions. Well that is what the stage does for me. It is an escape from life's burdens. To be so engrossed in another's dreams and aims, having departed your own being to become them, is indeed a transformation. You have cast off the weights pressing you, to become some other character. It is a new life you are embracing."

She used old Les as an example.

Les had been her father in the *Bertold Brecht* play when we met. Old Les, as all the cast knew him, was even to me, as a newcomer, a face I had seen scores of times on TV commercials. It was the most wizened face one could imagine, so much so that he was in high demand for commercials. In *Mr. Puntila and his Man, Matti*, Maggie was his daughter. They were the lead roles. He was aide to a Nobleman whose house they lived in. Father Les, as she began calling him, was distressed at his daughter's libertine approach to young men of the town. He was persistently advising her to lead a more virtuous life.

"I saw it as yet another lesson in real life," she admitted.

She knows me well enough by now, to feel safe on such a topic.

"As if it were," she continued, "I even made sure Old Les was made privy to my plans for a life with you, my darling."

We hugged for a long sensitive moment.

"It was like the time you told me, darling, unwittingly at the time, that 'when' I got to meet your mother, Lulu, I must never tell her about her cooking spaghetti. That was on but the second or third time we had met. I was just so amazed that a future together was so quickly in your subconscious mind."

"I didn't, surely!"

"Oh, indeed you did, darling. I could tell it was your subconscious talking, yet you did. It quite thrilled me!"

Bloody hell! Let's get this show back on today's road. At least on to the road when Maggie was playing Old Les's daughter.

"I was never so thrilled, I think, on some of those nights when I came along after dinner at Artarmon, to your rehearsals. It really was a new world for me. To see you on a stage being a different character, I was really torn as to which was the 'real' you. It was an astonishment."

It had opened at the *Live Theatre* in Sydney's Kings Cross and not only had I befriended so many of the cast, having often come to rehearsals after my dinner with the kids, but went on to 'after' parties, a regular thing at this one's or that one's room or rooms. We would call into late hour bottle-shops and pick up whatever we wanted to eat or drink and party on into the early and not so early hours. I got to know them all reasonably well.

Sometimes, after dinner at Artarmon, I would bring the kids to see the rehearsals, then later, the performances. I never, however, went on to parties in those instances. Their minds had each 'partied' however, while watching the stage; the 'that actress is my father's friend' sort of thing.

I had, then, quickly given up my teaching Friday nights. On meeting Maggie, my mind and sense of values had both become more selfish. I often harked back in those days, to how I would expect my kids to react to her if she should become a permanent part of my life. Yes, even from the first week of meeting her!

Paul indeed seemed headed in my sort of direction in life. Not commerce necessarily, but in finding satisfactions in achievement of whatever purpose he took aboard. Both kids being adopted, because after seven years of marriage, Kit and I had found that we could never have children. We adopted two; firstly Paul, then two years later, Leanne. Both had been but a week old. Paul was fair of hair which curled as he grew. Leanne was dark with straight hair. Paul was outgoing in a naturally expansive way whilst Leanne was severely introverted; a follower.

Maggie likened her to her sister Audrey when young. "She lives within herself. That's how I saw her grow up. In teen life, however, she broke out, became boy mad. Couldn't wait to be married and have a family."

"Oh! Subservience!" Maggie almost bellowed at me on that occasion.

She saw subservience develop in her sister, yet change.

Will my Leanne change?

I began absorbing the philosophy of acting that Maggie instilled in me. I could see how devoted to it she was—it was like a magnet. She was able to give herself to it without sacrificing the worldly needs of work and money for comfortable living. I saw it all as a most worthy attitude to life. Almost, in a way, with some envy.

So if I am to try winning Maggie as a life partner, where will that lead me?

I had the similar goal of wanting independence, yet also love.

How best to achieve both?

Maggie illustrated that she was achieving both. That is what I envied.

Or is it not envy? Rather a desire to join her in search of such an ideal?

I too took my work challenges seriously and felt, despite living apart from them, still remaining close enough to my children to be a guiding influence in their lives.

But could I ever envisage a life with both children and Maggie?

'I have no desire to mother babies, children or teenagers,' she had said on one occasion. It still rang in my ears.

The kids might not be of my blood, but I had certainly discovered a love for them. I realised the need to ensure they were properly readied for the world they must face.

Having found such a love for this particular woman, however, and my two children quickly growing into their teens, how do I juggle these into a manageable life?

Ah! Mais est-ce la vraie vie?

Seven

Maggie muses...

Darling Evan proves his love in so many ways. Not only the constant attention including the loving in bed, of which, by now, I guess, I should be considering myself experienced, it's his attention to little things like my clothing, choice of jewellery, even approach to housework.

The latter seems reasonably organised to the satisfactions of all three, Fred now seeming part of my new family. Even Evan's approach to my work is significant. He seems as interested in my satisfactions there as is he in his own. He just has that knack of making me feel cosy. He's even becoming to feel a housemate. There are odd things I miss from living with Jane and Liz because sharing with a couple of guys is in itself different, yet my mind seems to be adjusting. Not as if I still don't see Liz at least weekly, but Jane and I still catch the same train each morning.

Evan has business dinners now and again, including me when he can. I like meeting his workmates. Nor do I begrudge his occasional weekends on conferences. I trust him implicitly. Only too well do I know how some husbands play up when off on business matters—enough try coming on to me at business do's I attend.

Occasionally he has to wear a dinner jacket. I love it then. He looks so suave in it, especially with the ruffle-trimmed shirt I gave him for his birthday.

But the children? His attitude to them living at Artarmon is mixed. I certainly like them, particularly Paul. For a young teen he has a great sense of subtle humour. He even tries testing me in a jocular way, like Evan—taking a rise out of me while still illustrating respect. But Leanne? I simply cannot understand the child. She lives so much within herself that I cannot work out if it is me she doesn't like, or if she is like this all the time. I cannot reach her. Audrey and I quarrelled when she was that age, despite only three years separated us, yet we were simply such different personalities. We had learned to stick together in family crises, yet couldn't agree on minor things—and this is just how I feel about Leanne.

I would really be worried if I had to help raise her. It's also significant that I dislike the sort of person who does raise her, and this too, is Evan's worry. Lynn Stroud rules her family with the extreme narrow-mindedness I cannot abide. She is ruled only by her own sense of being—no sharing instinct. I feel so sorry for Norman. He even, in his way, admits total subservience to her.

Dear Evan realises it is a poor example for his children, yet remains insistent on keeping them together.

"Especially in that they know they are adopted," he told me. "I want them together. Each in their own way, lets me know there are things they like to talk about together, even to Leanne liking her life with the Strouds while Paul would prefer being with me."

Whether Evan means, in that, that it is not an option because it would split the children, or because he knows I would find responsibilities of motherhood a trial, I remain unsure. Yet I don't mind not knowing. If he wants to raise this with me, okay, I shall be all the help I can.

I love his beach-house. The little village has a Spanish flavour, so his cabaña as he calls it is truly of that aura, yet sensibly styled as a beach house. Even the roof now being erected has Spanish style tiles. While we have a bedroom, there are loads of folder-beds in the big open living-room, only other room in the house except for the bathroom and shower-room underneath.

"Every beach-house needs a shower-room where sand can be dredged off into the fall of the land," he insisted.

The main entrance is also off the carport, the stairway up to the living area also internal.

Beach, of course, is not my thing. I not only find sand on my skin hateful, but just the thought of entering an ocean filled with sharks, even if just to splash about, is abhorrent. Yet I do admire young Paul out with the 'mates' he has already befriended there, accomplishing amazing feats. Watching him through binoculars has me quite in awe at his skill. And Evan's skill in bodysurfing is as admirable.

"Sharks rarely come closer than the rising wave," he explained. "They lose control over mobility once the wave breaks."

I cannot, however, find that reason enough. If even one shark gets caught in the breaking wave, it would surely make directly for me in the shallows, anyway.

~ * ~

"What do you reckon about this furniture, Mags?"

We had got around to the sort of home we would like the Bay Road apartment to become on a long term basis, with or without Fred.

The location was wonderful, a hundred metres from the train and fifteen minutes to cross the bridge to downtown, Maggie's workplace and also her theatre friends. For shopping, it was a five minute drive to the big five-ways at Crow's Nest, also to a dozen or more decent restaurants.

And only a fifteen minute drive for me to the kids at Artarmon, then on to the beach-house.

"What furniture we don't want here, Mags, can go up there. If I start buying new stuff for here, I can progressively take pieces away on weekends. The builder has promised lock-up conditions in a month or so. For here, I have a yen for period stuff—wallpaper and furniture."

We began making lists. Maggie had no personal furniture yet we shared a liking for period pieces.

"It always bugged me in Luton, darling, that mum and dad took great pride in updating to keep up with modern styles. I so envied girlfriends' homes which, in similar houses to our own, their parents had gone for exactly what you want."

We began with the dining-room. It hadn't space enough for a sideboard but everything a sideboard usually held was stored only in the adjoining kitchen.

One Friday night we attended an open-house viewing for a Saturday auction. It had no dining-suite as such, but several tables we liked. We needed a rectangular one. The one taking my eye had bottle-shaped legs and stone castors.

"I've never been to an auction, Evan. Can we get an idea of what it might cost?"

"We'd be told it depended on what sort of buyer might be there on the day. If we were to ask an idea, he will quote less than he expects it to bring."

"Let's ask anyway?"

"Okay. You ask. Use the guile you trapped me with. You do it so well."

She drove a not too gentle fist into my ribs and glared with that raised eye-brow.

In a mock huff she stormed into the office, me trailing. Using her practised Royal accent, she quoted the lot number, asking what it might fetch.

"It depends entirely who comes on the day, my dear. Some days you can be lucky."

She turned to see the smirk on my face.

She turned back. "In your opinion, sir, what would you expect to pay?"

"Two to three hundred dollars, maybe?" He then plunged his head back into the pile of figures he had been working on.

"He'll probably open the bidding at three hundred," I whispered while returning to the viewing room.

I pointed to a set of four chairs. "I like those."

"With that dreadful gold paint? It cheapens them."

"They can be stripped. It's messy, but there are workshops that will soak them in acid then scrape and sand them. The carvings are beautiful."

"There are only four. We want six."

"There are several old carvers. Let's check them out."

~ * ~

With kids excited with their first auction, we jostled among what seemed like a thousand others. Leanne wanted me to buy a typical girl's dressing-table painted a ghastly pink and festooned with pink tulle. Paper-flowers had been dried into the paint while still wet.

"If you can buy it out of your pocket money," I told her, "It's just the sort of thing mum-Lynn likes, I'm sure. I need all I can afford just buying six chairs and a table."

It took a long while before people were hustled off the gold chairs when their lot number came up. Only four bidders were against me and I had them knocked down for eighty-five dollars.

"Cheap, because of the dreadful gold paint, Mags. Many of these bidders have antique shops and don't want the bother of restoring."

A little later, up came a pair of dining-room carvers, deeply carved in a gothic pattern.

"Once smartened up, can you see them at home?"

I didn't admit to being concerned about cost. Despite a pair, they were being sold separately. After strong bidding, I won the first for ninety dollars.

With five of the six, I'm sort of committed, now, to go all the way! I must keep my eyes off Maggie!

By the time ninety dollars was reached, the bidding was against the same four. One shook his head and another looked disappointed.

"If they have antique shops, they still have delivery, profit and cash-flow costs to add. I've only delivery," I whispered to Mags.

A third bid a hundred and the fourth dropped out. I raised it five.

My sole opponent bid a further five. I quickly raised a finger, depending on him realising that with the first of the pair, I would stay in the race.

He shook his head and I had it for a hundred and fifteen.

When the table came up, I asked Mags if she wanted to do the bidding. The kids, of course, were wild-eyed with excitement.

"No thank you, my love. Not only do I feel the bidding should be someone with at least some practice, but it's already clear today, that these other bidders have seen you are one to persist. That surely gives you an advantage."

"You learn fast, darling."

Our table opened at two hundred and fifty and after some brisk bidding, we won it at three-hundred-and-eighty dollars. I left Maggie with the kids and headed for the office to arrange delivery for Wednesday.

"Sometime after lunch," was agreed.

I would take the afternoon off. I needed to ensure all were the correct items.

We all were quite chuffed over the experience.

"Something more than seven hundred dollars is a lot of money, Dad," I heard from Paul as we drove home.

"Good that you got to seven hundred by mental arithmetic, lad. Can you try for closer to the total?"

Maggie gave my thigh a hard pinch.

"I think that was already a clever summation," she said aloud, giving me a wink.

"Like to try?" I insisted.

"I can't remember what that last chair went for."

"Fair enough," I told him. "Yes, it's a lot of money, but you just wait until we have them all restored. They'll look like a thousand dollars worth."

Fred undertook to recover the seats once stripped and lacquered.

"And I shall contribute a tablecloth and new curtains," added Maggie.

I bought a book on upholstering, another on stripping and lacquering and one for designing and fitting curtain tracks. Mags, thrilled at being part of designing things for her own home, began buying *House and Garden* magazine.

"I never realised what an exciting exercise it could be," she marvelled.

Deliberately in front of the children, I grabbed her tightly and kissed her deeply. "You simply make me the happiest man in the world," I told her.

"Sheesh," I heard from Paul.

I was sure neither kid had ever witnessed such affection at Artarmon.

Eight

Maggie muses...

Mr. Puntila and his Man Matti's great reviews were but icing on the cake. My major thrill in the entire exercise was Evan coming so often to rehearsals, then performances. I was so proud that he enjoyed not just the play, but befriending so many of the cast. And brought the children on occasions.

I enjoyed reminiscing on that because the entire experience proved a big part in learning to understand him. Bringing him so much joy simply thrilled me—joy enough that I moved in with him.

"The children don't seem at all jealous, Mags," he had told me. "They even express pride in you joining our family."

That's just the way I feel about it. Except I worry that they want to move in also. Evan assures me however, that that cannot happen.

"Leanne really feels part of the Stroud family now," he said. "She loves mum-Lynn as she calls her, as much it seems, as if they were mother and daughter."

Paul, however, still shows he would like to be living with us.

"Mum-Lynn and Uncle Norman are all right, I guess," he had said. "And Maggie will make a good mum-Maggie, I reckon."

Evan had had to explain that his and my relationship was as much business as personal, that we were career people, that I was not the domestic type. He used the fact that I needed time out to do things like acting on stage instead of housekeeping...

"That's why we have a woman come in to do housework," he had explained.

I can't help but feel it leaves Paul somewhat stranded on an island, yet Evan understands my side of it and keeps batting on my wicket.

"When the beach-house is finished will be your opportunity to be a foursome," he assured Paul. "And I still come for dinner at Artarmon as always."

And I liked Evan's quick answer when Paul asked the difficult question... "Maggie doesn't always come with you. Why not?"

"Because she has things to do at home, as do all career women. She has family in England to write to, has personal things like laundry to do, same as mum-Lynn—things that need to be done at home some nights."

So while things have not all been smooth and easy, Evan is open enough to tell me these trouble sides of our relationship, certainly an encouraging sign. I would feel dreadful if he were bottling things up.

Her mind flashed back to one night when dining with Liz and Jane.

"I am careful, however, in not openly admitting that I don't like Lynn Stroud. She is almost Puritan in her outlook, even prudish. She simply lacks qualifications to be anything but common."

"And her husband?"

"Oh, poor Norman. He is a good husband for her because he doesn't stand up to her. She runs the family. She is the one with money and poor Norman just trails along. Lynn has no style yet maintains rule. I agree with Evan that this is not a good environment for his children, yet nor can we see a better option."

"You feeling sorry you bought into all this?" they had asked.

"Not at all, Liz. I dearly love Evan, more and more every day. And I like the children. Paul idolises his father and I like the lad immensely. Leanne is already, however, beginning to become the Lynn type; not at all a promising future for her, yet she seems happy living there."

"You rethinking your own life in some little way?"

"No, Jane. Life with Evan continues to dominate how I feel and think, but it doesn't include his children. He keeps assuring me that he has no problem pursuing a life with us living as just a working couple. He has his domestic family life on week-ends. He even changed things in the weekender so we can have our private moments, or for me to hibernate while they do their family things."

"He is not jealous of your time with theatre?"

"Not at all. He finds it a thrilling new experience. For the first time, he is meeting people with such different outlooks on life. He calls it 'a real-life pull-through'. At the after-theatre parties, he quickly got to know the cast, even became a favourite of 'old Les'. And of Zoe, who has 'foresworn more husbands than I can count'. She jokingly tells everyone, 'because theatre gives me more thrills than any man has ever come close to'. Evan loved that.

"I watched Zoe follow him into the toilet one night, wagging a good natured finger. He later told me she had kept wagging the finger, assuring him that she was my surrogate mother and he would have her to contend with if he ever caused me hurt."

I just loved the way he told me after that, that such incidents only made him love me more.

~ * ~

Evan muses...

Occasionally Mags and I snatched a social evening out with either her friends or mine—work-mates or simply social friends. Coming up was the occasion of what my workplace called its 'annual ball.' She brought from Toongara Road, two long frocks.

"I'm not a long-gown person, darling, but 'acquired' these two magnificent formal ball-gowns."

When she held each against her, I gulped.

"Beautiful indeed, my darling. But absolutely overkill for this night. We call it our 'ball' yet it is quite informal. It calls for something chic—a night-club effect."

But I ogled the gowns.

"These must have cost a fortune, Mags."

"I can see in your eyes, darling, that you are thinking how unlike me they are. The blue one is a *Balenciaga*. The lilac one a *Givenchy*. I have never worn the *Balenciaga* and only once, the *Givenchy*."

"Why buy them?"

She answered with a hearty laugh. "I never bought them. They would have cost thousands. Kay gave them to me. They were left over after some promo thing she had been part of organising. Neither is new. Both had come from a Once Loved store. She was too tall for them as well as too skinny, so gave them to me. I've ever since thought it was her way of helping me out of a tight financial period at the time, expecting I would sell them back to the same store. Yet they are just so beautiful that I've kept them for some other needy friend. They aren't good fits for me, anyway."

She had told me about Kay. Kay lived and worked in Canberra, part of the Prime Minister's Press Corps. Maggie ever referred to her as the sort of sister she had always wanted.

"Fortunately, I have chic stuff. I will let you choose what you want me to wear."

She laid out a series on the bed.

"In any one of them, darling, I shall be proud to have you on my arm."

~ * ~

"Saw a leather divan in a shop window, Mags. I think you'd like it."

"Like what?"

She shuffled an omelette around the frypan while I chopped mushrooms. Fred was in the shower.

"A deep brown leather, still in excellent nick, all heavily studded in a mahogany frame, wing-backed, or 'cosy-cornered' as I've heard you call them. It would fit our sitting room pretty well."

"How much?"

Don't know. Wanted to sound you out first. We can go look at it on Saturday?"

"Where?"

"Glebe. Just off Parramatta Road."

"Fine. Can we look along Glebe Point Road? Girls at the office know an antique jewellery shop I would like to check out. I'll ask today, exactly where."

"Sure. What are you looking for?"

"A necklace to go with my new red leather."

Maggie had bought a formal suit in a red verging on maroon, all in a brushed-suede. I loved her in it. She capped it off with high-topped boots in a deep tan suede.

"I want you to wear that gear every time I'm to be seen with you," I told her.

Come Saturday, being winter and too cold for surfing, Paul was in a parade with his school, and Leanne and foster sister Sue were clothes-shopping with mum-Lynn.

We left early for Glebe. Mags loved the divan and I bought it. She found her jewellery store and bought a choker-pendant—an amber bauble set in beaten silver.

While she fed the washing machine and drier, I made sandwiches to eat in the car and took off alone for my beach-house inspection. I was beginning to get annoyed with the builder over the slowing progress.

Other jobs are for local people who keep hounding him. He can be harassed by them on a face-to-face daily basis, of course, while mine is but weekly. If I don't get there regularly, I'll likely find further delays.

I mulled threatening to with-hold regular payments until the job was complete.

~ * ~

Meanwhile, Maggie's mind was on other thoughts...

With him in that sort of mood, the washing machine promises better company, so I'm happy I'm not going with him. Also, of course, someone has to be home to receive the divan.

Which led her on a different tack...

"I'm pleased the old divan from his time with Kit is going to the beach-house," she told the drying machine. "It was pop-modern stuff for the time and won't live with our new divan at all."

Come Sunday, we shared the task of wallpapering the living room.

"I always understood paper-hanging is fraught with messy accidents, darling," she said, watching him 'wiping' over the pasted paper with a folded towel. "You make it look easy."

He had come home from the beach in a reasonably better mood, the builder having promised to finish all but the landscaping by March.

"Just long enough," Paul bemoaned, "to miss out being ready for summer!"

So with the builder's promise, he felt it a good idea to tackle the wallpapering while his mind stayed positive. With help from the kids, it was going well.

Nine

Maggie and I committed our lives to marriage.

Oh, what a lengthy stride in life that was!

So many times I had wondered if I might take that step again, but only until she chanced into my life. I had never since met someone I could imagine a lifetime partner, yet since Cat's farewell, I'd thought only of how happy Maggie made me.

Sure there are the odd times a question-mark raises itself, mostly on the kids. Each time I've come down to realising how much of a good influence she is on them. She has a clear picture of what life should be about, but is that only because everything seems to run according to how she wants them? Or is it that she is simply an amenable character? We certainly seem well suited in the cot, as well as socially.

My mind again strayed to Lynn Stroud, a habit I wished I could better control. I couldn't imagine her in physical contact with a man, let alone the adventurous sex of exploring and teasing. There simply seemed not that sort of goal in her life.

I understand Mags not liking her. Mags is a woman so compatible with everyone she's had to face, from those of the

London Diplomatic Corps to the theatre crowd, or Fred and his overnight lovers. Lynn has seldom looked beyond what Victorian morals demand of women. And Norman trots at her heels like a lap dog.

Can Maggie see me as one who shuffles love in different ways? For her? For my children? For my mother and sister? She knows how many letters arrive from Lulu, and phone-calls from Valerie, so clearly sees I am from a close family. With me having buried a wife, sister having buried a husband and Lulu buried three, I wonder if she feels somewhat insecure in marrying into such a family?

I had to quickly cast such a bizarre thought aside.

Maggie is certainly not one to pay credence to superstition. Such is but too vapid or banal a consideration. She has said she wants to marry me, content to leave the children where they are and I can have as much time with them as I want. She thoroughly supports the idea of me going off alone with them to the beach-house. She simply does not want children of our own and I certainly don't want more. What I want is a companion and I can imagine no other giving me the satisfactions I get from her. She is a gem. I see every reason why we should marry.

She indeed met every qualification in my understanding of the word marriage.

~ * ~

Arriving home from the office, Mags informed me she had made it clear to Fred that she was taking me out to dinner.

"She told me," Fred interrupted, "to keep my door shut and take no notice of any noise coming from your bedroom later tonight!" He grinned wolfishly.

I had no idea what might have happened to have my Mags in such a mood.

Certainly I'm not concerned about the consequences, but what brought it on? Why insist Fred must hide in his room wearing ear-muffs?

Something big was up, for Mags was dressed in her red leather and had a Bristol Cream poured for me.

"We dine at *Café Accogliente*, darling. I have booked for seven thirty p.m.

I took a quick shower, splashed myself with *Aramis* and pulled a tweed jacket over a sports shirt.

"Is this formal enough to escort a gorgeous blond dressed for the catwalk?"

I was given a deep kiss.

We were led to the quietest little corner of the restaurant where a tiny waterfall trickled over greenery and a lonely candle lit our table.

Our feet, each clad in suede, played footsies under the table.

We held hands whenever not eating or raising wine-glasses.

Donato and Gina served us, leaving the kitchen to their younger generation.

"I've taught them all I know and they now are putting it into practice," Maggie translated to me.

"Oh, does that put other thoughts in your mind?"

"Only that I want to further ravage you."

She did. There had been no answer to her mood, other than that she wanted a special night of loving.

~ * ~

"What sort of engagement ring would you like?"

Part of our 'practical outlook on life' was that it was less sensible for me to buy a ring she might like, than going together to choose one she did.

It was opal. "Unlike diamonds, my pet, the opal has such boundless variations in colour and soft tones."

At a city opal jeweller she chose a stone with the softest of light blue and orange 'swirls'. The setting? A teasing 'swirl' in itself. In gold—a fine thread weaving itself around the stone—entirely a 'made-to-order' situation.

Also decided was that our wedding would be private, just my close family and her close friends.

"I'm not a girl big on Wedding Bells and a long guest-list," she insisted. "To me, marriage is strictly a personal affair."

I had already had my big social wedding, black tie and tails at *St. Phillips* on Sydney's Church Hill, right at the city end of the great harbour bridge. It was the parish founded by the First Fleet settlers. But that marriage was a long way behind me now.

We came up with holding a pre-wedding 'bash' for social friends—a noisy big party. Fred would move out so the apartment became our private tryst. Because of his special relationship with us, however, he was the only one invited to both our pre-wedding 'bash' and our catered 'family' wedding breakfast at home.

"You are sort of family, my love," Maggie insisted.

Re the 'bash', we carefully worded up neighbours in our building's block of four, that we would possibly be making a little noise come Saturday night.

Wow, was that ever an understatement? We had as many from the theatre group as could turn up, even if only after their current performances had closed for the night. I had my four salesmen from work with their wives. Jane, Liz and their *beaux* came, many other personal friends including Mag's workmates and some of my mates, even dating back to school days. I made my special punch that really shook people's eyes open on reading the recipe framed on my kitchen wall.

My punch took three days to make. It called for not only hiring a fridge big enough to hold the largest garbage can, but buying the new can. Once scrubbed and 'sanitized' it required for its first overnight, sliced oranges, chopped apples and large chunks of watermelon maturing in a bottle of rum. Over party eve I added a half bottle each of Gin for the English, Whisky for Scots, Brandy for French, Vodka should any Russian gate-crash, two litres of white wine, two dozen Coolers and many splits of soda-water. On party day, not only were loads of crushed ice added, but six bottles of Champagne were on hand for topping up as the level subsided.

One incident I ever remembered of that night was when a mob from the theatre arrived about midnight...

"What's the punch like?" asked someone.

Zoe had arrived early and was, in that moment, supine on the sitting-room floor, head lost to view beneath the Grundig, my prized five-speaker Hi-Fi. The rest of her body was visibly stretched out, an arm protruding from under, its hand clutching her half filled goblet.

"What's the punch like?" came Zoe's voice from down-under. "I've had three and they're not doing a bloody thing for me!"

Others insisted it went down well.

"Anyone who sleeps over," we explained, "will find the fruit in the bottom of the can, prime for breakfast."

Ten

I talked with the kids at length about me marrying.

"It's about time," Paul exploded. "Several mates at school have been counting how many months you've already been shacked up."

Mags, when I told her, laughed. "What did you reply to your thirteen-year old?"

"I told him he should take bets with his mates and string the time out.

"That's not fair on the boy, darling. That's teaching him to cheat. When I next see, him, I will tell him so."

"Something else that he told me, Mags, made me happy."

She raised that one eyebrow.

"He wants to give up Rugby. 'I'm just no good at it, Dad.' was his reason, which pleased me. I knew it, for I'd seen plenty of his play and he simply hadn't been getting good training. I've been doing my bit, for as you know, I've been there as line-umpire and sometimes even match referee on weekends, and I'm the first to agree many of those lads weren't being taught the science of the game. But I'm thrilled he recognised it for himself. It illustrates a thinking mind."

"Maybe his mind keeps reminding him of your competitive swimming, darling."

"Maybe so. I've certainly told him that to take sport seriously one must train exhaustively. All he wants to pursue in sports, Mags, is surf-boarding. I bought him a board for his tenth birthday, having no idea what I was starting. He now thinks of little else by way of sport."

All that had little to do, however, with planning our wedding—when we could get time off from work, when Lulu and Valerie could come from Brisbane, when Kay could come from Canberra, when the kids' school timetable could fit in? All had to be juggled. We found it could work best if we went for our honeymoon before the wedding.

"Not a problem," said I.

Maggie had never travelled to Queensland and it would also be opportunity to meet my family before the wedding. We'd had the pre-wedding bash for friends, so now drove the thousand kilometres to Gold Coast, Australia's 'little Miami', staying at the *Surfer's Paradise Hotel.* Mags was content for me to get in some body-surfing each of our three days. She had no intention of venturing into a surf but purchased a swimsuit and the biggest floppy straw hat I had ever seen, its fabric band and tail, matching the swimsuit.

She looked great in it but spent her time relaxing on a king-sized beach-towel, under a big umbrella, reading.

We drove through Brisbane to the Sunshine Coast where we found Perigean, a mile-long empty surf beach. Twenty-five years later it was to be a Mecca with towering apartment blocks the length of it, yet in January Nineteen seventy-one was still in its natural grandeur; no buildings and no people.

We set our umbrella into the sand and spent the day naked, or at least Maggie nearly so. It was nothing new for me, having been a naked surfer since schooldays. Only people we saw all day were a mother and daughter, also naked. They waved to us from near the water-line where hard sand made walking easier.

In Brisbane, Lulu and Valerie took Maggie to heart. I had been worried about the meeting, yet they made her thoroughly welcome.

After several days it was agreed Lulu would ride back to Sydney with us. I preferred to drive straight through and she insisted she would be happy sleeping in back of the big car. She wanted the several days extra to visit sisters living in Sydney. She didn't enjoy flying and was keen to avoid a 'down' flight to Sydney on her own, as well as an 'up' flight home with Valerie.

We loaded the back seat with cushions for her. Valerie would fly down the day before the wedding, then they would fly home together, the day after.

During the night hours of the journey, Maggie and I chatted while Lulu snoozed.

When we could hear little snoring sounds, Mags whispered...

"I just had a thought."

"Yes, my darling?"

"We will be arriving a day earlier than Fred is expecting."

"So?"

"Hasn't Fred, when we have been away at the beach-house, used our big bed when 'entertaining'?"

I used my spare hand to slap my temple. "Bloody hell, yes."

It now struck me that the spare bed Lulu would be using was in the veranda-room, its only access through our bedroom. We would be arriving in the early morning hours, two or three a.m.!

"Oh, bloody hell," I said again.

We had agreed that mother meeting Fred would not be a problem. He was pretty straight in his way. Even knowing he was gay would be okay with her, yet in getting to her own bed, being confronted with him in bed with a naked gay lover could certainly be more than she could take with a shrug. Especially when it was our bed!

"We do indeed need give it thought, my dear."

Mmmm.

Our building was of only four apartments, two up and two down. We were an 'up' and the stairway lights were on a time-switch turning off at midnight. They were turned on by a switch that automatically turned off after two minutes. Our veranda-room faced the street, our bedroom directly behind it. Any light switched on in either, could be seen from the street.

"Is she still sleeping?" I whispered.

She turned to check. "Yes."

"When home, then Mags, you stay with Lulu by the car at the kerb. I shall tell her to wait while I go up and turn on lights so she can manage the stairs. Maybe you could keep her fiddling with luggage or something?"

We arrived at two-thirty and it was moonless. Nearest street light was outside the train-station a hundred metres away. Mother woke as we stopped.

"I'll see if I can juggle the stair light system so we can get luggage up. I don't like leaving things in the car overnight. You girls wait here, please."

I unlocked the boot for Maggie, then went in.

Turning on the stairwell lights, I ran up and let myself into the apartment. I knew the girls could see the glow from our vestibule light. Our bedroom was off to its left, the sitting room off to its right. The vestibule light would let enough glow into our bedroom for me to see the situation there.

Yes, Fred is entertaining in our bed.

I knew Maggie, as the delay increased, would realise the situation.

She will be smiling inside, I know, picturing what must be going on up here.

I shook Fred's shoulder. Startled, he looked up and saw me in the soft light.

"You are not due home until tomorrow," he stammered.

"Maggie is down at the car trying to keep my mother occupied while you and your friend get into your room and close the door!"

He quickly grasped the situation and began rousing his friend, a bewildered stranger obviously as startled as Fred himself.

The friend was grabbing his clothes, Fred trying to help, all at double-quick time.

"Michael, this is Evan. Evan, this is Michael."

Michael and I shook hands as the two naked fellows, still startled and in their haste, tripped over shoes on the floor. I gathered them up.

They were eventually, with all their clothes, closeted in Fred's room.

"Fred, please have Michael quietly out of here before six in the morning?"

He understood. I apologised to Michael and raced back to my room to make something tidy out of the mess the bed was in. I could imagine Maggie trying to find reasons to explain why lights were flashing on and off and what was taking me so long to organise the stair lights.

However, all was well. Next morning, Lulu was introduced to the lone Fred as the four of us sat for breakfast.

They got on famously.

~ * ~

The wedding was a quiet Registry Office affair. Valerie came from Brisbane, Kay from Canberra, the Strouds and three kids from nearby Artarmon, and Liz and Jane from Toongara Road.

Our Champagne Breakfast at home was timed that we would phone Maggie's parents in Luton so they could 'meet' me as son-in-law. We chatted backwards and forwards for some time.

Champagne choice had become *Veuve Clicquot*. It was fortunately not the most expensive but certainly Maggie's favourite. Even Lynn decided it would be bad manners to refuse, so she and Norman sipped at a shared flute.

One of the strangest things about the wedding was that Fred had come the previous night to present us with an electric frypan and gave us, with lots of hugs, many warm kisses. But he didn't show up at the wedding, nor leave us any contact number. Next day I phoned the only friend of Fred whose number I had, to be told he didn't know how to contact Fred. I knew it for a white lie.

We never heard from Fred again.

Had he felt that our marriage had somehow changed our relationship?

We never did figure it out, for it had all been so amicable, almost loveable.

Eleven

Three weeks after marriage, I arrived home with a problem.

"You are not going to like it, Mags."

She raised the devilish eyebrow. "What, my darling?"

"I've been given a marketing assignment. It will have me away several weeks."

DRC of Bristol, UK, five years ago, had bought out several packaging companies in Sydney and Melbourne, including the plant I had been with for twenty years. One of its Melbourne operations was losing money.

"They want me to spend a week in Melbourne swatting up on its product potential and equipment, and to assess its management weaknesses."

"To what end?"

"To then do a market survey of present and lost customers. It will mean visits to Melbourne again, then Brisbane and Adelaide. Then Sydney. I've to then recommend the company's future. Do we re-equip it? Replace its management? Sell it?"

She let out a great sigh. "Is that all? I've already told you, darling, that anything to do with your career is okay by me. When must you go?"

I bent down and kissed her. She was sitting over a cryptic crossword while the lamb chops grilled.

"Grant Gorman told me to try fitting it into a month, as quickly as I can arrange cover for my work here. My boss has been 'asked' to grant me a month's leave."

She knew Grant was CEO Australia. She had met him on two occasions.

DRC International was no small operation in the world's printing-packaging industry. It employed twenty-four-thousand people in twelve countries. Its only goal was to keep shareholders happy by increasing profits each year. Requests translated as Orders. It was always a matter of 'front up, or else'.

So during our second month of marriage, she would see little of me and nor could the children. Yet Mags was to prove of immense help in my assignment.

The most modern recording device was the pocket-sized microtape-recorder. I had made it a feature of my responsibility in company sales, indeed a revolutionary move to earn many a congratulation. The recorder mini-tape held an hour of dictation each side. By phone from Melbourne I had instructed my Secretary to buy a second transcribing machine and instruct Maggie on its use.

The office transcriber was used for Salesman's reports, so this would give me one at home also. My salesmen never wrote a word. I insisted their role was 'out there' in front of prospects, increasing both customer base and sales. Every time they walked in from the field they swapped their full tape with my secretary for a refreshed tape. From their's, she filled out the factory orders so the rep could get back to selling.

The transcriber was operated by foot-pedal and ear phones. Over weekends, Maggie typed up tapes I was daily despatching by air-courier. In that way I quickly had all my interview notes ready for editing my report.

"You are a gem!" I told her time out of number.

My assignment took five-weeks during which, as a surprise for me, she had had a company re-upholster our dining-room chairs.

That was to have been Fred's job, yet all was now done. She chose a fabric to match the curtain colours she had in mind.

Having submitted my report to top management, I was anxious to return to my normal routine. Only ten days later, however, another bombshell burst.

Whilst every one of my recommendations had received the 'Go' signal, a great boost to my confidence and prospects was announced when offered the General Manager position of the subject company. In Melbourne.

~ * ~

"I move to Melbourne, or say farewell to my DRC career, Mags."

I knew she would understand the ramifications, yet all must appear ugly to her.

And my career? I would need my children to come! The beach house? Leaving the Sydney I love? Maggie leaving the theatre and her many friends?

She knows enough of large companies to realise it a 'do it or else' situation. I know only that I cannot refuse. I simply have to find a way of suffering the pains.

She slipped an arm around my shoulder.

"I vowed to make whatever sacrifices I must, to help you on your career path, my darling. We shall simply move to Melbourne. We just have to talk around what happens re the children and beach house."

~ * ~

"Let me start by saying," she told me as we went to bed that night, "I realise that from your career point of view, you must accept. Also on the good side, Melbourne claims itself the arts centre of the country—its opera, ballet and stage are all more highly renowned than Sydney's despite the wonderful Opera House here. My attitude to leaving is positive. Didn't I move across the world on an impulse?"

I held her tightly and kissed her deeply.

"You again make me realise what a lucky bastard I am."

"And clever," she said with a wicked grin.

"Another advantage, of course, Mags, is the leap in salary. We can afford live-in boarding school for the kids. Surely there are such that cater for both boys and girls who can meet every day? I certainly need my kids under my control. Staying with the Strouds has too many drawbacks for me to sacrifice my kids to, without regular direct input from me."

"I understand that too. If you want them with us, it need not interfere with my finding satisfying work if we can afford a housekeeper. Don't yet despair. There can be lots of ways of looking at the difficulties."

"Copacabana?"

"Admittedly there is not much option on the beach house. Maybe rather than selling straight away, you can look at renting it out? That gives us time to mull the question further?"

"I must take the kids, Mags, but I promise to pursue the idea of boarding school."

"Of course you must. That is already behind us. How we live around having them is the only question. If I read them properly, Paul will be happy being with you, albeit sad at losing the beach house. I simply don't know how Leanne will react."

"She won't want to come. Nothing against you, my pet. Lynn Stroud simply has the child tied into that household. Now this option has forced me to a decision, I can admit that I now have opportunity of getting them out of there. Norman knows how I feel. He somehow transmits apologies for Lynn, yet he hasn't the guts to make a stand. He's already regressed into a man without confidence. He can't keep a regular job and even if he did, he could never progress. He's lost any ability to put up his hand to be noticed, let alone make any kind of decision. I'll be pleased to have Paul away from there. And Leanne, but yes, we may have problems there."

After my next dinner at Artarmon, I was able to tell Mags what was decided.

"What gives all some leeway in making the break, is that whilst I must be in Melbourne by July, Paul finishes primary school in December, to begin High School come February. I don't want him changing two schools and friendships in so short a time. Also, my pet, you and I are both going to have so many changes to adopt in our early days there; accommodation, a worthwhile job for you, loss of ready friends, a new company for me, a company in a big bloody mess. All will be easier to accomplish without the children. Letting them stay at Artarmon to finish out the school year makes the move easier on all of us."

"Was everyone agreeable?"

"Lynn wanted to wait until the children were abed, to then talk about it. I insisted they should be part of the decision-making. Lynn still believes children should simply do as they are told, without having input. I believe they would more readily adopt change if privy to its reasoning."

Maggie put a hand on my arm.

"Absolutely. However, this will give Lynn another six months to win Leanne even closer?"

In the back of my mind was the same rumbling—also a rumbling closer to home.

Is Maggie facing a possible conflict in life that is to only slowly emerge?

"Things are not so easy with Paul either, Mags. He raised a personal difficulty on something else. I hadn't realised how desperately important was the beach-house and joining the beach-club, part of his future. Unbeknown to us, he has had such an excitement in mind, a thrill desperately looked forward to. He also realises that Melbourne's nearest surf is some two hour's drive from the city—a city you and I must live close to."

~ * ~

On the train next morning, Maggie filled Jane in on the upheaval.

"Everything had been so well planned, Jane. I know how unexpected changes can simply drop in one's lap, yet I've always been able to face them. But I was the only person involved. I could quickly choose to stay on in Italy when you went home. I had you to come back to when I had the yen to return home. No dependent children were involved when you and I wanted to risk moving to the other end of the world. But his children do cause a problem for my man. Against his wishes, he needs to disappoint me."

"I know your fiercely independent streak, Mags. When changes have happened, you have been able to overlook negative aspects. I know you can accept risk. Yes, we've taken many together and you've taken independent ones beginning with leaving Luton. You make friends easily and you've adapted to all the changes I've seen happen in your life. I have confidence that you can accept burdens you are not happy with, given time to adjust. You've proved it."

She is right, of course. I've made my independent streak work! I do homework! And I'm lucky at Evan being a man ready to talk through problems. We've both seen enough of the business world to realise there can be only one best course.

"I guess, dear Jane, I've always been able to land good jobs. So I can do it in Melbourne. And I have a man who considers me. I can live with stress areas while he, with the kids, is limited. But yes, we can talk on such things."

"Liz and I are devastated at losing you, but we understand your now responsibility of going with him. We see how happy you are together, to realise it would be a great tragedy if you didn't."

Both had tears running down their cheeks.

"I shall brush up on my Shorthand again. I will return to Secretarial work."

"You'll seek an apartment?"

"Evan's been told not to rush into buying. He reckons it could take two or three years to turn this company around and I intend helping. At least he doesn't bottle up problems. I think I can help keep up his confidence."

Jane patted Maggie's thigh. "Great spirit, girl."

They were pulling into Town Hall. Jane gathered up her things and joined the throngs already shuffling into the aisle. Maggie turned off the welling tears and looked forward to the train bursting into the daylight within the next few minutes.

It caused her to wonder if Melbourne, a riverside city rather than harbour-side, a class-conscious city compared to Sydney's cosmopolitan trend, according to Evan, had underground trains that burst into blue skies of sunshine?

Twelve

We drove the long road to Melbourne, skirting the coast.

"Never having travelled in Australia, my sweet, you will see why this New South Wales' south coast is renowned for its beauty. We shall be three slow days, resting up in motels," I said.

Not only had Maggie never taken a three day car journey, she had never travelled in a car so heavily laden. Furniture was being shipped to Melbourne by pantechnicon, for storage until called for, yet we must bring with us all we would need before having permanent accommodation—every stitch of clothing and accessories, desktop stuff, even all treasured potted plants.

Three of Paul's surfboards were strapped on roof-racks because he wouldn't risk them with removalists, and our boot wouldn't fit even a one cent coin. The back seat area was full of garden pots and plants.

"Just as well you have a big car, darling."

"They told me to take not more than a two year lease on 'something nice'. They made a point of it being a home with an image befitting a General Manager. They will subsidise twenty-five percent of its rent."

We talked about the children's schooling. I was yet unaware if colleges made provision for company transfers, but otherwise, even getting a boy into a decent one would be almost impossible.

"I booked him into Shore, a Great Public School in Sydney when he was a tot, Mags. And I guess Melbourne's GPS schools are the same."

We talked more on the Stroud family, for it had become high priority.

"Lynn Stroud lives in yesterday's world, Mags. She has no friends. She lives in a cocoon. And Leanne is a vulnerable kid. Paul is more like you, Mags, can flow with the breeze and make the best of things—an adventurous spirit. Leanne is a follower needing guidance. She will never get it from Norman either. He's even admitted to me over a beer which he has to keep hidden from Lynn that he can never get out from under the woman's domination.

"I reaffirmed my appreciation for his taking the kids in. He can see they'll be better off in the long-run, removed from Lynn's persona. But I am really concerned about finding a mixed-gender boarding school, particularly when Paul is due for High School in the New Year and Leanne still has two years in primary."

She laid a hand on my thigh and gave it a squeeze.

It had been agreed amongst all, that we should 'play things by ear' until December when I would drive to Sydney to collect the children, or the Strouds would put them on a plane or sleeper-train.

"By then, Mags, we shall know about the school situation."

~ * ~

On arriving in Melbourne, we were in for several pleasant surprises.

First was that the company had booked us into a hotel on a gloriously impressive tree-lined boulevard.

"It reminds me of the magnificent *Champs Elysées*," opined Maggie.

Second was that the hotel staff raised no qualms when requesting plastic floor coverings for their carpet, for our indoor plants, nor for having to carry some score of the ceramic pots with advanced foliage up in the lifts. They also happily stored Paul's surf-boards in their 'left luggage' store. We also gave them five portmanteau-sized bags to store there. None seemed phased by our large amount of luggage.

"No doubt, they'll be used to company transfers, Mags."

Third was when, at the rental company recommended by the hotel, discovering that Melbourne rentals were considerably cheaper than Sydney's.

"Grant's 'Get something nice'," instruction still rang in my ears.

I left Maggie to inspect houses while I dove straight into my new responsibilities, first being to assign a man to take my car through a car wash while I sat with Dawn, my Secretary, getting to understand each other.

Maggie called on the hotel's recommended Job Option consultants. She had her updated *résumé* and glowing references tucked into her luggage, along with her still current British Mensa Certificate. She left it with them.

"I shall inform you once finding accommodation," she advised them.

On only our third day, Mags told me on arriving back at our hotel suite that she had found an absolutely divine house.

"I want you to see it by daylight, my love. It is something I am sure you will love. I've beaten, not the agent, but the owner, down to not a penny more than we were paying at Waverton."

"Where?"

At my suggestion, Maggie had, on her first day there, purchased two copies of the latest Melbourne street-directory, one for my car and one for the house when we found one. I drove us to it on my next day's lunch-hour.

"St. George's Court, Toorak, darling. It's a half-house. The widow owner lives in the other half."

My breath caught. "I know enough of Melbourne to know that Toorak is where the Prime Ministers and Chairmen of major corporations live. They don't live in mere houses, they have mansions."

"This is not a mansion, darling, it is indeed a house—a half house with two bedrooms and bath up, a living room, dining-room and kitchen down, along with a maid's room with shower that will be ideal for Paul."

We arrived in what was certainly a cul-sac of elegant homes. When Maggie pointed, I thumped a hand to my temple. It was indeed elegant, a modern house right in the end of the Court. As I opened my car door, the house door opened and a graceful grey-haired woman emerged.

I reckon she wants to meet me to see if I pass muster too.

She stood between a pair of potted Bay Trees standing sentinel each side of the door, watching us walk down the path.

Mrs. Carmody shook my hand and stood back to let us enter first.

"It is a very quiet neighbourhood, Mr. Robson Just three doors around on St. George's Road was the home of Prime Minister Holt until he was lost, poor man, just after my own husband died. Dame Zara has recently sold it and bought a smaller place, just a street or two away."

All Aussies knew about Harold Holt's 'loss'. The Prime Minister had dived into the surf near his weekender south of Melbourne, never to emerge. His body was never found. His mansion was just a hundred or two metres away.

'Our' house was unfurnished. Both living and dining rooms had bay windows, the first to the front garden, the other to the rear. The large kitchen was well-appointed.

"You will find a double garage into the back street, Mr. Robson. You may have full use of it, for I do not drive, so have no motor-car."

I turned to Maggie. "Are you sure of your figuring. Maggie? On the rent?"

She put hands to hip like Liz and raised her eyebrow, saying not a word.

Mrs. Carmody smiled at the silent reproach.

I turned to the lady who had all the appearances of having just returned from her hairdresser and beautician. "You see where I stand in some matters, Mrs. Carmody. My wife is, I continue discovering, highly apt in a great number of areas. And I've yet to fault her. However, I shall take her silent word for it. We both like your house. A two year lease?"

"Yes, Mr. Robson."

"You've no objection to children? We will be fetching my son and daughter from Sydney at end of the school year. They are fourteen and twelve?"

"That is already established with Mrs. Robson. But I do not want pets in my house or garden. A bird in a cage would be no problem."

"We have no pets, so shall acquire none."

Having enquired of my work situation, satisfying herself that we were moving on a company transfer, she seemed wholly satisfied.

"Thank you, Mr. Robson. Having met you both, I am pleased to have you taking the house. The telephone here is operating, so may I call the agent in the village so you can agree a time to see him, sign the agreement and arrange with him how you will pay your rent?"

She is a lovely old lady, well into her seventies I should think, with a quiet, slow voice. She has as much said, 'I've checked you out and found you satisfactory, so am now brushing you off on to the agent.'

I phoned Dawn to let her know I would not be back, that I was seeing to a lease agreement. We visited the agent and formalised the lease, then arranged for our furniture and other chattels to be delivered on Saturday.

"What we still need do, darling," I proffered on leaving the agent, is go into the city and open an account at Myers, Melbourne's top department store. Tonight, we can have a celebratory dinner."

We parked the car at the hotel and took our first ride in a Melbourne tram, across the Yarra-Yarra River, the ten minutes to downtown. We called at Westpac and affirmed they had our transfer of bank accounts in hand, and could now give them our address. We not only opened our Myers account but placed there, an order for name cards at our now 'home' address.

We enjoyed an amusing incident at Myers. On quoting our address, the clerk suddenly squared his shoulders, raising his chin an inch. He inflected a considerably more businesslike manner in his speech and excused himself. Maggie and I looked at each other, shrugging shoulders.

Next minute, the clerk returned, trailing the Accounts Manager.

"My name is Morgan," he introduced himself. The clerk furnished him with the paperwork to date and Morgan asked us to follow him. We completed our mission in his large office and he bowed almost obsequiously on seeing us out.

"Do not hesitate to call me personally if you have a hitch in our accounting," he farewelled us, having given us his card.

Going down in the elevator we had quite a laugh, wondering if that would always be our reaction when quoting our address. And walking down the street for the tram, I explained, "Melbourne is considered Australia's Old Establishment city. Whilst Sydney is developing into a cosmopolitan centre, Melbourne retains its British interpretation of Class."

At the hotel, I phoned Grant Gorman, my now direct boss, a Melbourne denizen.

"Our furniture is being delivered on Saturday, Grant."

"Great news, I'm happy for you. Where is your house?"

I gave him the address.

I had to wait, shrugging shoulders at Maggie.

"Everything has gone silent," I whispered.

"Did I hear right?" Grant asked.

I repeated the address and held the phone out so Maggie could hear.

"Fuck! How much are you paying?"

I told him, and waited while he did some mental calculation.

"That's bloody good. Is that the monthly rental showing on your lease?"

He sounded flummoxed.

"The monthly rental, having allowed the twenty-five percent subsidy that Bristol advised."

A further silence followed.

His pencil is flying!

"Okay. Wow, Evan, that will really give you impetus both in the works and with your clients. Make sure you quote it offhand. But only once. People never forget being told an address like that."

"Veiled message received and understood, sir."

He giggled. "What is your phone number?"

We chatted for a few minutes on things at the factory. I liked Grant Gorman. He was a professional manager. He had been CEO of many large combines and always moved when each was on a high. He was father of six children and a ruthless Managing Director.

I could see that Maggie too, had a big smile on her face.

We needed a new mattress. We had donated our old one in Sydney, to the Salvation Army.

"Did you notice both Mrs. Carmody and the agent pronounce Toorak as Trak?"

I explained that that seemed reserved for those who lived there.

Toorak was Melbourne's premier suburb, the Mayfair of London. Even the local shopping centre was designated: 'Trak Village'.

We had one more call to make. We knew exactly what bed mattress we wanted, having decided on it when quitting our old one. Maggie phoned Myers bedding department and ordered it, agreeing delivery for Saturday. When she gave the fellow the address, she told me on arriving home to the hotel... "I could swear I saw his spine straighten and his shoulders push back a notch."

We drank *Veuve Clicquot* with dinner that night.

Thirteen

Saturday was a mad, mad day.

The furniture arrived early. We had, on Friday evening, arranged with the hotel to hire, on our room account, a carrier to bring Paul's surfboards, the potted plants and our several portmanteaux on Saturday. I nominated the rear entrance into the big garage, to avoid the chance of two pantechnicon vans arriving at the same time.

Mrs. Carmody had left a large bouquet of flowers for us on the only table in the house, the built-in breakfast nook. She left a note asking us to return the vase when convenient—a very nice touch, we thought.

I bought cold beers in the village for the removal fellows once they'd finished, and had conscripted a couple of my own guys from the factory to help shuffling furniture about to Maggie's satisfaction.

"Thank God our dining-room chairs aren't still that awful gold," she told me. "I'd have died of shame."

But Myers failed to deliver the mattress.

"Not to worry, darling. Maybe it will come tonight, sort of after hours?"

It didn't.

"They won't open Sunday, of course, but we can call them first thing Monday."

"We are to quit the hotel tomorrow."

"You can sleep in Fred's old bed in Paul's room. I shall use a sleeping bag."

Leanne's bed was yet a note on a shopping list.

"I shall hate sleeping without you, darling, but I agree, Paul's bed is a crush."

"I reckon by tomorrow night, we'll still feel too damned exhausted to care."

~ * ~

We didn't rush into anything come Sunday.

After a leisurely breakfast we quit the hotel, calling at the Trak Village *Safeways* to stock up on food and various bits and pieces. We were both happy at so readily finding an ideal house and already our own things installed.

We talked about the types of packaging my new plant manufactured, and agreed that before she began working, she would come to the plant with me one morning, to be given a tour, then taxi home.

"It will make me feel more a part of your work, darling."

"And you will meet some of my people, too, my love."

"Yes, especially to take a look at this Dawn who you reckon is a 'bit-of-all-right'. I've personal experiences in how bosses word up secretaries."

We giggled over that and come Monday, I had a ten o'clock city appointment, so idling over breakfast, we tuned into the radio news.

In Federal Parliament on Friday, there had been considerable rumpus. Prime Minister Sir William MacMahon, popularly known as 'Billie' MacMahon had got himself involved in a colourful debate over trade. Assertions and counter assertions flew backwards and forwards. MacMahon was short of stature yet loud of voice when needed. I was keen to see if the Monday news had more on it.

So was it coincidence that Billie MacMahon had been so prominent in our minds when Maggie phoned Myers?

By now, of course, I was well acquainted with her ability to suddenly invoke her stage voice, a 'jolly good royal' British accent. She now gave me a wink when the Myers switchboard answered…

"Bedroom Furnishings, please."

I watched while she waited. Then…

"My husband and I ordered a mattress to be delivered Saturday. You let us down."

I waited.

"Robson, 9 Saint Georges Court, Trak."

She held the phone so I could hear the response.

"Oh, excuse me just a moment, please *madame*."

We waited until a slight click signalled the other end picking up.

"Good morning, madam. MacMahon here. Can I help you?"

Maggie winked at me, then slowly raised her eyebrow, to say in her most theatrical diction…

"Oh, Shit! They've put me on to the fuckin' Prime Minister!"

~ * ~

"I've been in giggles all day over that, Mags," I said on arriving home for dinner.

"I've had more than a few giggles myself. It arrived, of course, with a hand-written note of apology signed simply, Cedric MacMahon."

"Did he address the note, 'Dear Bitch'?"

"No, but I'm sure he would have felt inclined."

It was a moment I knew I would always remember.

"And your day?"

"House-tidying, darling, so I can tomorrow get on to looking for work. I rang the agency. The ever so chick woman of about forty or even more, who had interviewed me, said she was impressed by the resume and file of references I left with her. I…"

"I should think so, my dear."

She blew me a kiss.

"She asked my home address now that I have settled."

"And?"

"She was chick enough to make no comment, just asked if she could make an appointment for any time tomorrow. A prospective employer had seen my resume and is interested. Only ten minutes later, she called me back with a Collins Street address for a 10 a.m. interview."

"Company?"

"Melbourne Stock Exchange, no less."

"Mmm. Any more to add to that? Hint of what sort of position?"

"I have only his name and floor number. She told me that is all I need."

I held up crossed fingers, then went to the fridge.

I returned with a glass of wine each.

"Collins Street is a long street, but has trams. Can you collect those calling cards?"

"Consider it done, darling."

Fourteen

Five months later...

St. Georges Court continued an advantage to our kudos.

Also by then, the upsurge in the confidence of my people at the plant, especially as we had to increase staff and often raise a night-shift, was noticeable. As was the bottom line. I had introduced a quarterly Sunday barbecue in the factory's garden where employees could bring family. Many spouses met for the first time. It was but one of the morale-lifting systems used in the plant I had been with in Sydney.

"It all began from your visit to the plant, Mags," I told her in a joking way.

I had also had Maggie out to dinner evenings with my Accounts Manager with her husband, Production and Despatch Managers with their wives. The first had been to a pub near our plant and the other at our home, having that evening, catered.

I also had the accounting department post monthly spoilage rates in manufacture, for all to see.

"For every percent saved in spoilage over the previous month," I announced, "there will be a wage increase of one percent across the board in that department."

Soon, departments were vying to keep increasing their good record.

When I asked Grant Gorman for a guide to entertainment expenses, his canny answer was, "Spend what you consider reasonable, Evan. I will quickly tell you if I think it unreasonable."

I asked him to also note that only fifty percent of my entertaining expenses was spent on customers, the rest on my employees—lunches and social events."

Maggie gasped when I told her that. She had met Grant on several occasions and liked him, yet realised he would be a very hard man if tested too far.

"What did he have to say to that?"

"He quietly rose to his feet, picked a pencil from my desk and drew a little tick on my office wall."

"And your reaction?"

"I had Dawn buy an empty picture frame to mount over it."

Mags also was doing well. She was hired on her first interview, no less an honour than Personal Secretary to the Chairman of the Melbourne Stock Exchange. I took her out for a big celebratory dinner that night. *Veuve Clicquot* again.

She was sitting at my right hand rather than opposite, a habit we had developed since *La Pistache*. On this occasion, following my toast, she reached her left hand into my lap and grabbed my balls. With her right hand, she drank, then gave me a gorgeous smile. An expected side issue of her new position was that Insider Trading took on a whole new dimension in our lives. Spying into her boss's personal portfolio, however, wasn't needed. She was responsible for its recording.

"It's just that I have a good memory, darling," she gloated when informing me how well she was doing on the Stock Exchange. And she was as happy there, with her work situation and colleagues, as was I at DRC Bags.

Maggie also liked my Secretary, my 'bit-of-alright' Dawn, a grandmother returned to work until her husband retired.

~ * ~

Come December, end of the school year, I had agreed with Lynn and Norman that the kids share a private sleeper-train compartment. Maggie and I would meet them at Melbourne come Saturday morning.

We were there in good time, to be met by a tearful Paul.

"Where is your sister?"

"She jumped off the train at the last minute. She wanted to stay with mum-Lynn."

In a sort of stupor, we collected both his and Leanne's luggage, plus two more surfboards from the guard's van. On the drive home he told us a number of tales about mum-Lynn.

"She kept telling Leanne that you, Maggie, couldn't make a good mother. You were a bad woman for living with dad before you married."

"When Leanne jumped off the train, was mum-Lynn still on the platform?"

"Yes, Dad."

"Was Uncle-Norman there?"

"Yes. Then when the train started moving, only Uncle Norman waved good-bye."

Oh you poor little bugger, I thought, knowing Maggie was thinking the same. *To have to live with that stress all through the night!*

Paul started crying again. He was in back on his own. With Maggie not a driver, I pulled off onto the freeway verge, got out and climbed into the back seat with him.

"Did you get some breakfast, son?"

Between his sobs, he answered, "Yes, Dad. The conductor showed me last night how to get to the dining car for dinner. And you know what?"

I waited. The sobbing stopped and he was all excited.

"After breakfast, I walked all the way from our front carriage to the back. And gee, Dad, some people right at the back had to sit up in chairs all night!"

We got home, keeping up a running dialogue so he wasn't brooding on the dreadful night he must have spent. Also trying to make him feel welcome.

I could imagine what was going through Maggie's mind. She had several times put a hand on my thigh as we drove, and several times turned and talked with Paul.

Paul was not only amazed at the house we lived in, but thrilled to find he had an en-suite shower-room.

"Nice house," he summed up. He was quick to ask where were his surf-boards that we had brought on the roof-rack. He'd searched the house but couldn't find them. I told him to go look in the garage.

I was quickly on the phone to Artarmon. Young Sue answered.

"Is your father home, Sue?"

"Mum is here."

"I don't want to talk with your mother, Sue. I want to talk with your father."

"Just a moment, Uncle Evan."

"Hello, Evan," said the timorous Norman. "There was nothing I could do. The train was already moving before Lynn and I even saw Leanne running towards us."

"Fair enough. I can imagine the screaming and realise you were helpless with the train moving."

"You know Lynn. She was filling Leanne's head with all the wrong things even as we drove to the station. Lynn was driving and had Leanne in front with her."

"I was conscious of Paul coming back in, standing by Maggie who had her hand on his shoulder.

"Yes, I know Lynn, Norman."

"I will put her on, Evan. She is right here.

"NO! I don't want to talk with Lynn or Leanne at this stage. Just you, Norman. I want my daughter on a plane tomorrow. All I want from you now is to call me back within the hour to tell me what flight I must meet tomorrow. I don't want to be forced into legal action. Please write down this number and read it back to me."

I spelled out our phone number.

"Either you or Lynn or both come with her. Please call me with the flight details."

I hung up and pulled Paul to me. "Come with me, lad, pour yourself a Coke while I get Maggie and me a glass of wine. I need one."

~ * ~

Lynn actually flew. It was she, who phoned back, telling me she would fly down with Leanne. She gave me the airline, flight number and time of arrival yet insisted I do not go to the airport.

"Give me your address and we will come by taxi. I want to talk with you."

Once they'd hung up, I told the others what had been said.

"I have no intention of talking with Lynn. I am still too full of anger. However, I want her to see this house so she cannot add 'in poor surroundings' to her gripe."

We watched for the taxi and I alone went to the kerb.

Maggie and Paul waited in the opened doorway, in full view.

I spoke first to the driver, telling him that his fare would be going straight back to the airport. I told Lynn, who wanted to come in, that considerable water had to flow down the river, that we needed time before airing thoughts.

I hustled Leanne down the path and into the house before she could even wave Lynn off. She hadn't been crying, likely too frightened.

I hugged her then and so did Maggie, and so did Paul.

"Wait till you see your room, Sis. It's cool," he told her.

We had her room as ready to receive her, as we could, including fresh flowers. All her luggage had been unpacked and her clothes put away, and the treasured dolls and old teddy-bear she had obviously packed as too precious to leave behind, sat on her pillow.

We talked much throughout the day and through dinner.

After a time, Leanne was ready to talk. She understood the unusual situation we all were in, realising too, that she had no option but to be here. We other three made not too much fuss of her, yet carefully avoided talking about Artarmon.

"Would you like to just sit with Paul for a while, sharing your thoughts on things, when Maggie and I depart for bed?"

Paul smiled.

"That would be good, Sis. We never got much chance back there, did we!"

And oh, we learned a lot from that remark.

How lonely Paul must have been in that house! My guilt hurt.

Fifteen

Come February, we had had six months of Melbourne experience and were happy with it. Paul began at Melbourne Boys High, a GPS qualification. I had been given excellent references by a number of the company's clients and was granted one of the vacancies under the school's 'Company Transfers' policy. That I had had him booked into a Sydney GPS school was sufficient qualification.

"I'm inclined to think our address was a significant reference too, Mags."

After considerable talks between all, Leanne chose to enrol in a government experimental school. It allowed students to leave any class they were not enjoying, so long as it was to join a class of their choice. This way the student decided which subjects best suited themselves. All teachers were available for consultation with parents. She seemed content there, claimed to be making friends although none were brought home. We also met some parents and made a point of arranging evenings of get-togethers to talk on how the school's unique policies were reacting on our respective children.

I was suddenly struck by Maggie's seemingly natural instinct to take to Leanne like a lost friend.

Not natural, of course, I told myself, *very much consciously acquired yet passing it off as natural. Truly it is an affectionate way to prove her love to try helping me in my dilemma in this thing— automatically jumping in to be of assistance.*

I talked with Mags about it. Let her know I recognised her 'sacrifices'.

"Making them entirely out of selfish need, Evan darling. The child is trying to be brave about it all, even if her natural desire is to be there, and not here. She recognises that you have legal rights and she seems to be really trying to be part of our family."

"Despite the letters pouring in from Artarmon?"

Leanne received frequent letters from Lynn. Maggie and I decided it must be better in the long run, not to hide them.

"That would quickly, somehow be discovered and we would have declared ourselves deceitful. Better to just leave them on the hall table and make no comment. That will keep it clear that our objective is open rather than secretive."

We spent considerable time helping both kids with homework and talking through problems. Paul made many friends, obviously seeking out those 'into' surf-boarding.

An extremely welcome visitor was an African Peach-faced Lovebird that arrived on Leanne's window-sill. She wanted to keep it. We immediately bought a cage, yet told her...

"Let's watch the local weekly in case it's someone's pet."

We fortunately found none. Nor were there ads in any local shop window. So it not only stayed, it was granted run of the house despite the poop it left in the most unwanted places. The cage hung in Leanne's bedroom, its door open. It occasionally got out of the house yet always returned to the same windowsill. Leanne took it to school one day to show friends and teachers.

When we took Easter holidays on Phillip Island on the surf coast, the parrot came too, dangling in its cage under our beach umbrella, squawking to be let out. We knew its language by now and it was undoubtedly a "Let me out of here" squawk.

On another matter once back home, after dinner when the kids are in their rooms with their homework, Maggie passed the local rag to me, pointing to a large ad.

I read it and looked up.

Damn and blast, that I cannot raise just a single eyebrow!

"So?" I asked. "You want to go back on stage?"

"Not me," she said. "You!"

I read it again.

"*Boys in the Band* is a gay play. And I'm no actor. Do you want to work front of house? Or backstage? If I recall the movie, the cast has no female."

I was feeling almost incensed. *What on earth is she on about?*

"Besides, I've a full-time job and I repeat; I'm no actor. What are you at?"

She raised her eyebrow. It said a barrel-full. "It's because you are thinking work all day and all night. It seems a phobia. It tells me you need a drop-out interest."

"A gay play? There's golf. There are chess clubs, there are…"

With a distinct flourish of annoyance, I put the paper on the coffee table.

She got up from our antique divan, went to our little mobile bar, an old 'traymobile' we'd found in an antique shop, to pour a *Courvoisier* for me, sweet vermouth for herself.

"You would be amazed how much relaxation a busy mind can find in departing your present life for a few hours—become someone else! It is a wonderful pull-through for your mind! I was talking about this only yesterday with Julie at work. She plays a little in amateur theatre and agrees entirely that it is an escape that works wonders for a person's mental balance."

"An escape having to learn hundreds of lines?"

"You told me you used to spiel off a score of pages, word perfect, when a Freemason, darling. The part of Alan in '*Boys*' is a straight part. A joint lead with the Michael role. It's a demanding part. No one is ever sure if Alan is gay or straight, although he is married to a society wife and lives a straight lifestyle."

"Are you hinting something?"

She laughed openly.

"No, my sweet. Haven't I decided to spend the rest of my life with you? All of it in bed, if you like! Think on it! Take off your priestly mitre and look squarely on it this way; playing the character most unlike your normal self is the most wonderful challenge of all! You literally become a stranger to yourself. It's what you need right now. I know enough of gay people to know they are not looking to convert you. That's a Purist's misunderstanding of the entire sexual scene. In this play they are looking for a straight guy trying to justify instincts. That is the Alan role. They don't want a gay guy trying to play straight, they need a straight guy looking in on their scene. There is no danger to my Evan in that. Think outside the box, my darling! See stage-work as a dropout from the daily grind—it is a let-out to pent up tensions. Take it from one who knows and has you at heart."

She was staring so intently, I worried that she was trying to change me.

"Finished?"

"Yes. And I want you to do it. You've been working so hard without odd hours of relief that I am worried about you. Please audition? Please?"

I could see she was not going to give up.

"You've made much to me, darling, of your admiration for Old Les," she continued. "And Zoe. Both are old troupers who have played every sort of character one can imagine. They've so often had to call on guts, believing they couldn't do it. Are you less a person?"

"Can I call you a darling bitch? You really know how to drill holes in a man."

I suddenly felt this was our first ever sign of a pending argument.

"You are a proven salesman. Haven't you felt like a bastard at times, angling to get the order? Why did DRC select you to do that marketing exercise that landed you this job? You're not on trial. A company that size doesn't promote someone on chance. They know you will succeed. You have all the qualifications for stage work."

~ * ~

"I was given a script, Mags, with three passages marked. I am to read them at audition tomorrow night."

She leaned over and kissed me. She had done so when I arrived home late after beers with staff.

"The guy who interviewed me is as straight as a die. It was at the radio station's offices. Simon had just come off air. He does the morning breakfast broadcast. On his desk are photos of he, his wife and baby. He is playing Michael. He said if I get the part, he and I have many scenes together. Two other troupe members are also auditioning as Alan."

"Does the troupe have a name?"

"No. It's new, a crowd of theatre guys who reckon the time is right for this play to make a comeback. They've already booked Melbourne University's theatre for June, so it's a long way off. Mostly gay guys, but with loads of talent, so Simon says. They will decide on a troupe name once the entire crew is chosen."

"Read these extracts for me now."

"Eh?"

She prodded a finger towards the chair across the breakfast bar and sat with arms folded. The kids were in their rooms on homework, so she had me to herself.

I read the first and she suggested different ways I should try. She gave some examples and had me stand. I did them again, trying to mimic her examples.

"Much better." She took the script and pencilled a couple of words.

"Say these with more emphasis. Don't just read them, deliver them! Stand erect, point with your finger, then do a throw-away toss over your shoulder, sort of thing."

She got to her feet and illustrated the movements.

We were still at it when Leanne came down.

She screwed up her face. "What's he doing?"

"Practising for a lecture he has to give," Maggie told her."

"Use a wagging finger when you say something like that, Mags," I said with a swagger.

She gave me exactly that line back as she reckoned it should be given on stage, flourish and all.

I gaped. "That lived, Mags, It had soul!"

"Rehearse your lines while under the shower and again in bed. Try to dream about them, darling."

Sixteen

A Maggie chapter, a month later...

My work was going well as was Evan's. He was well past training new staff and was chuffed at how his market had increased.

The healthy side of each of our jobs was that challenges were being met.

One lucky thing I found at work was a new friendship—a girl not unlike Jane in many ways, except newly married. Julie's husband was Hungarian, emigrated with his parents about the same time as me. We had them for dinner one Saturday night and Evan hit it off quite well with Olaf. I think Evan was pleased that I cooked a recipe he'd taught me, a pudding of spaghetti baked in milk with loads of garlic, onion, tomato and cheese—a great taste sensation.

My biggest thrill was shopping for a new suit for my man. He was now making regular interstate trips, his product line unusual for Australia, printing and forming the square-bottom bag used as supermarket check-out bags, retail packs for pet-food, domestic garden fertilizers, coffee, flour, sugar, etcetera. His was the largest supplier of that type of packaging in Victoria. He was now winning back business from interstate manufacturers. I reckoned his position demanded he have an upmarket new suit. Not that he wasn't already a careful dresser, but I had greater plans for him.

"I want to buy my man a new suit," I told him. "The stock market is being very good to me. Meet me one lunch hour and we'll see what Myers has on its 'Gentlemen's Floor.'"

"I don't need you buying me expensive clothes, Mags. Yes, by all means help me choose one, but I will pay."

"For your birthday," I insisted.

"My birthday was January."

"For Easter, then."

Easter was also gone, yet I'd made my point.

It was a floor in Myers where neither had ventured. It smelled wealthy.

"Seeing it is my gift, will you let me choose it?"

"I have absolute confidence in your impeccable taste, my love."

Of the twenty jackets he tried on and the three full suits he 'modelled' for me, I chose a light brown, small diagram visible only with considerable searching, a silk-lined *Ermenegildo Zegna*. I glanced briefly at the price tag and many muscles cringed. But he was the man I loved and I wanted it for him. I would cheat on housekeeping bills for a while and eat only a piece of fruit for lunch for a month or three. I simply wanted my man to have it.

He was thrilled and pandered to me even more affectionately.

He took me to a Champagne dinner on the strength of it.

~ * ~

Evan's stage 'career' had him in thrall. I could sense what he was experiencing.

He had won his Alan part and my knowledge of subtle physical manoeuvres helped accentuate particular lines. Nuances of facial expression and how fast or slow movements upstage as a line was delivered, could also give emphasis. I had him pacing about our living-room delivering lines as he felt they deserved while I, script in hand, played sometimes Michael, sometimes the 'screaming little queen, Emory' and sometimes the Director correcting the phrasing emphases of his lines.

"Never feel Mart Crowley should have used a different word, my love. Your prerogative is not to change what a playwright wrote, but seek his reason for choosing it. Your expressive expertise must find how to make the word sound as he intended."

The cast numbered only eight of whom three had sought the Alan role. We never learned who were the other two. Evan, however, reckoned his major objective was to convince whoever they were, that they couldn't have made a better Alan.

Another admitted goal was to show me that my confidence in him wasn't wasted.

Yet another was that he wanted to prove me right in claiming his efforts would prove a healthy break from constant concentration on work.

His honesty in admitting all that to me, means a lot.

He learned his lines well, practising in the car when driving home from work and back from appointments, he told me.

"Why not also when driving to work, and to appointments," I challenged.

But the darling had his answer pat… "Driving to work I am planning my day, ticking off in my mind, all I must do. Driving to an appointment I am rehearsing my spiel, seeking the detail thing that is going to spring his mind!"

"But driving back from an appointment, wouldn't the results of that interview have you plotting their course through the factory?"

"No, my love. Every word uttered during the interview is safely recorded on my Phillips. Once into the office, Dawn has all that at her fingertips and is by now, trained in what needs doing. My mind is already on other business."

I gave him more kisses, realising that it all helped pay for the life I was enjoying.

One night at rehearsal, for I attended many, happy amongst the camp crowd, up came the matter of choosing the group name. It was near time for promoting our opening night. Name after name was suggested. I tossed in *Rhombus*. All eyebrows shot skywards.

"What is a rhombus?" was the question on all tongues.

"It is a Greek word," I explained. Rhombus is a square on a slant—a bent square."

OH. It blew so close to home for every one of them. They loved it.

"Oh," screamed the brilliantly cast flamboyant and effeminate Emory. His arms flapped everywhere. "It's gorgeous." He rushed to give me a sloppy kiss on the cheek and a hug. Jamie didn't 'play' Emory, it was written for him.

Rhombus was to launch itself on conservative Melbourne late next month.

~ * ~

Leanne wanted to join a riding school, no doubt emanating from girls at school. We had been giving a half day every weekend to taking her there. Both kids we had often taken to *Rhombus* rehearsals and both had responded positively in terms of interest. They illustrated that it was sort of a highlight in their lives. It had reached a stage when hiring of stage props was severely testing the group's living on a shoestring. Fortunately the only specific costume required was Alan's black-tie dinner suit and he already had one from his Lodge days. So that was a saving.

Evan had made a point of involving Leanne in a play at her school, but she simply refused to try out for an acting role. She was happy to take on back-stage work. We just hoped it might help her gain more self-confidence.

I held doubts but withheld them from Evan. I needed to let yet more time run out.

Letters from mum-Lynn remained frequent. We still didn't interfere. It was something we must leave Leanne see as her personal prerogative, yet her silence persisted. The not knowing was a tedium we had to overlook with fingers crossed.

Surely those letters will continue uncomplimentary about me. Surely too, Leanne must be answering them; yet deliberately keeping everything secret. Deliberately secret is counter to the happiness she illustrates, so why be devious about the letters? The reasons can only be furtive. It all smacks of an insincerity that her smiles belie.

I just have to be careful to ensure concern over this doesn't mar my relationship with Evan. Conflict hovers somewhere but I cannot put a finger on it.

I simply dread something emerging from all this.

Seventeen

During May, Grant Gorman phoned.

"Can we have lunch tomorrow, Evan?"

"Bloody hell, Mags," I told her that night, "my heart near dropped. Can he have discovered I am cast in a gay play? Am I to be dragged over hot coals?"

"But his tenor? Surely it indicated something?"

"No. The bastard's left me stewing. That's why I think it's bad news. Rumours in the factory that the boss is secretly playing on a gay stage could prove devastating in a conservative city like Melbourne, not only with staff, Mags, but with customers!"

Grant often took his GMs for lunch, or for dinner with wives. I always had the feeling he was never quite sure how to relate to me. I am a tad taller than him, and knew my reputation of seeming to look down on people even taller. It was simply me being me, but did he always see it that way?

On this occasion, however, his news was good news.

"Your appointment as General Manager of DRC Bags is affirmed. Sir God in Bristol is satisfied with your progress and agrees with the appointment. I also have his nod on the new equipment you recommended. The order must go through head office. With their fire-power, they can screw down the price."

"I added too, Mags, that it also prevented me having to pay graft sums under the counter here. He agreed. Sir God is Sir John Cameron, Chairman of Directors, DRC International. You will get to meet him later in the year when he visits. There will be a function for senior management and wives."

She came around the table and kissed me. The children were witness and had the message that it was all good news for their dad at work.

"There is more," I told them. "Such good news made me rethink hiding secrets on my personal life from my boss. When in his 'good book' was surely the appropriate time."

"What secrets, Dad?" Paul asked.

"It went something like this, son,..."

"Something I'd rather you hear from me than via the grape-vine, Grant..."

"Spill it."

"I'm rehearsing in an amateur-theatre production opening next month."

"Is it interfering with your work?"

"I would never let it."

"Maggie is happy about it?"

"She screwed me into it."

"Then best of luck with it. Just don't tire yourself out. How long does it run?"

"Five performances over two weeks."

"Good. Shakespeare? Tennessee Williams? Where?"

"Mart Crowley. His: 'Boys in the Band'. Melbourne University Theatre."

He nearly choked. He eventually said, "Monica and I saw the movie. Loved it. Which character are you?"

He still held the smile on his face, still shaking his head more than a little.

"Alan."

"*Which part is that? I don't remember the names.*"

"*Not the screaming queen, Grant. Alan is the pseudo-straight guy in a dinner suit.*"

"*He makes that telephone call near the end. Monica cried at that, as I recall.*"

"*You don't mind?*"

I wanted Mags to hear how he spelled this out. I turned to her.

"*So long as I don't even get the hint of a feeling that personal distractions are interfering with your work. When you open, Monica and I might even come along.*"

A Home for Old Ladies

BOOK 2

Stanford Lodge

Eighteen

Affirmed Melbournians, it was time to buy our own home.

"I can arrange time off," offered Maggie.

"If I make afternoon appointments to visit what the agent considers likely, I can arrange to leave the office and tram to Trak Village. He can then take me to the viewing. If I see something suitable, we can see it during your lunch-hour next day."

We had specified something in the Toorak, Malvern, Armadale arc and given him our price limit.

"We prefer older houses," we told him. "We want to decorate in period style and don't mind if it needs some renovation."

Maggie and I had earlier agreed that only in dire emergency would we telephone each other at work. Many times, of course, when I foresaw a pub session coming up after work, I would leave a message on the home phone to say I would be late, stuck in the pub with the boys. These were my Factory Manager and my two sales guys.

"Just don't forgot those guys also have wives, dear," I was frequently reminded, "who may not be as forgiving as yours."

Now, however, we had to find additional time.

As well as depending on Mrs. Carmody's agent in Trak Village, we scoured For Sale ads during evenings and lunch hours. The 'arc' we nominated gave access to tram and train for getting both kids easily to schools and Maggie to the city.

A first day site was *Stanford Lodge* in the very desirable Stanford Road, Malvern.

"I hesitate," the agent advised, "because while this was once a glorious home, of latter years it's been a Home for Old Ladies. It is now in such poor condition that the health department has refused to renew its licence. It has closed."

Mags and I looked at each other with raised eyebrows.

"Let's not cast it off without a look," I said. "It's but five minutes from home."

~ * ~

At first sight it simply bloomed with Federation elegance.

The sign on the cast-iron gate read *Stanford Lodge for Ladies.*

Inspection, however, revealed faults galore.

The lawns were overgrown with paspalum and other weeds. The formal rose-gardens were full of weeds, most of its roses dead. The many veranda posts all had peeling paint and for the want of pruning, trees were even fouling guttering. A huge holly-tree was so overgrown it entirely blocked the entrance to a side passageway. Inside, double-doors between living rooms had their upper glass panels boarded over. The turn-of-the-century kitchen was putrid, walls and ceiling grease-stained and most cupboards beyond repair. Also in the bathroom, wall tiles were dreadfully stained, chipped and even missing. Plumbing throughout was all very old. The once glorious Brussels carpets were, in places, exceedingly worn.

Everywhere and everything was tainted with the odour of ill patients.

The Estate Agent was blasé about it.

"In good condition it would be far beyond your price range. But built 1901, year of Australia's Federation by a master-builder as his family home, its foundations are broad and deep. The house is structurally sound. It is currently owned by a husband and wife, she a nursing Matron, and he owner of an electrical installation business. The wife ran it as an old ladies home until retiring. He had recently rewired the entire building, so everything electrical is sound. But that is all. As you see, it needs considerable restoration."

Maggie's and my hungry eyes could see beyond the squalor. It had loads of potential.

From the front gate, if one could overlook the poor state of the out-doors, the ochre brick façade of the house with large bay-windows projecting into fret-worked verandas, was indeed elegant—the seven chimney stacks in the complicated roof gave the whole, something of a Wuthering Heights appeal. The roof-tiles of genuine turn-of-the-century Marseilles Clay seemed in good condition.

The entrance hallway was seven feet wide and the branch hallway the length of the house, five. All rooms were large. Each of the three living rooms and master bedroom had spacious bay windows, the living room two bays. Every window in the house was of stained glass lead-lights in glorious floral designs. Double doorways opened between all three living-rooms and vestibule. It had three bedrooms. Every room had twelve-foot ceilings, marvellous for Melbourne's hot summers. Every room had a built-in fireplace for its winters. A large Octagon was where hallways met and doorways led to various rooms. It was graced by a once glorious chandelier. The pattern in the old Brussels carpet followed the odd-shaped rooms throughout. It had been woven in Belgium to exactly fit the house contours, leaving in every room, a twelve-inch border of black-stained hardwood floors.

"This huge old kitchen, Maggie, must be gutted and built anew. Already I can see opportunity of turning it into a bedroom. That strange rear bedroom-come ward that takes an L-shape, would make a good modern kitchen-come-breakfast-room."

I was already seeing it made over for modern living, yet retaining all its charm.

The entire back veranda had been cheaply turned into the hospital staff-quarters.

"That entire area needs scrapping, made over into a flag-stoned terrace and barbeque. Can you envisage grape-vines growing over a wooden trellis here, Mags?"

"You seem sold on it, darling. But oh, everywhere my eyes look, so much work needed. And the expense? And this sickening smell?"

Beyond the kitchen was a huge scullery, the 'wet-room' of previous century cooks. Off the mid-house hallway were a larder and a linen-room.

The old scullery would be an ideal laundry with washing and drying machines in this corner and plenty of space left for gardening gear and workshop.

It had its own direct entrance into the back garden.

"And, Mags, that larder is big enough to become a second bathroom for the kids."

"That awful switchboard in the Octagon? How thoughtless putting it there!"

"That bathroom door can be bricked up, Mags, to open instead, into our bedroom. The switchboard was installed by the owner, so he will know the simplest way of moving it onto the bricked up doorway. I can easily build around it with shelving, to make that entire wall a walk-in linen-press, the switchboard hidden. Folding wooden doors can be wallpapered to match the rest of the Octagon."

She put her arm through my elbow and marched me into the main bedroom.

"Yes, a door to the bathroom can go through here."

"It will be an easy house to get bank finance on, my pet. It has 'site' advantage—a wide street almost a boulevard with its kerbside trees, and the agent says, is right around the corner from Sir Robert Menzies' home. He had been Australia's most popular Prime Minister, personal friend of the Royal Family, no less."

The house certainly seemed structurally sound. We would need to go to council only for the second bathroom. I could do the rest. Having grown up under the wing of a master-builder stepfather, building was a sort of second nature. I envisaged the restoring of *Stanford Lodge* being a magnificent adventure.

"These wonderful high ceilings, though Evan. All the cracks would need to be professionally done. They are too high for us."

She has Bay Road Waverton in mind.

"I know how to erect simple scaffolding. Old 'Pop' as I called my step-father, was restoring many of these sorts of houses. There was an embargo on building houses all during the war, Mags. Sydney's Mosman had many houses like this. I helped Pop wallpaper ceilings to cover a multitude of sins. Same with the walls. Most here have been poorly patched when pulling out the old gas-lamps. Better sanding is all they need, before papering. You can choose the paper."

"Paper twelve foot ceilings?"

"Now there's a bloody challenge, ain't it, my love!"

That night, we talked many more details. A bottle of wine each over a long dinner seemed barely enough. The kids, who hadn't seen it, were part of the conversation. They were intrigued with its age. They asked about the likelihood of secret passages.

"It's not a castle," Maggie assured them. "It doesn't even have a second story. It is just a rambling old house that can be made comfortable."

"It could have a little cellar, however," I said. "Many houses in those days had a 'cold-room' under the kitchen or larder floors, for keeping dairy products, accessed through trap-doors in the floor."

When the kids had gone to bed, we sat with our brains pulsating on all the adverse things we could come up with. We both, then, took sleeping pills. Tomorrow was a Saturday and we would get a key from the agent and take the kids to see it.

"It is but five minute's drive," we told them over breakfast.

We listed things to take, like note-books for all.

"Most rooms are big," I told Paul. "Put a long tape on your list. Should we decide on the house that will be a must for our first visit to a hardware store."

I turned to Maggie. "I shall slip my chequebook into a pocket. I already want to vote 'Yes'. I'd like to at least pay a returnable deposit giving us first option while the bank makes inspection for a mortgage. It also gives us opportunity for second thoughts. What do you reckon?"

She couldn't help but nod; it still left all doors open for a change of mind.

"It is certainly in a street of fine old houses, Evan darling. And that it had been a home for old ladies, somehow gives me the same sort of feeling I had when the Girls' Choir gave concerts in hospitals and old people's homes. I could not help but feel that I might be helping those old people travel to their afterlife with music in their ears. I wonder if now, we could help the old ladies from *Stanford Lodge* know someone was taking the trouble to restore it to its old splendour."

"I can envisage it not only a fine home for our family, Mags," I said with eyes deliberately on the kids, "but it would do my heart good to consider how often those old ladies must have wondered what their home would have been like in its youth. We have the chance of showing them."

"You sound like you've already bought, it, Dad," said Paul.

"Wait until you see it, boy. And you, Leanne. See what you think it can become with lots of loving work and, yes, more than a few dollars. But the asking price, with potential in mind, is within our pocket."

"Why was it let get so old and messed up?" asked Leanne.

"It was a home for old ladies who could not be looked after by family," Maggie explained. "Many may have had no family. Maybe it was poorly run as a business and went broke? Maybe only the present owner can answer your question."

Paul disappeared and returned with the street directory.

"Stanford Road?"

"Yes, son." Number one-twenty."

We let him do the searching.

"The street directory has it marked 'Hosp'."

"Well there you go. It seems we might be buying a hospital."

I brought my camera and called on the agent for a key.

"Happy that you want a second look. I'm due now, at an auction, so you just help yourselves. Leave the key and a note for me here, if I am still not returned."

"He is not interested in the house at all," I told the kids once back in the car. His interest is only in the commission he makes if he sells it."

One twenty Stanford Road had no car entrance. The original garages and before them, stables, had obviously been on the side-street where had also been the house's tennis court. The property had since been divided, the small corner block now having three modern single-storied town-houses, modern yet still fitting well into the streetscape.

The house's front fence was a delightful five-foot crazy-stone wall, except only for the pedestrian iron-gate. Behind the wall was a high hedge.

"It would seem such a pity to break into all that, just to push a car access through." said Maggie. And I so like the sudden impact of the house as one emerges through the gate and up the few steps to discover this spacious lawn with its formal rose-gardens."

"Mags. I'm not fussed about the company car being parked in the street."

The formal rose-gardens were built in matching stone to the front wall. The side 'fence' to the town-houses was tall and smothered in wisteria vines. The other side fence couldn't be seen for jungle.

"The holly tree reminds me of England," said Mags. "It is huge," she told the kids, "biggest I've ever seen."

Both had smiles on their faces once through the gate and hedges that hid everything from the street. Leanne was first to comment.

"All those chimneys!"

The pathway wound around the large sweep of rose-gardens and down by the fret-worked veranda to steps up to the front door.

As soon as it was opened, the smell of disinfectant again assaulted our nostrils.

"Paul," said Maggie, "please skirt around the yards and see if you can find a stone large enough to hold this door open."

"Stones for all outside doors," I challenged him.

We busied ourselves opening windows while Leanne dashed off exploring.

I showed Maggie how the unsightly power-box could be moved and she gave me the thumbs-up. Another wall of the Octagon included the door into our bedroom. I measured the inside.

"Mmmm."

"Meaning?"

"I was thinking in bed last night that this entire wall could be built up like my wardrobes in the Sydney condo, with doors of sliding mirrors."

She checked that neither child was within hearing.

"Good thinking, darling. I'm all in favour of mirrored walls in bedrooms." She waggled that eyebrow of hers.

I slapped her bottom and she kissed me.

I pointed through the bay window.

"That old holly tree is pressing right against the leaded panes. It needs urgent pruning. We should get a man in to bring the entire gardens into better trim."

"I want to buy roses, darling. Those beds need refreshing and I want them full of roses again."

"You too, sound convinced. Do you feel it?"

"You just pointing out these changes makes so many of the problems seem surmountable. A lot of work, though."

I checked the ceilings. "Yes, wallpaper will cover that crazing."

"With that?" She pointed to the large moulded centrepiece.

"Centrepieces must be painted, Mags. The flat areas can be papered."

On searching, we found that the lounge, the dining room and Octagon, as well as the major bedroom, had large and heavily moulded centrepieces.

"Maybe we should get tradesmen to do the ceilings?"

I didn't answer. *I won't pursue it now. Everything must take its turn. Even before moving in, the second bathroom must be built. Getting the kids ready for school and each of us for work, will be pretty damned impossible with only one bathroom.*

Each kid seemed thoroughly satisfied with the large space each bedroom offered. We told them they could each design their own room layouts, but general décor must match the rest of the house. All were putting thoughts to paper.

"We can 'sterilize' other rooms for sleeping while we work on bedrooms. If we have to change that old kitchen to your room, Paul, it must be well down the list. But there are other rooms aplenty in the interim. Just pick one."

After a hectic morning, all agreed it would make a great home as well as a family adventure. It was only around the corner from trams to schools and city.

We called back to the agent. I told him that given a thousand dollars off the asking price, we would pay a holding deposit and sign his 'intention to buy'.

"The bastard accepted so readily," I complained while driving to St. George's Court, "that I should have demanded more."

"I reckon you are highly delighted with our purchase, nevertheless, darling."

"Don't tell the kids, yet, Mags," I told her when alone, "but I'm going to sell the beach-house. I want as big a deposit as I can manage, for *Stanford Lodge*, while still having cash for renovations."

We used mealtimes for general discussion. Early agreement was that once the bank approved the loan, we convert the larder to a second bathroom. Meanwhile, we would 'sanitize' the old kitchen ready for temporary use. Next we would clean the dining room that must initially be for both living and eating.

What we were calling the 'third living room'—that behind the presently nailed shut double-doors between it and the dining-room, would start as a bedroom shared by the kids. Eventually it would be our TV room as I objected to television in any room in which we ate.

"Meal times are family discussion times," I insisted.

Meanwhile, however, yes, the TV must be in the dining-room.

First room to be restored to its finish would be Leanne's bedroom. Not only did it require no restoration other than decoration, but would the quicker, give each a room of their own. We were both keen to prove to Leanne, right from the start, that we saw it important she have her own room. She had never had such.

What would eventually be our lounge-room, would in the interim, be a storeroom for all our spare furniture. It would be last on our restoration list.

~ * ~

The bank didn't hesitate in granting the mortgage.

"Let's face it, Mags, they not only have me putting down a larger than required deposit, but have access to my bank account into which my significant monthly salary is directly paid. And aren't I already renting a house in one of the most elegant addresses in the country?"

The previous owner and electrical installation professional, was the obvious one to ask about a builder to convert the old larder into a bathroom. I already had a sketch of the layout we all had agreed on. I phoned my builder at Copacabana, requesting he submit his account for work-to-date since the last payment, so I could put it up for sale. He made an immediate offer. "I can then finish and sell it on Spec."

"The offer he made, Mags, gives me a small profit, so it had to be a good deal. As soon as the lawyers have raised the paperwork, we will have the cash needed for our Great Restoration here in this Home for Old Ladies."

Nineteen

Everything seemed to be falling into place. A good omen?

Paul found his disappointment at the beach-house being sold, difficult to swallow. He realised, however, the pointlessness of having a beach house a thousand kilometres from home. I promptly rearranged our programme that he and I, while that bathroom was being built, scour the old kitchen together, talking about how he wanted it decorated as his bedroom once getting to that stage.

"It also ensures, Maggie, that the kitchen will be cleaned ready for us to begin using. The washing and drying machines must also come into it for the nonce, so I can have the entire scullery as my tool-room and workshop. I'll have the electrician add more power points in both as he does the new bathroom."

Every night for the rest of the week, when not at *Boys* rehearsal, I joined the family in 'think-box', that all ideas be discussed. Paul wanted assurance there would be space for his surfboards.

"For the nonce, they can fit in the lounge. You will eventually have a big enough room to hold them. Then you can keep your eyes on them," I teased.

Leanne sought Maggie's help in decorating her room.

"Of course, darling. We are family. Everything to do with the house is doing things together." She slid her arm about Leanne's shoulders and gave her a hug.

Leanne didn't pull away; a great sign.

Maggie asked, "Is there a projected date for finishing the second bathroom? We need to think about giving notice on our lease here. It still has several months to run."

"Good question, girl. Why don't you throw the pleading question to Mrs. Carmody? We may even have to call on her good services to stay on a little longer if the bathroom runs behind schedule."

"I've called you a crafty bugger in the past, dear. And here you are twisting what could be a difficult question, into putting poor Mrs. Carmody into making an awkward decision?"

"Just trying to wedge doors open should a squall start, dear. I have every confidence in you getting the answer we want from Mrs. Carmody."

Maggie turned to the kids. "Your father believes in keeping doors open."

"Just tell her, Mags, that we will be desperately trying to have enough done by the time our lease expires, that we aren't left in the situation of having to find somewhere to live just for a week or two extra. If I judge Mrs. Carmody correctly, she will be patting your shoulder and assuring you she would never put us in that situation."

Maggie answered by raising that meaningful eyebrow.

~ * ~

In bed that night, I went back to square-one.

"Are you sure, Mags? Once we sign the contract and pay our deposit, there can be no turning back."

"The kids like it, you like it, I too can see the potential. And the joy of doing it will be fulfilling. The only question is, are we taking on too big an 'out-of-hours' project? We both have time-consuming jobs. Can we afford outside tradesmen?"

"We can, yet I would begrudge every cent and bemoan the fact we are not doing it ourselves. And our commitment to the old ladies? Isn't that our driving force?"

"Of course. I realise creating a bathroom must be a professional job. Once moved in, of course, we can pick and choose what next needs doing."

"We should have the plumber, while doing the new bathroom, install a new tub in the front bathroom, also hand-basin and make-up bar into what will be our en-suite. It would be good to have that when moving in. Walls, ceiling and floor can be slotted into our schedule as it suits."

"Good thinking, my love."

"While the bathrooms are being done, I will rig up temporary plumbing for the washing machine and drier once bought, in the old kitchen. We can also buy the cooker you want and I can rig these temporarily into existing benches. Once in, we can then immediately start on Leanne's room. Has she shown you what she wants?"

"She told me you had it in hand."

"Only in respect of her wanting to use her fireplace, and that one of her windows won't close properly. I told her to put them on her list."

"All right. I shall take her to look at wallpaper and carpet. I shall also convince her how ugly were Lynn Stroud's plastic flowers in every room."

I gave her a playful dig in the ribs.

We rolled into a cuddle and made love.

~ * ~

A Maggie moment...

I have faith in his judgements, yet remain thrilled that he continues to include me in making decisions—proof of his trust in me too, I guess. Yet I still have every intention of trying to get him to call in cleaners to do the initial 'sanitizing' as he calls it. The sooner the smells of disinfectants are driven out, the more pleasant a workplace it will be.

"What if we get cleaners to do the sanitizing," I asked over the breakfast table.

I had often found that jumping in with both feet can work with Evan. "It would give us a more pleasant atmosphere for doing the rest of the work. We could maybe, then, be able to spend a few more Sundays at the riding school?"

Leanne was quick to smile.

Yes, the right timing works on her too!

"You guys seem to have made up your minds about buying this house, then?"

"Yes, Paul. Your father and I talked it through last night. We both think it will be good for all in the long run. Your dad's career will see him tied to living in Melbourne and the rent on this house is considerably more than the mortgage we are committing to. Not only is buying a house a financial advantage, such a house as *Stanford Lodge,* once restored, will indeed be a home we all can enjoy."

It was Sunday. Leanne and I walked to the Real Estate office for a key. They also gave me the name and number of the previous owner so Evan could enquire about a builder for the bathrooms and to get a price for moving the switchboard.

Evan phoned him and he agreed to come look that very day.

Percy, a big man, arrived in overalls as if to start work right away.

"I have to move this doorway first," Evan explained, "and brick up this wall. It is right here, on the new brickwork, that the power-box is to be mounted."

Percy also recommended a builder for the bathrooms.

"It will be no trouble with council. If Bob and I jointly give them the plans, it'll be just a rubber stamp job. Show me what you want there and I'll have Bob give you a price."

He was excited about our plans to restore the house as a dwelling.

When he'd gone, I began working my way through all the rooms that had been 'wards' in the 'hospital', palms held as if in prayer.

Evan caught me at it. "What are you doing? Making blessings?"

"I am telling the ladies that we are their new nurses, seeking permission to smarten up their surroundings. So far all seem happy at the prospect. The idea is from a play I did in London. An old man who had been a lay preacher was blessing all the rooms in an old hospital being torn down for a housing settlement. I am telling the old ladies that they are our inspiration in restoring this house to its original glory."

He kissed me. "A lovely thought. Tell them for me that we will be doing it with the utmost care and will have their peace and welfare in mind at all times."

Paul wanted to take down the 'For Sale' sign.

"That belongs to the agent, lad," Evan told him. "He will take it down when the last signature has been made and we have full title. Maggie and I will be joint owners, then we don't have to ask permission any more. We can do what we want with the place, except only where the law says it needs council permission."

"Why not just do it and don't tell the council."

"Because, lad, that will save you and your sister bringing food to Maggie and me in prison."

We spent the rest of the morning scouring the property.

"Can we get a dog now?" Leanne asked.

"As soon as we move in," I told her. "You can choose it and name it. And you can bring Hairy Legs."

Hairy Legs was the unlikely name given to the African Peach-faced Lovebird.

"Of course you may lose Hairy Legs. Many birds are territorial, regularly returning to their place of birth. Many creatures are like that. Pigeons, Salmon, even many people. So if given freedom of the house, he can be lost any time any one of us opens a door or window."

She agreed to accept the risk.

Come lunch time, we agreed all should walk the length of Stanford Road to Malvern Village on Glenferrie Road, to see what offered.

"I want to find a hardware store. We are going to need a good one," said Evan.

We found that Glenferrie Road was not one for hardware stores. However, it was well endowed with high-grade fabric shops, art galleries galore, clothing boutiques for the upper-class, restaurants, beauty-parlours galore and gift-shops galore. It seemed a very galore type of street. It did have a lone newsagent who delivered free to members, the cost of membership reasonable. It also meant a discount on books and magazines. I gave it top marks for its quality of stock. We became members.

We found what I explained was a European style café with chairs and tables strewn along the footpath, and it being a Sunday, a day the government relaxed laws and allowed leniencies, onto the roadway yet not too close to the tramlines.

What wasn't acknowledged by the authorities, however, as is so often the case with bureaucracies, Glenferrie Road was one of those chic areas defying convention. Many shops stayed open to trade all day Sunday which made the roadway more condensed with traffic than any week-day. Yes, the same Sundays when the roadway was invaded by chairs and tables.

Are some of these customers enjoying imbibing alcohol on Sundays in broad daylight, the very same bureaucrats who make the laws? Likely, I guess, but then, of course, it is not their responsibility to see laws upheld. And who dares question it?

We took a table. They served a wide selection of *hors-d'œuvres, fromages, patisseries, quiches* and *pâtés* along with an infinite variety of milk-shakes, coffees, liquors and wines. But no beer.

Is beer considered too uncouth by Toorak and Malvern social standards?

Both kids ate up big, of course, and so did we.

Sated, we took in a number of galleries, twigging my mind into wondering about things to grace our walls. I raised it as a question.

"It is a beautiful old Federation house, darling. I think we should consider prints of Australia's 'old masters', paintings of the goldfields during the eighteen-hundreds? Wattle-trees and eucalypts?"

Evan smiled. "Why is it I am unable to raise a bloody eyebrow when given such an opportunity?"

I raised one for him.

"A DRC company here in Melbourne, my love, holds world rights to reproduce many of what are considered Australian Old Masters. Most in fact. Do you recall me twice being taken to the MCG to see Aussie Football played to seventy-thousand roaring fans? Well the guy who took me there, Trent Harris, is its Marketing Manager."

"Well you should be able to get a discount, shouldn't you?"

"Maybe they cannot sell direct. You will have an opportunity to meet him soon. Grant told me the other day that a company function is coming up. With all this house thing, I forgot to mention it."

"You forgot? That should be a black mark against any General Manager."

"General Manager of a small company, dear. Trent is Marketing Manager of a large one."

I yawned. "Tell me about it later, dear."

We were walking back to the house down the other side of our delightful street, wide and heavily treed. Many local residents walked dogs, several older men touching hat-brims to me. Some houses were glorious. Only a few were two storied, yet all of a period several generations old.

Yes, I cannot but feel I shall be happy here. And Evan clinging on to one of my elbows, is surely, in the moment, thinking the same.

~ * ~

Evan...

Maggie's and my most querulous task in the Restoration, a word raised to capital R because of its now significance in our lives, was deciding what to do with the Brussels carpets. Choices were simple—keep or quit them.

The decision, however, was difficult. It rested with us; we had no-one to pass the buck to, should we later be sorry.

"My mind holds no doubt, dear husband," she told me, "that the Old Ladies (she having elevated them to capital-letter-status for similar reasons), must have seen something quite beautiful in these carpets, faded in places and heavily worn in others. They would have seen in the pattern been made to exactly fit these rooms and hallways with their awkward shapes, that they had in themselves been someone's dream of what they wanted in life."

It had yet no dangerous threads threatening to trip us up, but whilst the once bright colours were now dull, the carpets remained a distinctive feature. I was all for keeping them but realised they could never survive being lifted while I tore down brick walls and barrowed rubble over them.

"I agree, Mags. However, 'restore' is a finite verb. We are not talking about restoring carpet, we are about restoring the house. You are the Mensa member, my love, the one to come up with logical argument that we are restoring the house by throwing out a specific feature of its history? Surely the house would be losing something of its character. The Old Ladies would surely vote to retain it."

I could see her mind musing, so waited before adding...

"Everything else in the house reflects its era. The matching chimney stacks are intricately crafted to live with the Marseilles tiles, themselves features. The intricate fretwork of the veranda woodwork also reflects the era and remains in remarkably good nick but for peeling paint. The windows, every one is a coloured feature to cherish. All over the house the original brickwork retains its aura. All fall into exactly the uniqueness of the carpets. Isn't the carpet the most striking of all the period features? It is in itself an antique."

"How many years do you think they can survive we four living here?"

"We are but a small group compared with not only a dozen patients shuffling or being wheeled over them, let alone the nursing staff backwards and forwards all the time over twenty years. So maybe three times that long?"

"They must yet be very hardy, darling. And another thing..."

She held up her hand while it seemed her mind fought for some particular expression...

"Somewhere in my mind I feel the carpets and building are a couple living through a love affair. They were made for each other and have been together all their lives. We are not 'restoring' this home by separating them. Just think of the memories trapped in their mesh—a togetherness that surely the Old Ladies will have sensed. They would surely hate to see them parted. We must keep them together."

"Certainly their blue and black with the odd hint of gold will live happily with what we have chosen for wallpaper."

"You sound like you are looking for excuses."

"No more than you, my sweet. We can cover them with plastic and planks before trundling wheel-barrows of bricks and brick-dust over them."

"I'd already thought of that."

"Then why are we arguing?"

"We are not arguing, darling. We are trying to solve a problem."

She leaned back, hands ahip like Liz.

"You men can seldom see the difference."

She threw her arms about me.

"I shall carefully creep over these carpets all the years of our lives," she whispered.

Twenty

A setback to our life arrived in the form of a letter from the headmaster of Leanne's school, asking us to contact him.

"I shall call him," said Maggie.

"No, my love. We agreed that you would concentrate on your career and be financially responsible for things 'Maggie'. I would take responsibility for the children. You have already conceded a great deal in having them live with us. Once I know details, we will talk it through."

I know how much of her chosen life she's set aside without complaint. She didn't try hiding her determination to release Leanne from the strong hold of 'the Stroud woman' as she refers to Lynn. I know too, that she will as readily give more of her time in this direction if needed. Surely if there is a problem, the fellow would have given the reason in his letter.

I called.

"I would like to talk with you and Leanne's mother, Mr. Robson."

"I am afraid that right now you must be satisfied with only me."

We settled on five o'clock.

I left a message on our home answer-phone that I had the appointment but would be home before seven.

I was on time.

"Leanne constantly changes classes, Mr. Robson. She makes few friends. She prefers to live in a world of seclusion."

I explained about her background; her emotional ties to the Sydney family.

"Ah, that does help explain her attitudes. What is needed is agreeing how the situation should be handled."

I explained about our house project and our Think Box; how we discussed every project as a team and that she illustrated positive interest. He seemed unimpressed.

"What is her relationship with this mum-Lynn, as she calls her mother? It seems she feels her own mother has deserted her."

My heart dropped to rock-bottom. Bump!

~ * ~

"For the next hour, Mags," I told her while the kids were doing homework, "we talked over detail. He accepted my insistence that you were conscious of how sensitive was the situation, also that it seemed on the surface that you, me and the children being together, was the more natural setting. I explained how happy Leanne seemed about having her own room for the first time, and that you had insisted she design her new room's layout and decoration.

"He recommended Leanne visit 'with her step-mother', a child psychiatrist in the city, a free educational service. He said the normal course in such a situation was that the psychiatrist would seek private interviews with each parent alone or together with Leanne. I have his phone number."

"Evan, darling, that confirms it is my time to jump in. His office is in the city and so is mine. Leanne needs only to take the tram and alight in Collins Street where I can meet her. She can return to school the same way."

I mulled for a moment, my office being in an outlying suburb.

My views on her not being overburdened with this, remain valid. But why should I go against both Maggie's and the Head's advice?

"I submit, Maggie my love. But promise me that whatever the outcome of your meeting, you will close no doors. I'm not sure about shrinks, Mags, but let's give it a try and see what happens. It is Leanne who needs the help. Tell the psychiatrist for me, that I will give him all the time he needs."

"I'm not sure about shrinks either, darling. I've never had personal experience of them, but Kay has strong views. She found how, with their salary based on hours, they invent reasons for more consultation. It is an over-service, 'an absolute rort', she called it. I agree we first do what they ask and see how Leanne reacts. We have yet to discover, of course, what Leanne thinks of it. Unless she is onside, it must prove worthless. But I agree we recommend she takes her school's advice."

I nodded and topped up her glass.

"I am learning to love her, darling," Maggie continued. "She is a sweet child, just unfortunately, secretive. I've read about the various stages of this thing called autism—it hints of introspection being a symptom. Do you think I should ask the psychiatrist if this should be considered?"

"I would give that time. Firstly, see what he recommends. I thought autistic people showed a selfishness and rejection of others at an early age, that even as tots, they forsook speaking. Let's give her time with this fellow. Just hold nothing back. If it is me having been somehow remiss, I need to know."

She kissed me and promised.

~ * ~

"Dad there are just so many things coming up at school."

"What things, boy?"

"Well many of my mates are joining the School Cadets and trips are being organised. Trips to all sorts of places around the country— things to do with our lessons. Then there's Rugby? Cricket is out, for I find that boring, but there's trials for entrants in a swimming team, and I reckon you should be a soft touch on that."

"I admire your sentiments, boy. But you cannot do all. And you have responsibilities to your family. Last week you were all for *Stanford Lodge.* I need some muscle-power on occasions. Let's look at what time you can devote to things at school, and what time you give your family."

I could see that had him flummoxed.

"Would you like to see where doing your room is on the priority list? Maybe we can talk about what your share of the work is reasonable? I'm having to share my time between that and work, and so is Maggie. If you want the benefits, you must share."

"I didn't have to work at St. George's Court."

"That wasn't a home. It was somewhere to live while seeking a home. You had a full vote deciding on *Stanford Lodge*, knowing work must be done. Yes, if you want to join the School Cadets, we will do that. But just roll up your sleeves this weekend and I'll show you how to scrub walls. Then we can look at what else is offered at school."

~ * ~

While I worked with Paul, Maggie and Leanne talked on sharing the housework. Their trip to the Psychiatrist had much to do with opening communication channels.

"The guy has great personality, Evan, one with considerable appeal to kids. Yet I can't be sure about his other professional abilities. It has to be given time, yet I am prepared, for an assessment period, to follow his lead."

I nodded.

"I'm not saying I am happy about it, Evan," she told me while the kids were washing dishes, "yet I feel a responsibility in seeing how things go. Certainly it's outside the agreement we made, but I am the only person around who can help both Leanne and you in this situation. Nor do I begrudge the time. Well, not so far anyway."

I agreed we must give the fellow some time.

"He wants to see Leanne and I again in a week. He explained to Leanne that the situation calls for her to be with you and me in Melbourne rather than with mum-Lynn in Sydney—that surely is something in our favour. He seems to realise that his role is to make her happy with us. He told her that this situation happens to many children—that families break up and people, children included, have to make allowances. He also wants to talk with you alone, maybe next week."

Mags then told me something quite significant that Leanne had confided.

"I have no idea, Maggie, where to start thinking on sharing the house-work. Mum-Lynn did all my thinking. She told me when I'm older is when I will have to think things out."

"So this, Evan darling, is what we are up against. That woman's reasoning is beyond all logic."

"What did you answer?"

"That her future is what she should be working towards—and that takes planning—that only she can best know her interests. I asked if she wanted a lifetime of simply being told what to do? Asked her what satisfaction she felt just waiting to be told; that doing things her own mind engineered, is what gives satisfactions. Like my theatre work. Like your interest in theatre now."

"What did she respond?"

"She was still a child and should be doing as told. To do otherwise, was deceit."

We both threw palms up in the air. We had to accept that the kids were both changing from kid-stuff to teen-stuff. They'd yet to reach the stage of realising that everything is not simply given to them—that they must earn everything from privileges to lucky breaks. We were using 'home-making' as a means of getting them to feel a contributing part of family.

Paul certainly was responding better, yet Leanne still floundered.

"When both kids were at Artarmon, Mags, it was the other way around. Leanne was the one responding to that domestic situation whilst Paul was unsettled."

We both had home-work to do.

Twenty-one

Over the next weekend, all four fell to scrubbing walls, floors and ceilings of the 'third living room'.

Destined as TV Room, it would be bedroom for both kids until Leanne's room was done. A small desk was planned for the old linen-room for Leanne to do homework and another in the 'third living room' for Paul to do his.

I was off to *Rhombus* rehearsals only infrequently. We'd been rehearsing for a long time and were down to performing the entire play only once a week. Director Milt was concentrating on each and every face-to-face scene, so needed only some characters some nights.

Paul's and my first shopping list had been buckets, brooms, scouring pads, mops, aerosol disinfectants, polishing wax and band-aids. By Saturday evening we had the third sitting-room clean enough for the kid's temporary bedroom. We were now ready to begin cleaning up the old kitchen for instant use as cook-room-come laundry. Next week, Bob would have his plan for the second bathroom ready for council. I pencilled in to my schedule, the ripping out the wall in the front bedroom for the new door to the old bathroom, then bricking up the old, ready for Percy to move the switchboard.

Sunday we made a duty call up-country. Maggie's boss was throwing a barbecue garden party at his weekender.

"I just have to be there!" she insisted. Neither kid minding missing out on a second day of scrubbing, nor me if daring to admit it. After Saturday's shopping I had spent the rest of the day high up a stepladder scrubbing the ceiling. My neck muscles were giving me hell. Maggie tried her best at massaging it as I crashed into bed that night, yet the neck remained sore for days.

"Getting old," I explained to the family. So Sunday was a relief.

Plumpton? Kurunjang? Those sort of names struck me as we drove into the hills.

Maggie had a map across her knees, Paul and Leanne had another in back. Sure, I occasionally had to pull off the road to await a consensus, but we arrived at a delightful hideaway still friends. Beer and wine flowed more copiously than I expected of a man in his position, when his people had to drive home. He was Peter to most staff for the day, rather than as Mr. Stirling at the office.

"The Chairman of the Stock Exchange exudes a vastly different personality here than there," Maggie whispered. "He is in his relaxed mood here."

"I am sure he will expect everyone to front up on time tomorrow, all bright and bushy-eyed?"

All however, it seemed, arrived home safely, even if not being bright and bushy-eyed come Monday. Monday was also my appointment alone with the psychiatrist. Over dinner I winked at Maggie before turning to Leanne.

"That psychiatrist fellow, dear daughter, is a most unusual fellow. How do you find him?"

Leanne screwed up her face as if either having no idea how to answer, or not wanting to divulge her real thoughts. She looked not at me, but to Maggie for help. Maggie simply waited, both eyebrows raised at her.

"Aw. He is all right, I suppose. Why? How was I supposed to find him?"

"I doubt the school even considered how you would find him. They are concerned that you too often walk out of class to join another. Psychiatrists are trained to find out why. His chances will be better if you feel right with him. Will you feel happier when he asks questions about school? Or other things?"

"What other things?"

"I don't know. But he works for the Education Department so should know how to win information from a student, how to help them with personal problems."

Leanne didn't respond. She kept looking at Maggie with pleading eyes.

That she is seeking help from Maggie is a positive sign. It at least indicates that mum-Lynn's letters haven't fully poisoned the child's mind against her stepmother.

"Maybe it is too soon for us to have opinions on him," said Mags. "Leanne and I met him only once. What did you make of him, darling?" she asked me.

Paul was keeping a low profile, eyes darting backwards and forwards.

I smiled. "He quite impressed me as a typical public servant."

Maggie's eyes smiled. I could almost read her mind, agreeing that the guy was so young that he depended entirely on the ritual course taught him.

~ * ~

When the bank loan came through, money was paid, the contract signed and Percy and Bob had their council friend rubber-stamp the plans for the second bathroom. While it was being built we sanitized the master bedroom.

Maggie and Leanne went to weekly meetings with the psychiatrist. Sometimes he interviewed Maggie alone, other times Leanne. He never requested another interview with me. Maggie told me how she ensured Peter Stirling noticed she came to work early most mornings, to compensate for her times absent.

"He is being quite tolerant, darling. I've told him enough that he realises it is something serious for us. He explained how his own kids 'gave my wife and I a bloody hard time too'. 'And let's face it,' he added, 'you accomplish more work in any day than any prior secretary, so don't feel guilty about needing family time off'."

I laughed. "Congratulations on having instilled such confidence in him."

"Yes, it almost made me feel I was falling in love with him."

I put on my *pseudo*-suave look and quipped…

"Maybe that might be a good thing, my dear."

She put hands to hips and raised her eyebrow at me.

In front of the children, I grabbed her, kissed her and smacked her bottom, then turned to Leanne.

"Did you ever see Uncle Norman do that to mum-Lynn?"

Paul threw a hand over his mouth, to nearly burst out laughing.

Leanne smiled, and said only, "No. Never," smiling in a bemused sort of way.

Maggie leaned up and whispered in my ear…

"Top marks for that little bit of salesmanship, my dear."

~ * ~

Three weeks later, Maggie approached Mrs. Carmody.

"We are ready to move into *Stanford Lodge*. We are six weeks short of our two year lease, but will pay you rent up until then. We have indeed been happy here."

She patted Maggie's arm.

"You will pay not a penny, dear. You have been ideal tenants. I was afraid when your children arrived, but they quite renewed my faith."

We made sure the kids were told that. We knew too, that she already knew how well we had looked after her place, for our cleaning lady was her very own. She had recommended her once Maggie began work.

Stanford Lodge had its first remodelled room, an old larder having become a sparkling bathroom with tub, shower recess, toilet and wash-basin…

"…a wash-basin backed by all the mirrors a growing young woman could want," Maggie announced to Leanne.

It was hardly Restoration, of course. It but paid homage to our comfort while getting on with the main chore.

Mrs. Carmody's maid's sister Evelyn accepted a post to come in each weekday to tidy up kitchen and bathrooms at any time she wished, before evening.

So having installed laundry machines and gas cooker with overhead exhaust, we moved into our Home for Old Ladies, paying them due deference by setting up a large vase of roses on a cardboard box in the vestibule. We had the children join us in a little ceremony of obeisance.

First meal in our new home after the removalists left, was a bought fish and chip finger-fed dinner on paper plates, a newspaper as 'table-cloth'. The roses were brought in to adorn the table. It being winter, we risked the likelihood of a blocked chimney by lighting a log fire in the grate. The chimney was luckily clear enough and we sat around that corner of the big room, feeding the fireplace with clap-board torn from the walls of the old staff quarters.

Maggie was amazed when the kids announced that the roaring fire was a first in a lifetime experience.

Next morning, being Saturday, Maggie took hammer and jemmy, the baby crowbar, to wrench off the three-ply sheets covering the leadlight panels of internal doors. They had been added, obviously for privacy, when all rooms became wards.

"I've been dying to do that," she told us.

She was in raptures, once the massed cobwebs were washed away, at the beauty of the stained-glass patterns, all of roses in various colours and all in surprisingly good condition.

"I shall definitely restore those formal rose-gardens in the front," she announced. "Then we shall have roses blooming both inside and outside."

All rooms seemed even bigger with those doors now admitting more daylight.

"Next weekend, Leanne, love," she then happily announced, "we shall shop for your puppy. You can choose the dog, the leash and its bed cushion. I will choose the kibbles and fresh meat that every well-kept dog needs every day, okay?"

That went down extremely well.

Twenty-two

Boys in the Band was soon to open. The eight-man cast was ready, the backstage crew primed. Director Milton and Light Technician Eric went into a scrum huddle, wrapping arms about each other, happy at the prospect of a coup for *Rhombus*. We still had ten days to perfect things.

I remained terribly nervy on two fronts. I had never faced a live theatre audience. My public-speaking experience, apart from some election spiels in earlier Sydney years was limited to my sales class teaching. *Boys in the Band* would be a critical audience, mostly gay, expecting something as professional as the successful movie. My big scene, the long telephone call near the climactic end, was still pressuring me. It was neither a Shakespeare monologue nor a scene in which I could stride about to attract audience attention. It was one requiring me on my knees at the very front of the stage, all alone with all lights spotted on me.

If I don't pull that off properly, it will ruin the entire show!

I had lost count of how many times Maggie had put me through the scene, coaching me on body-language—not easy when on the floor clutching a telephone, so close to front of stage that all I had to look at were faces in the front row. It was a tender scene where I must tell deliberate lies, questioning my very sexual make-up to my wife? Or at least, Alan's wife. I was a maybe-straight guy caught up in the whirl of gay bitchiness and unnatural lusts. A major objective of the play was that everyone, audience and cast, could ever truly know if Alan were gay or not!

Maggie had known that in moving to a city of strangers, she would miss her stage work, so had thrown herself into this opportunity of working with the crew from the very day of my audition. She felt quite at home with it all and had quite befriended Director Milt. He was thrilled at the experience she brought to rehearsals.

I had no background and depended on her help too. She insisted I take every notice of Milt and he too had worked hard on building my confidence.

The theatre's sound equipment was excellent. We realised this when taking our first rehearsal there. So close to opening night, however, we realised we needed cash for hiring stage props and lighting equipment that Union Theatre lacked. The *Rhombus* purse was again empty.

We decided on holding an auction come Saturday. Everybody must not only invite as many as they could scrounge, but all attending must bring an auction lot.

Where? We reckoned there could be sixty or seventy people. No-one knew where we could get a free room to hold so many.

Maggie and I looked at each other with raised eyebrows. She raised a finger.

"Evan and I have somewhere," she announced, "but everyone will need to bring cushions or pillows to sit on."

The Home for Old Ladies, in all its dishabille, was offered and accepted.

At least it was easy to find in any Melbourne street directory.

We had but our six chairs for any old and decrepit soul who should turn up.

"And bring your money in small notes and plenty of coinage," I insisted.

With gay crowds, 'purse' was most times a problem.

Well, what fun was in store. And Leanne and Paul were to be part of it.

I gave each five dollars over their weekly pocket money so they could bid on something they felt worthy. Being part of the host family, each was given chores. They had attended a few rehearsals so had some idea of the wild sort of crowd expected. They also remembered a few of Maggie's workmates from the reasonably recent barbeque, for several from her work were invited, including Julie and Olaf.

Mags was the first to realise that such 'strangers' to *Rhombus*, provided they enjoyed this evening, were likely to pay to see the show.

Sixty-two people turned up.

First to arrive, tinkling the bell on the gate was Tim and his wife of the moment. Tim was to play Donald, an ambivalent friend to leading man, Michael. In the play, Donald keeps threatening to spurn New York for the countryside 'where there is no homosexual life'. His 'wife' on this occasion was Sylvia. Donald's real-life reputation was keeping a girlfriend as wife until she fell pregnant, then swapping her for another—and double-dating gay lovers along the way.

"This just happens to be my lifestyle," he would impart to all and sundry, including current 'wife'.

"Wow, look at this," he said walking up our front path. "You said you'd bought a house, but you didn't tell us it was Buckingham-fuckin'-Palace!"

People began arriving in numbers. Howard, a sixty-year-old queen dressed in drag far more flamboyantly than any real woman, also with more jewellery, and more perfume, was playing Harold. The entire play was Harold's birthday party, so Howard pictured himself lead player, despite it was a bit part.

Maggie's and my minds seemed to be everywhere. So many times our eyes met as each flitted about seeing that no-one was needing help. Leanne seemed the most flummoxed. It was her job to present every arrival an *hors-d'œuvre* or cookie. At one stage she was standing quite mesmerised by the sight of Howard in his ostentatious drag. I could see the serving tray she toted, with her mind so distracted, beginning to tilt. I had to almost dive through the crush, to snap her back to consciousness before everything fell to the floor.

Oh my God what is this lesson going to teach my children?

All the action was in the dining-room, biggest room in the house, with overflow through double-doors on one side into the vestibule, and through the matching doors on its other, the kid's room. We had a modest fire burning in the dining-room grate and the house's only table was quickly filling with items donated as auction-lots.

Russel brought his parents and a grandparent. Russell was to play Larry, an outgoing gay guy with hots for Hank. Throughout the play, whatever the scene, Larry is trying to hustle Hank aside. Simon, the breakfast radio host and wife Beverly, arrived with baby daughter. Maggie saw to putting it in what would be Leanne's room, on one of the kid's mattress, for our bed was set aside for everybody tossing their out-door winter gear. Simon was the lead part of Michael, host of the *Boys* gay birthday party for Harold.

Cyril arrived with them. Cyril was Cowboy, an attractive blond prostitute, Donald's overnight birthday gift to Harold. Bernard and Maurice were next, two young guys who in real life shared a half-house, by amazing coincidence, on Stanford Road. We had unknowingly passed it the morning we walked the length of the street. Another unique coincidence was that Bernard, a Sri Lankan, played the part of Bernard, a Negroid gay who lusted after the son of a rich woman he had worked for. Maurice was playing Hank.

Many unknowns came, having heard by word of mouth. "I experience auction never," Olaf informed me.

Wow. Is he ever in for a shock.

Maggie was collecting auction lots.

I was simply relieved that none of the unknown visitors turned out to be DRC business acquaintances!

One of the last was Jamie, or in the play, Emory, the screaming little queen, he who would draw most audience laughter—or so we hoped.

Leanne nearly fell about in giggles when he flounced through the door, flapping wings, insisting on kissing everybody. The casserole he'd half-cooked as an auction lot was quickly passed on to Maggie for stashing on the table. Its label read, *Bake thirty more minutes.*

Isn't this one ever a natural to be playing Emory?

Everyone, of course, wanted to see through the house. That was Paul's job.

"Make it quick, son," I had schooled him. "Few will remember anyway because they don't really care. Gay guys are extremely self-centred so don't try working them out. Just see that they have a glass of punch in their hand, and answer the call when the auction starts."

Late arrival was a bevy of four girls Maggie quickly twigged as lesbians. They seemed to know all the cast in *Boys.*

The auction was a scream from start to finish with raises sometimes as much as two cents on an aged toothbrush. Decent lots were few, Jamie's casserole, for instance; "Loaded with oregano," he shrieked as it was announced. "My mother never cooks anything without oregano," he assured all, just letting us know this was an Emory line in the play.

Leanne and Paul sat on pillows in the vestibule, looking in on everything, bemused at the eclectic variety. The room itself was naked. Nothing had been done with it but sanitize the rawness. The walls were montages of stains and cracks in the plaster, signs of where wall-sconces for gaslights had been ripped out and the holes badly patched. We had already taken down the two small crystal chandeliers that had graced the ceiling, along with the huge one in the Octagon, storing them away until time for their turn in the Restoration. The present lighting was two naked light bulbs dangling from untidy holes in the ceiling. What still featured proudly were all the nine-inch architraves and twelve-inch skirting boards of moulded cedar, albeit needing a repaint. Also the beauty of the half-windowed double-doors. Maggie had the stained-glass in the doors glimmering as if lovingly polished.

Except for the older or more portly bidders, all perched on their cushions or on the especially scrubbed Brussels carpet.

Simon, as auctioneer, had people in screams of laughter at his outrageously pompous descriptions of worthless lots—a lone pedal off a bicycle, a stylish woman's hat with ostrich feathers donated by Howard, a yellowed bridal gown, remnants of a toy train-set lacking an engine, a plastic meerschaum, three Waterford crystal wine-glasses, and such—as eclectic an assortment as the guests themselves.

When I was relieving Simon as auctioneer, Maggie deliberately chose to pass me as the next lot, a packet of condoms. I had to ignore her snide smile. My brain whirled, seeking inspiration. I slid one little ring out of the packet and held it high.

"When retiring, just slip one of these under your tongue and keep it there. It will keep you safe from all the nasty things in life."

It was bought by Margo, one of the lesbians. I could never imagine why.

When all lots were sold, all accepted coffee in paper cups while Maggie, Julie, and Beverly counted the takings. We made four hundred ten dollars and eight cents, a fortune in *Rhombus* values.

After a telephone call from a neighbour reminding us it had become Sunday, we called a finish to the fun-filled evening. Partings of the several friends kerbside were as noisy as had been the hilarity inside. Jamie's screaming laughter was particularly evident, echoing back and forth through the chilly night air of Stanford Road.

~ * ~

Over a late breakfast, Leanne asked...

"Is today the day we buy the dog?"

"Um, yes. We did say come the weekend, didn't we?"

"There's a gorgeous little puppy in the Glenferrie Rd pet-shop. Can we go there?"

She's already been there on her way home from school, to suss it out!

I looked at Maggie who was both nodding and smiling.

"Of course, love. You need wash your hair, so maybe you should ask Paul and your father to do the dishes? I'll help you with your hair and we can go early in case your puppy gets sold."

She admitted to having seen the puppy yesterday afternoon.

It was still there, the tiniest black Labrador with a white crest on her chest, so young that I was amazed she was not still suckling.

We bought Baby Kibble and minced-steak, baby leash, rubber bone, sleeping basket and a milk-feed bottle with rubber teat. Leanne carried her home in a shoe-box lined with tissues. En-route home, the pup spewed all over herself and the shoe-box.

"The excitement of you having chosen her," Maggie told Leanne.

"I'm calling her Tiffany," we were informed as I drew up at the kerb.

We congratulated her on the choice and once indoors cleansed Tiffany of her vomit, then took her to the front veranda. There we put her inside a white tea-cup, her little bottom fitting nicely, her front paws dangling over the rim. Maggie took several photographs of Tiffany in her 'cup and saucer', Leanne attending.

"You will like to keep this in your album," we told her. "She will grow up surprisingly quickly."

"Can she sleep in my room?"

"Dogs piddle everywhere," said Paul. "It's my room too, you know."

I was thankful at Paul saving me from being the one to say 'No'.

"It's important for pets to recognise a place entirely their own. Same as Hairy-legs insists on returning to his cage to sleep," said Maggie. "Let's make it in the scullery so as she grows, she can let herself outside for toilet."

I get the message. Cut a hinged dog-flap in that rear door, Evan!

"We should choose a spot for her toilet also," I added. "Get her used to going in the same spot. That will make it easier, Leanne, when you clean up her droppings each evening before dinner, eh?"

Leanne looked askance. Maggie was quick to remind her, "Even humans have our special places for going to the toilet."

Leanne seemed happy with such logic and agreed.

Tiffany was already proving a big drawcard in Leanne wanting to stay with us!

Twenty-three

I was all nerves leading up to *Boys in the Band.*

It was to open Tuesday, then play again Thursday, Saturday, then again, Tuesday and Thursday.

"Be prepared for take-out dinners every performance night," Maggie told the kids.

"Great," both shrieked.

"Don't forget my school's visit to DRC Bags on Friday," Leanne reminded me.

"I wouldn't dare, my dear."

I had obtained from Grant Gorman, approval for Leanne's school to make a plant visit next Friday afternoon. Enough teachers would be along to ensure children didn't get too close to working machinery.

"Working parts of every machine are safe-guarded, of course," I almost recited, "yet, as every parent knows, children can be... Yes."

I didn't bother finishing. Both kids had grins across their faces.

Mags had thought the adventure a brilliant idea.

"Not only will it be educational, darling, but kudos from peers will brush-off on Leanne."

The psychiatrist fellow had thought it a great idea, as had the Head of School.

"There will also be a brush-off in morale for me, Mags. Pretty well every one at the plant is a mother or father, some even grandparents. All seem excited about it. I have arranged that school-teachers will be responsible for controlling the children, so all my people are available, at each work station, to answer questions."

"And who is meanwhile running the machinery?"

"The way I have my plant running these days, darling, the machinery will run itself—the ultimate proof of good management!"

She covered her mouth and yawned.

I had a rehearsal fixed for Wednesday night. We were running through the entire play, then come Friday night, all cast would pick faults with any difficult passage or awkward stage movement.

"You are lucky *Boys* doesn't call for scenery change," said Mags.

"Huh! But that means, nor do we get a break except for between the two Acts."

Each scene change was but ten seconds of black-out, during which we fumbled our way to our places for the next scene. Whoever had the first line must be exactly on his spot, for Eric will have the spotlight directed on it. Poor Simon, playing Michael, never left the stage; he was in every scene.

"So are you, once making your entrance," Mag had said on that point.

My testing 'phone-call' came right near the end. It was a dramatic part, but Milt and Maggie between them, had me well primed.

The children wanted to come to final rehearsal Monday.

"Only if you have finished all homework. You will be on your honour in that!"

"And only if you get Milton's approval for them to be there," Maggie threw in.

"Milt doesn't mind, darling. He is seeking an audience."

Maggie put on her 'terribly, terribly' British accent, "It is professional stagecraft courtesy, dear. He would appreciate your realising it. He would also hold it against me for not reminding you of it.”

Leanne looked almost frightened, but Paul was beginning to read Maggie pretty well. He laughed.

I sighed deeply, “I shall call him tomorrow, dear.”

The kids enjoyed such exchanges. They were our nearest moments to arguments.

Saturday was sworn for shopping for Leanne’s wallpaper. With some input from us, she would choose it herself. On Sunday we would attend Paul’s first School Cadet Parade, at least first for him.

“Leanne,” I announced at Friday’s breakfast, “you know this is a busy week. Only thing to be done in your room before hanging paper is to scrape and sand old paintwork. New paint can be done only in stages because each of four coats needs overnight to dry. And Paul, with all of us attending your parade on Sunday, I expect you to help me tomorrow. We must take up the old linoleum in her room. Okay?”

So Leanne was committed, and Paul obligated.

Maggie had a smile on her face.

Before retiring, she said, “I’m just so envious, my dear husband, in the way you can twist orders to sound like needy pleas.”

“It comes naturally to some, my dear.”

Our weekend went smoothly. The Monday night rehearsal was a riot of fun. Even Maggie, who by now knew every line by every player, so anticipated what was coming, couldn’t help but laugh and applaud when the stage movements were added.

“What I call the ‘tender’ scenes when the gay guys are pouring out their hearts to whoever cares enough to listen,” she pointed out, “are all such clever writing. Milt has recognised all the nuances. He has the cast, in my opinion, all up to the mark. Especially you, darling. Your telephone call had even your two kids spellbound.”

She got a great kiss for that.

Many people had sat around the little church hall loaned for rehearsals. Many friends and family of the cast had come along to see the final run through. They had been asked, as an audience, to hold nothing back, that if they felt like applauding any line or even shouting something distracting, they were free to do so.

"Every player must be able to cope with interruptions," Milt told them.

"Your phone call, my darling, was heard in dead silence. Even I had a lump in my throat."

"Oh, what a great review. Do you reckon you can string that out in lights all the way up Collins Street?"

Twenty-four

Tuesday morning, the mess of Leanne's room hidden by a closed door, was guarded by a Robson heirloom. The old iron shoe-last my father had used to repair my shoes, had been *his* father's. It was now my 'Do Not Enter!' sentry.

"I reckon, my darling," Maggie said, watching me soak breakfast dishes in the sink, ready for Evelyn, "that you are right now suffering what actors call 'Opening Night Pains'? Doubts always seem to plague actors at this time. Are you right now thinking of all the things that could go wrong?"

"You're dead right, girl."

"What in particular?"

"Physically moving during blackout, to that corner of the stage. Hank and I have to be sitting on those ottomans ready for our duologue as the lights open. Even in rehearsals with lights on, we have been bumping into others."

"It went fine last rehearsal."

"That doesn't mean it will be fine in every performance. Eric will have his spotlight concentrated on that stage corner. We have to be there on the ten second mark."

"You have the opening line of that scene. If the spot comes on before you are posed, simply wave a hand as if frustrated and begin your line. Just let it seem natural. Nothing says you must be already sitting when the spot comes on."

Thinking around that, it made sense.

"Many times in theatre, darling, glitches happen. A good actor covers them up. If caught on the hop, worst thing you can do is falter. Simply make any natural movement, a shrug, or the heel of your hand to your temple. That gives you seconds to recover. It happens often. I have been there many times."

I didn't answer, but Maggie, old trouper, diverted my worries.

"Where are you going to ditch the old linoleum from Leanne's room?"

I grinned. She was changing the subject.

"Leanne must have to wait for her room. "That rotten old back veranda is going to have to come down. We've already decided a flagged terrace for that area, a terrace needing filling with solid junk and old linoleum qualifies. So does the old iron roof from the back veranda. The hole will need an outer brick wall. If I don't build it now, that old linoleum must be moved again."

"A big hole there will close off our back door."

"The back door also has to move when I build the new kitchen. Once the terrace wall is built, less than a metre high, I can rig up a plank walkway across the hole. That retaining wall needs building now."

"Such a big hole will need more filling than rubble from our renovations?"

"Yes. I'll have to work on that."

As from that day on, the Big Hole was to earn capital letters.

"Shouldn't a brick wall be laid by a bricklayer?"

"Not this one, darling. I will be facing my rough brickwork with crazy paving to match the street wall."

"Nobody can see the back wall at the same time as the street wall."

"I am sure one of the Old Ladies would notice the difference. We must consider their peace of mind."

She rolled her eyes and gave me another cuddle.

I called Leanne as she emerged from her bathroom.

"To make the hole needed for burying the old linoleum from your room, darling, I need time. Can we leave your door closed for a further week?"

I noticed the surprise in Mag's eyes and the pensive frown on Leanne.

I knew it would be all right with her, because of the *Boys* commitment.

"Of course, Dad. The play is important. I can put up sharing with Paul for that long."

It was the first hint of humour from Leanne.

"Phew," we heard from Paul, heading for the bathroom.

Leanne pulled my head down and gave me a kiss.

It made my day. I chose not to choose now for reminding her she hadn't cleaned Hairy Leg's cage.

Twenty-five

Melbourne University's Union Theatre…

"There's police all around the theatre walls," exclaimed Paul seeming in a state of shock. "Is this play illegal? Can you be in trouble, Dad?"

I sat in front of a mirror, Maggie applying my grease-paint.

"Son, our language calls for, 'There *are* police'—not 'There *is* police'. But no, no problems. Nothing is illegal. It's just that being gay is something not talked about. This is a University campus and students could maybe hold a protest."

They were the days when homosexuality was considered both blasphemous and socially obnoxious. The university insisted it must avoid a riot. It was agreed a review would be made after the first two nights. Meanwhile, twenty policemen would line the walls inside, and another twenty, control front of house and rear exits.

The kids had their seats booked, so Maggie had brought them backstage for a few minutes, to see what went on in real theatre. She now scooted them off to their seats alongside Julie and Olaf.

My mind quickly sprang back into *Boys* mode.

I wouldn't be in the least surprised if Maggie doesn't try influencing Leanne into theatre. I just know she is trying everything to help bring the child into our family of her own volition. She certainly doesn't like this young shrink fellow, and I think even less of him.

My mind wandered around so many things.

I was trying to concentrate on anything but the play, yet, like a coiled spring, the mind kept switching back to things *Boys*.

Grant and Monica Gorman? Did they get their tickets? Can't remember now, if he said they had them.

Shit! How many sides of a man's life is one supposed to keep in fine detail?

I have a life in which I am sure my wife loves me, and that at least one kid seems to, and a job in which I get every vibe that most things I do at work, I do well.

The things that still bugged me were the last things I needed to be brooding on now.

But acting? Taking the stage? Shit again! Maggie says I have it at an acceptable level, but is that just to build up my confidence?

I was saved further distraction by Milt offering final advice.

"When coming on stage, just recall your opening lines and concentrate on them. You will be conscious of the police lining the walls, yet must see them as no more than audience without seats. Audience is not part of the play, they are there to simply cough, sneeze and generally try distracting you. Just ignore everything but what your line is meant to achieve. Just concentrate on what Mart Crowley expects of you."

It got the nods he wanted and we got the confidence he intended.

Then, suddenly I realised that not only Paul and Leanne had gone, but Maggie.

"Break a bloody leg, mate," rang in my ears as being her parting words.

I was alone. And scared.

~ * ~

It went famously, with only a few minor glitches.

Harold had picked up Donald's wine-glass instead of his own and Donald, a minute later put out his hand but his glass wasn't there. He was quick enough to shrug shoulders as much as to say, "Where did I put the damned thing?"

Michael too, was pro enough to pick up another and hand it to Donald with a, 'Here it is!'

"Thank you, darling," answered Donald, and everyone was able to then resume lines.

It being my first time on a real stage before a real audience, Milt had warned me against letting my eyes rest on any face beyond the footlights.

"Their very expression can distract you. All must remain just ghostly visions," he had drummed into me. "Your thoughts must be focused on your own facial expressions, body movements and lines. Remember all the time that no-one is more important than the other characters on stage."

At one point, however, when I knew I had no lines for a few minutes, had only to stand by an aspidistra sipping my drink, I did sight Grant and Monica Gorman. Next to them were Graham Holmes, Head Office Accountant and his wife.

Simply more people to my challenge of doing a good job?

A challenge to be bested! my alter-ego replied.

I had some strong lines to deliver, yet I continued thinking only on Milt's and Maggie's coaching. By the time my telephone call came, I was feeling not too easy, yet aware I'd done well so far. The audience had laughed at the right places and I noted how the more experienced among us would dally their next line until quiet had all but resumed. That next line quietened the house anyway.

It not only felt so good that they were wanting to hear every line, but we had them picking up on all the nuances the playwright intended! So I fortunately had no negative feeling gnawing at me.

My phone call was my biggest moment.

I was conscious of all the cast being behind me, all in deep shadow because all spots were on me. It was the time in Alan's life when he had really lost his sense of self-security, stumbled into this gay party and was questioning his own sexuality.

Did I really have a gay love for Michael? sort of thing.

This had Alan doubting himself. The part called for every player, in a bitchy parlour game, calling a past lover or someone with whom they were in conflict, declaring their love. I had such lines to declare to an old schoolmate—I couldn't lose face by quitting the dare. A drunk Michael had thrust the number into my hand and pointed to the phone; my every word must sound as if I was talking to that guy, yet, instead of the number Michael gave me, I had dialled my wife. Alan's wife. The audience knew it but the boys in the band didn't. And Alan's relationship with his wife was that he was considering leaving her, anyway!

Alan, right here, is truly indeed vulnerable, and I'm bloody Alan!

Maggie had spent a long time on this scene—it was a crux period in the play. She had coached me on every word, every pause and every damned itch of nervousness that must stay hidden. If I were to come out of this night well, it was Maggie I needed to thank most.

Yet here I must appear as if trying to deceive a wife! This is my torment. How can I do this with feeling?

I came through it okay. Everyone came out of it well. With so many of Melbourne's gay crowd present, we received an incredibly noisy reception! Even some of the police were clapping.

Grant and his party were on their feet clapping. Only at curtain-call did I let them see I had noticed them. I had been dreadfully afraid they could be sitting, hiding faces behind hands in case they should be recognised.

Julie and Olaf offered to take the kids home so we could go partying with the rest of the crew, every one of us on a hype. The kids promised to lock up carefully and go straight to bed after cocoa. Both gave me great hugs, Leanne with tears in her eyes.

Press reviews gave us good inches, one declaring it a credit to Melbourne's theatre amateurs and the hope they would be seeing more of *Rhombus*. Others declared it high time the gay community demanded a right to be heard.

Could things have turned out better?

Twenty-six

The planned five performances became six when, by night four, night five was a sell-out and reviewers were still full of praise. By then I felt confident enough to let some of the folk at work know about it. Several, including Dawn with her husband and my senior managers with partners, came to the final night. And oh-boy, did the news quickly flash around the factory next day!

It had all been such a wonderfully camp experience.

By then my terrace wall was half done. On the odd evenings I mixed small batches of mortar and under electric light, laid bricks. I was anxious to have physical work to keep my mind from dwelling on the play. The wall grew quickly because I had only two courses of footings to lay. All original footings were of five layers, having to carry the weight of not only brick cavity walls but the roof. My wall was but a retaining wall for the solid fill. The filling itself would support the crazy-paving cover.

"Just don't tell the old ladies, I've taken a short-cut," I pleaded with Mags.

Leanne was excited when we moved the shoe-last and began her room.

The stripped linoleum, much of it reduced to shreds, was now wheeled along planks laid over the carpet and dumped into the Big Hole. Planks now extended from the back door to the terrace wall.

In Leanne's bedroom, all timberwork had received over the weekend, their two undercoats. She agreed to wallpapered door panels, as I would be papering door panels throughout the house, same as the walls. I made regular checks as we progressed through gloss-coating of woodwork, as all were giving time to it. I threatened all who didn't wipe off splashes from areas to be papered, or on the window-glass, with the sack.

"Sack from what?" all wanted to know. I told them that was my secret.

Tiffany, when we were waiting for the final gloss coat to dry, got into the room and managed to get white gloss streaks across her little backside and black fur stuck in the drying paint.

"Sometimes we have to be cruel in being kind to those we love," I insisted to Leanne when Tiffany complained piteously at having her backside drenched in paint-thinner. I accepted the onus of scraping the black fur out of the skirting board, sanding it down again, and patch-painting its two coats.

With subtle hints from Maggie, Leanne had chosen wallpaper of a floral design in lemon and olive-green, the colours of wattle, Australia's floral emblem. She was surprised when informed that these were also the country's sporting colours.

"So you will be in good company with walls in these colours, girl," I told her.

Glenferrie Road prices were a tad higher than elsewhere, yet at the gallery specialising in wallpapers, murals, curtains and upholstering fabrics and hardware, the emphasis was on quality.

Twelve feet, both length and breadth of her room, was also high for erecting scaffolds. Reaching up from an arched back to be able to see what one was doing, made it easy to lose balance, especially after several hours. I bought the tallest of stepladders and hired two more, one for easier access on to the planks, when toting on the shoulder, a twelve-foot length of pasted paper.

"What holds the end you have pasted, from falling as you move along the plank?"

"You, darling. You will have a long-handled broom holding that end against the ceiling while the paste inter-acts with the sizing. Once I have all the length wiped with my towel, I'll come back to the start, wiping it all again."

"You didn't paper the ceilings in Waverton, but I was impressed how you wiped all the walls as you went. It all ended up looking so professional."

"I've done ceilings before, albeit not so high. They will be awkward."

I found an excellent hardware store on Malvern Road and purchased brass doorknobs enough for every door, also brass 'swing-flaps' for every keyhole. Many of the old wooden flaps were either missing or broken. I purchased enough for all, not wanting to risk finding later, that the particular design had been superseded. Same went for the wallpaper for the lounge, dining-room, Octagon and hallways. Mags and I had chosen a reasonably dark blue and white, with hints of gold; what she called a 'traditional French period' design.

In Leanne's room, the large mouldings where walls met ceiling were painted acrylic white, I re-blacked the fireplace ironwork and eased the window that had been sticking. We were ready to start papering.

My factory used huge reels of thick white paper to make flour-bags. Waste ends made excellent floor coverings for pasting wallpaper. We covered the vestibule carpet with plastic, then the thick paper. I taught Maggie and the kids how much paste to apply. Leanne mixed, Maggie and Paul pasted. The ceiling was already sized.

Each length had to be carefully folded concertina style, with no edges letting paste touch the front side of the paper. I then had to hoist it on to a shoulder then get myself up the ladder and on to the scaffold plank. The 'roll' got increasingly floppy as the paper absorbed paste, so time was as important as care.

I warned all to expect several "damns" and "bloody hells" as well as worse, should I get paste either on to the wallpaper surface, or in my hair.

Maggie's broom had a length of bamboo lashed to its handle, Paul standing by should she tire. The work was slow and tiring. Many times I cursed myself for overconfidence when ignoring Maggie's pleas to let professionals do at least the ceilings.

But we got there some three hours later, without too much cussing.

"Time for beer," I called. Paul went to get it. Leanne, nursing Tiffany, stayed, staring at her ceiling with a great smile on her face.

"It looks beautiful, Dad."

Maggie massaged my neck with Tiger Balm that night, and I admitted defeat.

"Yes, my love, you were right. I will maybe get in professionals to do the rest of the ceilings."

"Maybe?"

"Well, this massaging is great. If I don't do more ceilings, I won't get the massage."

After that, the walls proved easy. We again stood around, admiring our first room, Maggie and I sipping wine, the children, sarsaparilla.

Maggie had an arm around Leanne's shoulders.

"I wonder what the two Old Ladies sharing this room, would now be thinking?"

Leanne didn't hesitate. "They would be thinking themselves the luckiest Old Ladies in the world."

Oh what added balm to my aching back!

~ * ~

We had agreed that while Paul went to a school-friend's birthday party on Sunday, Maggie, Leanne and I would shop for carpet.

"Will you choose it for me? Leanne asked Maggie over breakfast.

"Sure, my dear. I've a feel for something with a pattern. Spills on plain carpet leave obvious stains. We need something with a pattern."

We dropped Paul off at his friend's house in nearby Glen Iris and headed for the carpet gallery. An ochre Axminster, a darker shade of the wattle in the wallpaper, in a floral design with olive green leaves, appealed to all. It would be delivered and laid next Saturday. At the lighting gallery Leanne gave the nod to a simple brass pendant to match the doorknob and window-clasps.

For her looming birthday we bought a small writing desk from a wonderful little store called *This'n That*. It bought and sold all manner of things. They also had a replica brass 'paraffin' lamp for it.

We subsidised Paul in buying her a framed Van Gogh, *Bedroom in Arles* for a wall, and the first room in our Home for Old Ladies was restored not only to our satisfactions but hopefully too, the Old Ladies looking down.

We shared a bottle of *Veuve Clicquot* with the kids that night.

"I think it would be nice to send photos of it to Sue in Artarmon, darling," Maggie purred. "I'm sure she would love to see your room, despite no plastic flowers."

Twenty-seven

Maggie muses...

I am happy.

How many girls my age can say that?

Sure, there are things that disappoint me, things that could be better, yet nothing devastating—nothing that makes life really miserable, despite I hadn't planned the situation I'm in.

Never had I imagined one like this. A mother of sorts?

I would have expected to flounder. Evan, however, keeps me feeling confident that I am succeeding, yet I don't see my major trouble quickly righting itself. Things between Evan and I remain fine and I guess a girl has to consider herself happy with that. Only a few little things he overlooks in being attentive, as do all men, yet a busy businessman can't be expected to note everything. None are major enough to disappoint me. In bed he can sometimes be aggressive and at others, gentle; yet unless really pressured in his work at the time, I can bend him to my needs. He never seems to mind my calling his attention to them, certainly a big plus for me.

In the social scene he is ever conscious of me, particularly those at his work whom I don't know so well. I was just so thrilled for him on that first day at the office after the opening of 'Boys'. His first call was from Grant Gorman, the second from Graham Holmes, congratulating him. I know the feeling of something like that.

He was so worried that Grant might have felt he was neglecting his work.

As soon as 'Boys' was over and Leanne's room finished, he was on an early flight to Brisbane. His appointments there are always over a weekend, seeing clients Friday and Monday so he has the weekend for Lulu and Valerie. He then flies to Sydney for three days so he can be back in the office Friday to check things at the plant. A week later he would service Adelaide and Hobart with just an overnight. I tell him the Old Ladies will understand that he has other commitments.

My only real concern is Leanne. In so many ways she illustrates happiness with us yet puts things into words only unintentionally. I can only treasure those rare occasions. Letters from Artarmon are less regular, yet she still never mentions them. That really bugs me. They simply disappear from the hall side-table, yet never does she give us feedback. Her silence makes me both suspicious and frightened. She is obviously happy with Tiffany, Hairy Legs and her bedroom, yet is she also fretting for Sue and 'mum-Lynn'?

Dare I ask why the letters are now not so frequent? Could it be because other evil letters are being sent via friends at school or something, in case Lynn thinks I might be opening them?

I simply cannot believe Lynn Stroud is losing interest. That she could snare the child off that train was an action I can never forgive. It proves how deceitful she can be. Can Leanne have asked her not to write so often? Oh why cannot the child take us into her confidence? That she doesn't, I cannot but believe she has a deep reason she dare not divulge. Which adds up to a lack of trust?

Evan's attitude to bringing the kids up isn't what I'd ever depicted as usual. I so often get the feeling that he raises them the same as he brings on his people at work, outsiders who need cajoling into seeing themselves as part of the operation family. Only time I've ever seen him taking either child into his arms and cuddling them is when Paul arrived on the train without Leanne. It's not as if he hasn't a love for them, but I always thought families should all be physically loving. My parents were. Treated my fears and problems as their own. Evan seems to only want to oil the squeaks so the squeals of pain subside, then he's back on his programme.

Am I being too unkind to him in this? It seems not to worry Paul because he has a positive approach to his problems, talks with Ethan about not liking school, wishing he were in that rather than this, learning trade skills rather than economic or bureaucratic. But Leanne doesn't confide in either of us and Evan doesn't seem to face this seriously enough. Should I then, be doing more with her? No matter how I pry, trying to reach her thoughts, she never responds.

And the psychiatrist fellow is hopeless. The Head at school recognised Leanne's problem and took the regulation course, but it isn't working. The man he referred us to is simply not up to the job— cannot even give me a lead how I should respond to situations— tells me that Leanne misses 'mum-Lynn', that she answers 'Yes' to his every question on that, yet he cannot get her to elaborate. When asking should I be approaching her with such a leading question, he tells me it could be the wrong thing.

"Just keep paying her the attention you are doing."

I'm beginning to believe Kay is right, that some, anyway, of these people are more interested in receiving payment for extra services than helping the child become more outgoing.

Paul at sixteen is developing an independent streak. Evan insists that breaking away from family shackles is part of every boy's life around his age. I remember brother Martin reaching that stage. It caused Mum and Dad considerable concern. Evan hasn't conceded Paul such license yet, but I worry in case it might draw the lad into a more insular frame.

"I remember, Mags," Evan told me, "when I was that age, and without a father, Lulu calling in uncles to try putting halters on me. I never realised how much worry I was loading on to her; even illustrating belligerence at feeling so confined around the house."

Paul certainly hasn't showed belligerence. But does Leanne talk to him about her thoughts on family? Should I raise this with Evan? Or Paul?

But then, am I making too much of all this? Is my sense of being torn from the philosophy of life I wanted going to start causing problems between me and my man? I cannot blame him for having to retract on our agreement, yet I have certainly been drawn into it, coerced or not.

~ * ~

Mags had lamb chops waiting to put under the griller when the phone rang.

"Will you please answer that," she called to the kids who were setting table.

One of Paul's school friends again? Plans for the weekend again? He seems to be getting invitation after invitation lately. Other families doing this or that and their sons wanting to bring mates. All attractive to Paul, of course, considerably more than working on the Restoration.

But it wasn't for Paul. He arrived in the kitchen.

"It's for you, Maggie. Some bloke."

"He didn't give a name?"

"No. He just wants to speak to Maggie please."

She wiped her hands on her apron.

"You should ask for a name, Paul."

She walked up the hall. "Hello, this is Maggie."

"Maggie, I want you," said a strange male voice.

She waited, wondering what sort of hoax it was.

It wasn't. He laughed.

"It's Milton, Maggie. How are you, my dear?"

"I'm fine, Milt. Evan isn't home yet. He shouldn't be long."

"I don't want Evan. I want, you, need you. Do you know Mrs. Mercy Croft?"

She had to jolt her memory. *That rings a bell. Ah!* "The Killing of Sister George?"

"Yes. *Rhombus* is going to do it. I already have 'George' cast, and I want you for Mercy Croft."

"But that's a play on lesbians. I'm no lesbian, Milt. And besides, I now have three jobs—running a home, that we are busy restoring, plus I work days. I could not possibly do it."

"You can play anything. I know that. I watched you work with Evan and you are just the actor I need. And you are simply made for this high-rolling, stuck-up Brit! Your royal-voiced accent is perfect for this part."

"What's this 'stuck-up' bit?"

"You know what I mean. You can play this part. I've seen you waylay nuisance people with a vicious sting in your voice, albeit in fun, but this is the very voice and manner of Mercy Croft. Please talk with Evan on it? I'll make all the allowances you need for fitting it into your busy life. Please? Please? Talk to Evan and call me back?"

He hung up.

She returned to the kitchen, her mind roiling.

The kids had finished their chore and were watching TV.

Mrs. Mercy Croft? A great part of course, and yes, I too think I could do it. It certainly needs a British touch. But the lesbian scene? That I doubt I can do. I know Evan felt so out of his space in a gay play, but he wasn't looking at playing a gay guy. I recall that the entire plot of killing off George was jealousy, bitchy jealousy. Mercy Croft was trying to win Sister George's girl-friend from her. It just ain't me!

When I arrived, Mags had a *Bristol Cream* waiting. She was on her vermouth.

As I passed what was now only Paul's temporary bedroom, both kids were lounging in bean-bags watching the telly.

"Hi kids, Haven't you homework?"

"Finished," they called in unison.

Maggie and I kissed and I reported, "A nothing unusual sort of day."

Mags had pushed the chops under the griller and was mashing potatoes.

Shelled peas were on the boil. She clapped her hands.

"Come on you two in there, TV off please, and go wash you hands. Dinner in two minutes."

"Ugh-ugh," or some such sound greeted her, yet off went the TV.

"Toss Ya," we heard from Paul, followed by, "Ah, ha. You first."

We knew they tossed by the Paper, Scissors, Rock method.

Leanne was mumbling as she crossed the hall into their bathroom.

A beaming Paul came into the kitchen, hand extended towards me.

"Welcome home, Dad."

I gave him my hand and he shook it.

"What homework did you have today?"

"Easy stuff. All could be done with Logarithms."

"No English, no Geography, no History?"

"No. We only get one subject each day now. Today was Maths."

"Bloody hell, boy. When I was at school we…"

"That was during the war, Dad. Things are more modern these days."

"What do you mean by that?"

"We do all our learning during school hours. After hours is for sports training, or giving our brains a rest."

Maggie and I simply looked at each other, both rolling eyes at the dirty ceiling.

Over dinner, Mag's told me about Milt asking if she knew Mrs. Mercy Croft.

"And do you?"

She laughed. "Yes, dear. She is a lead player in the Frank Marcus play, *The Killing of Sister George*, all about lesbians and their bitchiness."

"Dare I say you might be just made for it?"

"That's exactly what he told me; that I was 'a natural' for it."

"Did you hang up on him?"

"I could but laugh. I told him I would talk it over with you. Tomorrow I will tell him I cannot do it."

"The play is what? A murder mystery?"

"Not that sort of killing. Sister George is the lead role in a radio serial, a gay nursing sister in a London hospital. Mrs. Mercy Croft is also gay, an absolute rogue of a British woman high up in the BBC. She wants Sister George killed off from the part. Unbeknown to George, Mercy Croft lusts after her young girl-friend, Bridie. Croft wants George killed off the show, discredited in Bridie's eyes."

I was now openly smiling. "Oh I do agree with Milt. You are a natural."

She feinted at throwing her glass of vermouth over me.

"I would throw this, husband, except I don't want to stain the Brussels carpet."

"Tell me why you don't want it. You seem to know both story and characters."

"Jane and I saw it on stage in London."

"Why not?"

"It's just not me. The only similarity is the 'high and mighty' royalist accent I can call on. Like the night Cedric McMahon phoned me from Myers. Grandstanding was her trademark in the play."

The kids were all ears, awaiting the outcome.

I explained that a lesbian was a female 'gay guy'.

They dropped jaws, amazed that women could be as 'untoward' as they'd found the fellows in *Boys*.

"Maggie, my very heterosexual wife, who has yet to illustrate any bitchy attitude, let alone a lesbian one, are you not the very lady who convinced me I could play in a gay production? Why are you different? Especially when you are the professional amongst us? 'Professional actor'?"

She let down her guard enough to laugh. "Of course."

"Did he give you a script?"

"No. I simply told him I haven't the time."

I reached over the table and took her hand. "Are you not in the same difficult time situation as when you insisted I should simply manufacture time to go on stage? How long since you have done some acting?"

"Oh dear. Three years? Not since *Man Matti*."

"And was I wrong in noticing, throughout *Boys* that you were missing it?"

I turned back to the kids. "Can you two face a period of Maggie being absent at rehearsals for a few months, then opening in a play we can go see?"

They jumped up, both cheering!

"Bastards. All of you!"

Yet a bemused smile seemed to underlay the taunt.

Then suddenly, so unlike Mags, she burst into tears.

I asked Leanne to bring tissues.

"You will do it?"

"I'm overwhelmed. I just feel so full of things."

She reached an arm around Leanne who stood there with tissues.

She began to say something, then pulled back. Then smiled.

"I suppose I shall just have to find the time."

"Who rings Milt?"

"Me."

"When?"

She sighed a sigh of both defeat and eagerness.

"It certainly would be a magnificent challenge. I shall phone him now."

We three embraced her, all at once.

Twenty-eight

The Big Hole in *Stanford Lodge*'s back terrace was quickly filling.

My mind had several times flown to the difficulty facing Maggie in exiting the back of our house. The scullery had a back door, accessed only from the old kitchen, its brick steps cracked with age, several dangerously loose. They needed breaking out and fresh ones laid.

The back door used during the hospital days now led straight into the Big Hole.

A plank crossed it now, but if one were to fall, it was near a metre.

I contemplated changing my programme.

"The only structural changes inside, Mags, are the bathroom door into our bedroom, and our bedroom door into the Octagon has to be moved three inches."

"What? The first I understand. But move our door three inches? That's madness."

"We talked of an entire wall of wardrobes, remember?"

"Yes."

"A wardrobe deep enough for hanging winter coats needs three inches more. I can give it that by moving the door three inches towards the bathroom."

"Move all that timberwork? Architraves and skirting boards? And brickwork?"

"Yes, on the bedroom side and Octagon side."

"That will make a lot of mess."

"Mess that will make rubble to help fill the Big Hole."

"I can suffer the dust. But the carpets?"

"I can cover them with drop sheets and lay planks again. Those doors must be the next job. Then the switchbox that worries you, can be moved."

"Oh how sad I must spend so much time at rehearsals, dear."

I slapped her bottom and we kissed. I made a sign to hang on the front gate...

Hard filling wanted.

Some neighbours rang the doorbell come evenings, wanting help to lift a broken toilet or a leaking bath-tub into my wheelbarrow, or asking should they just have a tip-truck empty its load of concrete chunks on the footpath. It was an area where many old homes were being restored—an area with *all* old homes. Local council frowned on modern buildings on several particular streets; a something we applauded.

Many such visitors pleaded a 'look around'. We every time felt almost akin to them. It was surprising how many commented on the carpet.

The footpath became, surprisingly quickly, a great pile of rubble—broken toilets and roof-tiles, old hub-caps, broken ceramic garden pots, old saucepans, glass bottles of all description, broken mirrors, an old battered bicycle, a car-wheel complete with tyre, a huge pile of broken bricks, soil and gravel.

Filling that I didn't want was also plentiful—broken chairs, although those could go into our firewood pile, a baby's pram, sacks of lawn-clippings, a cardboard box full of old clothing, hats, shoes with broken heels, an old bra for a size twenty woman, plastic coke bottles and old pillows.

A policeman called early one evening before I was home from the 'outer office' as I called the local pub near the factory.

"Complaints by neighbours about the rubbish," my darling informed.

"Did he make things difficult for you?"

"Oh, no dear. He was a young man, a real soft touch, told me it would not worry him if I left it until you were home next week-end. I told him you were…'away'."

"Did you raise an eye-brow at him?"

"Good heavens, no. But I smiled beguilingly. He became almost apologetic."

"Yes, my darling, I can well imagine."

I bribed Paul into helping clear the rubble.

"If you help me barrow it all around the back on Saturday, I'll take you surfing on Sunday."

He jumped at the offer—had Leon, a school mate, help, on the basis Leon could come surfing with us. We worked all day, not finishing until 8 p.m. Paul was nevertheless up at daybreak, banging things about in the kitchen so we were sure to wake up early.

I reckoned we should make it a family day.

A glum note sticking in Leanne's mind was that during my recent absence interstate, Hairy-legs had taken off on one of his jaunts and not returned.

"We waited day after day, Dad. He just didn't come back."

I had reminded her about the 'homing' instinct.

Paul too, took the opportunity of having me captive in the car, along with Leon present for support.

"Some of the boys at school, Dad," he informed when half-way into the ninety minute drive, "reckon they might be able to talk their fathers into taking a car-load to the beach all summer, on a roster system. Would you be in that?"

"How many fathers?"

"Five or six, we reckon."

"So there'd be five or six boys each Sunday? That's not only a big carload, it's a big load of surfboards on the roof, causing wind-drag."

"Yeah, that'd be right."

"And likely wanting to stop every twenty kilometres for a coke or something?"

"We could bring drinks."

"What if the surf isn't up? You'd want to try the next beach? Then the next?"

"There's a six o'clock radio report every Sunday on wind conditions. We'd soon learn how to read each of the beaches. Some of the guys already know."

"What do you think, Maggie? If I'm off on a Sunday every five or six weeks?"

"Well, if it helps Paul to get in some surfing, we'd find a way around it."

I turned around to see Paul's face. His and Leon's were both gleaming.

"We had an agreement, Paul," I added. "You would do your share of work on the house. If you are off every Sunday surfing during the summer, are you going to put every Saturday into helping me?"

"If it means getting to the surf on Sundays, then, yeah, sure, Dad."

Maggie nodded. "That seems fair."

"Okay, Son. But only on the basis of having five or six fathers involved. I couldn't be in it if it meant every third or fourth Sunday out of my work at home."

"Gee, thanks, Dad."

"And I'd want to first meet all the fathers so we can agree the system and terms. Also, if I get to hear you've abused the trust and been getting into mischief, or taking stupid risks, then the agreement's off, okay?"

"Yeah, sure, Dad."

I was conscious of Maggie watching me peer over my sunnies at Paul via the rear-vision mirror. She and I both knew Paul could read that okay.

~ * ~

"Shouldn't you be getting a bricklayer for that, darling?"

I had mortar mixed and was laying bricks for two steps from the back door, down to the terrace floor level. I had already built a solid foundation for them.

"No-one is going to see it, my dear. I will be crazy-paving all the wall, the terrace surface and steps."

"You told me this would be only one step. You are laying two."

"When building the retaining wall, I realised not only how many bricks would be saved, but how much time I would save by reducing its height two courses, another step level."

"Oh well that's all right then. You know how to do crazy paving?"

"I'll learn on the job, dear."

She waited, before rolling her eyes, until I looked straight at her.

"You are sure the Old Ladies won't mind?"

"I will let them know, dear."

~ * ~

A flexible rule was that Maggie or I would cook dinner, and the kids feed the dish-washer and finish homework before considering TV. That was made once Mags and I decided not to wait on the new kitchen before installing a dishwasher. This reduced the workload on all, even Evelyn's. Her work had increased, however, to keeping all windows clean, inside and out, even rooms awaiting Restoration.

"That way, darling," Mags had pleaded, "it just makes the place that much more liveable."

Dinners during the week were grilled chops or something easy to heat up. The summer's long twilights were great for barbeques. We were also great salad fiends. Sometimes we gave Evelyn the task of shopping for and preparing casseroles for our freezer. All this gave Mags and me extra time for Renovations. For weekends, Evelyn would prepare roasts. Leanne was encouraged to become adept in roasting potatoes, pumpkin and parsnips to perfection, and boiling up greens.

Tiffany grew quickly and was now being walked each afternoon. She was trained in her toilet hygiene and to alert us when hearing the front gate opening. In a corner of the Big Hole, I had built for Tiffy, a plank ramp. Leanne showed her, time after time, that this was the way to her toilet. A sand-pile was out back and each evening before dinner, Leanne would throw a shovelful over the mess.

Maggie acquired a gardening fetish. The *House and Garden* magazine we subscribed to had given her the urge. She made time between rehearsals for *George,* not only to read up on rose culture, dragging me around plant nurseries on weekends, but insisted on doing her own digging in the formal rose-gardens. Paul on occasions helped with the heavy digging along the front veranda facings. She had planned for there, in full view of all approaching up the front path, an English Garden of foxgloves, lily-of-the-valley, petunia, lavender and pansies in their dozens of colours. I had a man in to dig the soil over along the entire side fence, and fertilizing it ready for Maggie to plant hydrangeas, rhododendrons, azaleas, golden forsythia and camellias.

"I simply cannot wait until the veranda posts are painted so I can plant climbing roses and sweet peas," she kept hinting. "And a passion-fruit vine," she added for good luck.

"Next summer," I promised with crossed fingers.

~ * ~

"What do you think, Mags, of having that great holly tree pulled out. It prickles me every time I try cutting it back and…"

Oh dear, have I ever rushed too quickly into anything?

Maggie thrust both hands forward, palms upright.

Her single eyebrow raised and her eyes glared. For a dreadfully long minute she said not a word.

"I shall pay an entire team of men, if you like, darling," she announced so quietly that I had to lean forward, "to prune it back into manageable proportions so you can get through to that side passage. What think you of a tunnel high enough that you don't get your ears scratched, and wide enough so you don't get your broad shoulders scratched? But never can I condone losing such a dominant symbol of Great Britain."

Of course I found myself conceding.

Never was another word said about it until coming home from the office one evening. The holly tree was partly reduced, a great pile of off-cuts scattered about.

"It will take them three days," she told me.

She continued having gardens dug over, all around the verandas.

"I can just imagine several of the Old Ladies again sitting on the verandas in the spring, watching the garden bursting into bloom."

She was obviously trying to give all possible time to the gardens.

We were realising, however, that my driving her to rehearsals and except when choosing to stay and watch, driving back to the church hall again to pick her up, was robbing me of many hours work on the Restoration. One difference between gay sexes, we began to realise, was that whilst pretty well all the boys in *Boys* would go out of their ways to help us as friends if in need, the gay girls didn't seem to care about others at all. They lacked the 'family' feel prevalent amongst the *Boys*. All were as keen to ensure *George* was a success, but the endeavour wasn't personal.

"They clearly recognise your stage skills," I insisted, having sometime watched rehearsals. And there certainly seems no animosity that you are not 'one of them'."

"Oh, good heavens, no. We all get on famously—enjoy many jokes together."

"Even I can see, now, the difference in the way Milt appeals to those girls. The different types of nuances in the way they deliver their lines. He has quite a different approach to them."

Also Simon, the 'Michael' of *Boys*, was Stage Manager for *George*. He had the responsibility of acquiring props needed during the performance, ash-trays, drinking glasses, books for throwing, which was often, etcetera, and ensuring they were available and in the right place as each scene changed. I immensely enjoyed Michael's company, so ever felt comfortable during rehearsals.

At home, surveying indoor work to be done, I realised that not all ceilings were so crazed that they needed wallpaper. Study revealed bad bits could be plastered over and sanded back for painting. Of the heavily embossed mouldings in some rooms, Mags fancied herself picking out their flowers in colour.

"I would love the challenge," she declared.

"What? You up a ladder, painting twelve-foot ceilings?"

She shuddered and cringed yet felt determined.

"If you can build me a sort of platform between ladders, I can do it. I mean only to do little touching up in colour, the flower petals for instance—just in those three rooms, stems and petals with maybe a touch of gold here and there, to glitter under electric light."

The TV room ceiling had no embossed centrepiece and could be painted.

I was immensely pleased that I wouldn't have to paper all the ceilings, nor even hire anyone in. Painting was easy. Only the old kitchen ceiling would have to be wallpapered, for it was so stained that paint would never disguise it.

Twenty-nine

Early December, I was doing DRC homework in the temporary study, what had been the old linen-room, on dates for the company's annual Christmas Closing. All DRC operations shut down for the three weeks of annual leave, rather than employees taking time off at different times of the year.

The phone rang. I'd seen Mags pass with an armful of bedding, so hastened up the hall to the phone. It was Milt.

"Ah, hold on mate, I will call Maggie for you."

"No," he called. "I want to talk with you, Evan. It's about Alan."

"Alan of *Boys*?"

"Yes. Do you have plans for Christmas Eve?"

"I guess I'll be working on the house."

"I've signed up a performance in Trak Cinema."

After the call, I staggered into the kitchen.

Mags was feeding the washing machine. *Oh, he looks ashen. Bad news? Lulu? Valerie?* she wondered.

"Sorry Mags, it's not bad news, love. It's good in its way."

We were aware that Trak Cinema, an intimate little theatre, staged both amateur and professional short-runs. In between, it showed films both long and short from the various international awards held each year. It was highly priced yet with ideal sound effects right down to felt-lined walls and plush seats. I guessed the seating capacity somewhere around five hundred.

"*Boys* is booked to stage a one-night stand on Christmas Eve. A late start, but to finish by Eleven thirty. At midnight they are screening *Star Wars*. It will be a very gay night. Milt says every gay guy in Melbourne will be queuing up for tickets at up-market prices. He's already signed the contract and is just hoping to God that most if not all the boys can do the show. He pleaded with me, Mags: 'Please say yes, Evan. Please, please say Yes'. You know how he seems like he's about to burst into tears."

"I know it only too well. Who else?"

"I don't know. He said he checked Simon out first, then me. He said: 'You are the two major ones without months of rehearsal', which gave me a great thrill, of course. He is now ringing around the rest of the crew."

All the guys in the show had had an understudy. Simon had been mine and Tim had been Simon's. Milt himself was understudy for any minor role.

"So, Maggie, he is squeezing this in around rehearsals for *Sister George*. I told him I would do it."

"Is it to be an exclusively gay audience?"

"That's the plan. The place will scream!"

"Rehearsals?"

"If all the guys can do it, he reckons we will need only two. It will be advertised in the few gay rags around town and the gay clubs in universities."

"We have to help him all we can, darling," she demurred.

I felt like giggling at that. "No thought that it might inconvenience us?"

"Not at all. This is what theatre is all about, darling. You have your script?"

"Yes but, it's covered in autographs."

"It'll do for your brushing up. I still have mine. Go get yours."

"Now?"

"Why ever not? What were you doing?"

"Finalising dates for closing the plant. I was then going to measure up our wardrobes so I can order the timber."

"Finish planning your closure and let's run through the play?"

I kissed her and rushed off.

~ * ~

Next morning I phoned Grant with the plant's closing dates.

He had news in return. "Your car is due for renewal."

"Is it already two years?"

"Same procedure. Get it serviced and valued by three Ford dealers. You have first option to buy. If you don't know of a buyer at the highest bid, accept the lowest in the name of the company. You nominate your colour. Do it before end of December so it's not an immediate expense come New Year."

DRC International's fiscal year was January-December.

When I told Maggie, she had car news for me.

"I've been giving driving a lot of thought. I've decided to learn how and then buy a car. As we get further into our lives, darling, I find things could be easier for us both if I am not dependent on you for transport. I don't want your Fairmont. I want something small and easy. And not automatic."

"Eh? Not auto? Surely, Mags, that is the easier to drive. Especially in Melbourne with its trams."

"Automatics worry me. I'm an independent bird. I like to be in control. I don't want a car thinking for me."

"Oh darling. That is the first time I've heard that as a reason. Sure, I know your independence, but you are certainly the one in control when driving either."

She stood firm.

"Well, what will you buy? You know I'm no mechanic. I don't even know how many plugs or whatever are hidden under the bonnet. If it's not going right, I just have one of my guys take it to the Ford repair shop."

"You don't have to do anything, my love. I will get things done. If it's my car, I'll buy it, see to its servicing and everything else. When we married we agreed that you are responsible for everything…Evan and kids; I would look after everything Maggie. It won't cost you a penny, my darling."

"I don't like the thought of you owing money, paying off something month by month. That is an expense I don't wish for you."

"Thank you, my darling. But who said anything about time payment? If Maggie doesn't have the cash, darling, she doesn't buy. I have looked around car yards and talked to gals and guys at work. I already know what I want."

"What?"

"A Mazda three. It has a twin carbie, whatever that means. I bought it at lunch-time only yesterday. I was waiting for dinner to make it a family announcement, for only today did they confirm they will deliver it here Saturday morning."

She leaned up and kissed me.

"Bloody hell, girl, you are one of a kind, all right."

"It is three years old, belonged to a lady school-teacher who died. I doubt it was the car that killed her, so it shouldn't be unlucky. It's a grey colour. I'll pay one of the kids to wash it for me now and again."

"And driving?"

"I have my first lesson Monday. I've arranged time off from work for two hours every morning next week. The school will teach me on a manual Mazda."

I folded my arms and wagged my head.

"You really are the tops. I do commend your careful planning, however."

~ * ~

I scratched my head. The new metric-measurement bricks were fractionally different from those in the walls. It was no great difficulty, for the difference would be taken up between door and jamb, and certainly within the amount of mortar I would slap on the brick, whatever its age.

Anyway, three inches is an arbitrary sort of measurement. Three imperial inches is seventy-six-point-two millimetres according to pundits, so what the heck. I haven't a saw for cutting bricks so will simply split them with a hammer and cold-chisel.

Australia was in the throes of converting from British Imperial measurements to the International Metric standard for everything except money. We changed currency to metric Dollars five years ago. We were now converting all else, length, area, velocity, mass, volume and temperature. My mind when using tools seemed in some sort of quandary. I would be measuring this in inches and that in centimetres, milk in pints yet water in litres. Temperature was the one thing I was really standardised on however. Measuring temperature from one to a hundred, made simple sense—the same sort of sense as changing £.s.d into dollars and cents.

Fixing the architraves will be the difficult part. Might just have to drive rivets into fresh mortar and hope they bond firmly in place.

Our bedroom had likely been a ward for three Old Ladies who wouldn't have liked a slap-up job any more than me. So they would get a careful job. Our nearest timberyard, however, had exact copies of the Federation moulds of cedar timbers used in the house's construction—a sure sign of how much restoration of Federation houses was going on in the district.

I broke down the wall between our bedroom and the old bathroom, re-using the unspoiled bricks with some left-overs from my terrace wall, bricking up the old doorway. I'd give it a few days for the mortar to properly set, then have Percy move the unsightly power-board. Both doors remained in good enough condition, fortunately, to be re-usable. We now had an en-suite.

I could also now, install the timber framework of the wardrobe, eighteen feet of it. Three eight-foot high sliding mirror doors would front it. Once I had the framework done, I had the mirror company come in to take its own measurements.

Our wardrobe had six-foot high hanging space. Many shelf-drawer units were being made. Above the six feet was two-feet of shelf space and above that again, to the twelve-foot ceilings, was all additional storage; luggage and other paraphernalia.

All was achieved without wear and tear or damage to the Brussels carpet.

And we discovered that wine bottles made good filling for the terrace, a reason we reckoned, to up our intake.

Thirty

I was the family member most excited coming up Christmas Eve.

Every *Boy* made himself available for the Trak Cinema performance. Russell even cancelled holidays, and excitement was high. Major reporters would attend, ensuring the *Rhombus* name was being cast far and wide.

During the week prior, Milt hired a professional Staging Director to vet our stage movements and suggest improvements. Where Larry and Hank had stood quietly in shadows while something else was under the spotlights upstage, he had them behind the bar mixing drinks.

"No-one should be standing idle unless called for by the playwright," he kept insisting. "Everybody must be in action one way or another. It is an action-packed party!"

I was given two positional changes. Most significant was for my important phone-call. He had me not what I'd been calling 'front stage', immediately behind the footlight, he had a heavy plate glass placed over the footlights for me to kneel on. All other footlights would be turned off. For the entire phone-call, several minutes of it, he directed Eric to have every spot on me alone, and just those few footlights glaring up at my face made it the only attraction point for the audience.

My other was the scene opening with Hank and me on Ottomans in a stage corner. He quit the Ottomans to have us sitting on stage edge, dangling legs over the front. We would be that close to the audience!

Another change was the heated scene between Larry and Hank, which we'd done with Hank sitting on a sofa, Larry behind it, hands on Hanks shoulders. He instead had Larry, the aggressive one of the two, using the entire stage, striding about and shaking his fingers to make his points.

Milt adopted every recommendation and we could all see the advantages. At a last rehearsal we reran each such scene and could even 'feel' the improvement. The Staging Director got a kiss from everyone, although I don't think he was gay. He certainly knew his job and simply added to every crewman's confidence.

"Well! Front of house," Maggie told me in the dressing room, "especially when it was a sell-out, is Bedlam. Nine guys out of every ten are dressed in 'inflammatory' gear, some near naked whilst others are bedecked in glittering tiaras, sparkling gowns and stilt heels. They are flocking into the theatre now, every one determined to capture attention.

"Firstly the foyer and now in the stalls, my dear, it is screamingly camp. Police are making their presence felt, many of the gays planting lipstick kisses on their cheeks, or spiking sprigs of Christmas holly into their uniforms. I tried looking at their tickets to direct them into queues, but few cared. They just want to be seen. Most are gushing over friends. Even in London I had never seen such a camp demonstration. Cameramen are flashing shots everywhere. What journal they represent, I have no idea, but the cameras are certainly of the professional genre."

Then she added...

"Tickets are still being sold, despite we had sold a full house early yesterday."

From inside the curtains, we were peeping through, amazed at the costuming and the party atmosphere. Only those with numbered tickets were allowed to sit, so standing-room around the walls was filling. Reefer-smoke was already so thick it was seeping around curtains and invading backstage. Over the sound system, Village People blared out *YMCA*. It was all party mood, the spirit intoxicating.

Milt lined us up as stage-time came, telling us to take deep breaths and begin transforming minds and bodies into the characters who were to put foot on stage.

"You aren't you, now," he whispered. "You, Howard, are Harold. You, Tim, are Donald. You..." He went through the eight of us.

"Noise from the audience will likely be more than you have ever experienced. You must expect as the curtain opens, or when you walk on stage, that the air itself will be frenetic. Few of you ever get off stage, so those who do must re-adjust before re-entry. Do not let the mayhem distract you. Make it worth their while by your professionalism. We must pull together to get the name *Rhombus* up there in Big Bright Lights!"

~ * ~

It went amazingly well. The incredible noise the audience seemed loathe to let abate kept us on the alert. It was a play based on snide asides, bitchy one-liners and clever verbal nuances that demanded rapt attention by both actor and audience. And the audience appreciated it, even those uncomfortably crammed in the aisles, squashed in a mob along the back wall, and crouched on backsides not only up the side aisles but on the few feet of floor space between stage and front row.

The theatre seats five hundred fifty and we sold seven hundred and fifteen tickets.

Near everyone out there seemed under the spell of cannabis.

I was frightfully conscious of their closeness on those two up-stage occasions. When Hank and I sat on the very corner of the stage, legs dangling over the front, Hank telling me of his love for Larry and how things got twisted, some dozen or more of the audience sat on the floor, clasping hands around knees right below us. They were so close as to be touching our shoes as we concentrated on sensitive lines, trying at the same time to concentrate on throwing our voices to the back stalls.

Right towards the end was my phone-call. The stage-change had me again, almost into the audience looking directly into faces staring right up at me. Yet I felt so much alone. It was a scene essential to me making it so convincing that guilt must begin gnawing, guilt that I was betraying the cast in dialling Alan's wife instead of his old college friend, convincing either that I was madly in love with them.

Yet I am Alan! Again I felt the insecurity of having to act such a false personal situation. Had I been Alan in real life, I would be misleading her.

Me misleading Maggie? And Maggie right here in the wings? Witness to how convincing I can be in deceit?

Sure, she insisted I play it as written, hide my guilt and lie my way through it. She'd watched me do it many times, even instructed me on making insincerity sound sincere. In that sense, she was certainly on my side, yet wasn't I also giving her reason to lose trust in me?

In the real life sense, she sure as hell knows I am on her side, yet here I am illustrating a husband's unfaithfulness and trying to make it sound believable!

Oh what a risk!

Suddenly I was conscious of tears in my eyes, not Alan tears but Evan tears!

Only then did it hit me...

The audience doesn't know about Maggie. This is Alan and he is as distressed as I would be in his situation. So the tears are genuine!

I couldn't stop crying. I had to let them flow. I could feel them running down my face taking greasepaint with them because I was near melting under the spotlights. I was conscious, too, of the myriad of faces peering up, images clouded in my own tears.

Then I realised that for the first time tonight, the audience was silent. Everyone!

Eric's spots were on my face and tears were now bloody gushing! I was delivering my lines as taught, yet to Maggie, convincing her how much I loved her.

I made my final exit after hanging up. It wasn't a scene change yet the audience erupted in cheers and applause. We players on stage had no option but to freeze until it abated.

As I, only minutes later exited, the crew waiting in the wings, including Maggie, hugged and kissed me. Just as well I didn't have to appear again because my greasepaint was all over my face. And now all over crew faces, especially Milt's.

I had to appear for the curtain-call of course, but by then I didn't care how I looked. I wasn't Alan any more. I'd come home.

~ * ~

We didn't stay for *Star Wars,* not because seats were all taken but because Maggie and I, living only five minutes away, had all the cast and crew back home for *Veuve Clicquot.* The kids got up to join in.

Some then went on to parties elsewhere.

We had another Champagne, and crashed into bed.

Thirty-one

Nineteen seventy-four opened with a bang. It was mid-summer. DRC Bags was closed for three-weeks annual leave. I was free until mid January. The Australian Tennis Open was then played on courts in Glenferrie Road and began on Boxing Day. Paul was in school camp and Leanne was keen to see the tennis. It was indeed an exciting day.

She had finished primary school and was enrolled at Malvern Girls High, chuffed at the prospect of it being walking distance of home. She no longer attended the psychiatrist. She didn't like him and didn't want to see him anymore.

Occasional letters arrived from Artarmon so we only assumed Leanne was answering them. We still didn't probe, thinking it best to let sleeping dogs sleep. We rigged her out in her new uniform and ensured she had all recommended text books.

"Seek out what girls live near here," Maggie advised. "It will be company for you walking to school."

We would feel happier if she were not walking alone.

Rehearsals for *Killing of Sister George* were progressing but with Mags now having her car, I didn't have to desert work on our dining-room. We receiving more invitations out nowadays, so needed at least one of the living-rooms finished so we could reciprocate. It was also the room for which we had the most furniture for entertaining. It needed no restoration but decorating.

"I know exactly the curtains I'd like, darling. This is the biggest of the six bay windows in the house and quite dominates the end wall."

She fetched a *House and Garden* magazine. The curtains she liked were indeed impressive. We had already decided that the two major living-rooms and all hallways would be papered the same design.

"So our curtains should be plain light blue and headboards the dark blue of the wallpaper. It recommends here that to give the fullness required, even when closed, they should be made from heavy velvet."

The article had directions on building the headboard. I could make it.

"It also has directions for measuring up and cutting one's own patterns, so I shall make them. You bought all the tools needed in the house, Evan darling, so I shall buy a sewing machine."

For the long seat of the window box we would have a studded cushion made, covered in the same dark blue velvet.

"Ceiling?"

I coughed. "Yes, darling. Painted white with you touching up flowers in the centrepiece. No wallpaper on the ceiling."

Did I feel some guilt at having backed out of fulfilling my initial pledge?

"Oh, how sad, darling. I was looking forward to all the massaging it would need."

She fetched a different issue of *H & G,* the page she wanted, already flagged.

"I've since seen this. It's not colour, simply luminous gold paint tipped on random flower petals, that I want to paint. I like it."

She handed me the magazine.

"Yes, it certainly does look elegant."

I read further. *The Palace of Versailles*!

"If good enough for Marie Antoinette, my dear," she announced with a raised eyebrow, "It should satisfy the Old Ladies."

"And me, my dear. You will do the gilded tipping?"

"Of course. I would like to be able to tell friends it was my doing."

"From the tallest of step-ladders?"

"You told me you could build a platform."

I merely smiled.

"I'm having second thoughts on the light fitting here. The big chandelier in the Octagon is beautiful. I think the two old mini-chandeliers in this room will detract from it. Also, dining calls for a retractable pendant, adjusting to how big a spread of light we want over the table."

"We can check out antique shops, my love. Surely the pair of mini-ones can be sold at auction. And what think you of a dimmer-switch for this room?"

We began with plastic over the carpet, and while Mags was at rehearsals and with some help from the kids, I patched and sanded the ceiling, scraped paintwork on architraves and skirting boards and scrubbed the fireplace grate with emery-paper.

I phoned Percy and told him I wanted to install a dimmer switch in the dining-room and asked if it were a difficult task changing the ceiling light leads from the two spaced one, to a single central one.

"Easy, mate. Phone me when you've bought your dimmer-switch and light fitting and I'll send a lad around to do them."

~ * ~

Maggie's rehearsals were proving a problem.

"*Sister George* has all her lines down pat. She knows the life. She's being killed off and she's as shitty as any rough person can get. It's her girl-friend I am trying to steal from her. I sit with Bridie, stroking her hair, telling her: 'I want you to be my little girl'. I need to be literally drooling over her, pouring out loving phrases. Other times I can create the sense of being lesbian, satisfactorily enough, but this scene calls for real woman-to-woman emotion and I just cannot get it right."

"Try it out on me. I'll tell you what I think."

"That wouldn't work. I could do it with you because it would come naturally. It is doing it with a woman that just won't let me feel right."

"What does Milt say?"

"He tells me I'm on the wrong wave length in worrying about it; that the way I'm doing it, is fine."

"Well, if that's the director's word, it must be okay."

"But it bugs me. My confidence button just doesn't click in. I just cannot believe in what I'm trying to illustrate."

"Do you recall what you used to tell me about my *Boys* telephone scene? 'Let go of your instincts,' you would say. 'You are not Evan any more, you are Alan. You must wholly become that character'. So here, you are not Maggie delivering these lines. You are Mercy Croft."

She couldn't help but smile. I could see she saw the twist.

"Yes, I even recall reminding you of your mind-twist when trying to wangle a 'yes' out of a difficult prospect. You told me how you could call on all sorts of un-natural criteria to back up your claims."

"When I made my phone-call... No. Let me put it this way. In your scene, why don't you let your mind think it's me. That's not cheating. It is being practical enough to make your target, something you really have the hots for, like me when we first met. Let me be the one you are petting. During my phone call, it's you I had in my mind. I had to make myself feel that even though I knew it wasn't a real wife, I used you as the target. It was you, Mags that I was forcing myself to convince."

"It brought you to genuine tears."

A tear suddenly sprung to her eye.

"You realised your mind-game had you talking to me rather than Alan's wife?"

"That's when everything fell into place for me. It brought on natural tears. Next rehearsal darling, convince yourself that it is not Bridie you are wooing, but your Evan. You are having to convince me that you love me!"

Thirty-two

We reckoned the Old Ladies would have been as happy as us, at our dining-room.

"There would have been four in this ward," Mags estimated.

She had bravely, without a platform but on the top step of the stepladder, me a rung lower, holding on to her waist with one arm while grasping the ladder top with my other, tipped some twenty flower petals with luminous gold paint.

"It really does look like *The Palace of Versailles*! I feel almost transported," I assured her. We agreed too, that the curtains were as pleasing.

Apart from scrubbing the Brussels carpet, we gave considered thought to what we should do with its surrounding twelve inches of time-worn blackened floorboards. They indeed showed the scars of traffic over the years.

"But the black lacquer is original, darling. Only scars illustrate its age. Leaving them just as they are illustrates the atmosphere intended. Why not simply scrub them clean and lacquer them with clear gloss?"

It made sense. "You are right again, my love."

"Just like a glossy picture-frame around the carpet," declared Leanne when it was done.

At auction, we bought a sideboard and had a pro-shop strip and lacquer it to match our chairs and table. We installed it against the wall backing on to the hallway.

"The wall over it needs a large print in a gilded frame," Mags declared.

To grace the sideboard, she chose a ceramic vase from one of the Glenferrie Road galleries and we retrieved from our storage cache, my antique Tantalus, lacquered mahogany with silver-plated hardware and crystal decanters, a family heirloom.

"A matching print and frame for that empty space along the south wall? It's quite a large expanse of wallpaper needing something."

"Prints? God forbid, woman. This room deserves paintings. Do you recall meeting Freddie Barlow at last year's company dinner? The old guy at the Fitzroy plant who heads up our Art Studio? In private life he has acquired a reputation as an artist in oils, of pioneering days. One of the Glenferrie Road galleries sells them—ideal for *Stanford Lodge*."

We each bought one as wedding anniversary gifts. Their large sculptured frames in glittering gold indeed complimented Maggie's flowers in the ceiling.

We took lots of photos.

"It certainly is homey, darling."

We had arms around each of the kids' shoulders as all admired it.

"Don't you think it a clever design?" she asked with a teasing smile.

"And superior workmanship, my love," I rejoined.

~ * ~

February was finished and we yet had six weeks of summer to enjoy.

I reminded Paul that his room was next, that I would want him all day Saturdays for several weeks. We had been operating the Sunday Surf timetable all season and it was working well. The boys were enjoying it and so were the fathers who kept in regular touch. Every now and again one would need his Sunday off, so it was most unusual if another couldn't swap turns. We often had funny little stories to exchange.

"In fact, Mags," I told her while readying for bed on the Saturday night, "One recently joked about how much he was learning about his own son when having a chance to observe him with peers. I realised how, despite unaware, it had done the same for me."

We giggled about that while snuggling up. In summer's heat we both slept naked. Neither was in favour of air-conditioning; not only were they noisy contraptions but building them into walls or ceilings would belie any sense of retaining the pioneer influence in *Stanford Lodge.*

We also at that time, installed a movement-sensor burglar alarm. It required only a tiny sensor mounted in the ceiling of each hallway. Its control panel would be hidden in the Octagon linen closet once built. Meanwhile linen was stored in the shelving of the old linen-room. When Tiffany was the only one left home, she had to remain locked in her scullery. She had her dog-door letting her in and out of the garden, but had no access to the rest of the house.

The Sunday surf run began early. At six a.m. a radio reported surfing conditions at the several beaches within a two-hour drive. It gave wind and current conditions. From six fifteen to six thirty each lad reserved sole use of home telephones. Messages were short and sharp. Son of 'he who was the day's chauffer' would phone his five friends for their vote on which beach sounded best, then phone back to report the consensus. Meanwhile, all would be breakfasting so picking up all lads with their boards, could happen quickly. All would bring fruit and cans of drink, and a dollar for buying bully-beef for lunch.

Some would even remember, on a lucky day, to bring a can-opener.

At ages fifteen and sixteen, of course, all would consider themselves masters of everything to do with board-riding. Fathers, after driving so far with six largish lads filling the car and the wind-drag of six to nine boards on the roof-racks, was also quickly learning, not surfing techniques, simply the new language their sons were developing.

"It is quite an eye-opener," I would tell Mags at the end of my day.

"I had never learned that a surfboard's rudder-blade could have thirty-something shapes, each with a specific name. Or that wave tubes rolled at differing speeds according to both wind and current. And currents differed depending on the contours of each beach's headlands and shorelines.

"All fathers agree, darling, that we daren't ask obvious questions. This illustrates ignorance. And the reason Paul has five boards is that both board shape and blade are significant, subject to wind, current and beach contours."

"Your summing up?"

"That body surfers don't have those problems. We can manipulate our bodies to suit different types of waves."

"Paul's response?"

"With all his mates listening, he doesn't dare back down, he told me after dropping off the last lad: 'Cripes, Dad, you're just too old to realise what skills a board-surfer needs."

At such times, I too begin realising that I'd never get sensible answers to sensible questions, so simply shut my ears to the rest. On that day at Bells Beach, I'd packed a beach umbrella, yet found it difficult to snooze after body-surfing in the big swell. One time Paul woke me, thrusting a half-dozen cameras into my arms.

"The surf's up, Dad. Can you take photos of us?"

"With five cameras?"

"One at a time, Dad. Just keep your eyes on the surf and see which kid is on to one. It don't matter which camera, we all swap pictures around later."

"The expression is 'doesn't', son, not 'don't'."

"Thanks, Dad."

He dashed off, a different board under his arm.

Another thing I learned was how thirsty board-surfing made one. None brought cans enough. "Dad we need a few more cans. Can I borrow a couple of dollars?"

"Borrow?" I would ask.

"Well, you know. I'd hate my mates thinking you're a bit of a stinge."

By the time we'd got home, I'd have stopped each fifty or so kilometres for two or three to duck behind trees for a piddle.

"I found the day quite an experience, Mags. And Paul sure runs a mean tube."

~ * ~

Maggie muses...

Well, he's fallen off to sleep. But it is nice, I guess, for a girl who loves company to have a few moments to herself. There are always confidential things to ponder, and before dropping off is a good time. I feel guilty if my mind takes time-out in the office, planning things for the house, or on Evan, or on the kids, or on Mum and Dad. Let's face it, I don't give Mum and Dad as much thought as I should. We have the odd phone call, but mostly it's writing letters and these days I tend to begrudge the time that takes. There are always other things need doing.

Somehow I wonder when readying for bed, if tonight Evan will want sex—whether I should respond to kisses good-night by touching him up. Every time I've questioned him on reading his feeling, he answers with a sort of "You will know, my darling, I know where to touch you." If I start the touching, he seldom draws back. He knows I enjoy it more times than not. But I know he gets tired from working at night too, and quite often he is moody about problems at work.

There's no risk, of course, that we don't both enjoy it when it's on—he's as hot a creature as me when it comes to that and I still love his attention. I reckon he keeps a mental clock for when I've got the curse.

I know it worries him that we cannot get holidays together, to just get away to somewhere nice for even a week. Every year he must close his plant for high summer. It's up to every GM to see that no customer will be inconvenienced. It's part of their professionalism to ensure customers have full shelves to see them through that period. I sometimes cannot negotiate my holidays to suit.

But I guess that's all small cheese when one looks at life overall. I've many reasons to consider myself lucky, even got over wondering if we would have been better off not taking on the kids full-time. Working together to keep them happy has brought us closer. Paul and I continue on a harmonious chord, while I'm still trying to work out what key Leanne plays. Paul's a straight sort of thinker for a sixteen year old. I know Evan is in a bind now, having enrolled him in a school of commercial studies when Paul seeks a technical future. Huh! Here's Evan, bless his heart, deliberately chose technical High School, wanting to major in architecture, yet was confounded by the war ending. For the next three years, all university places were taken up by returning servicemen. He ended up in commerce. Maybe I should try ensuring Paul is aware of that switch?

But Leanne? We are both shattered that we cannot reach her. Yet I still wonder about Evan's attitude. In so many ways I am satisfied with my man, yet it is clear his two major commitments are to me and his work. Leanne seems to come in third. Not sure what I can do about that, other than ensure I think for Leanne and keep trying to hold Evan's interest there too. He's quick to react when I suggest something, yet so seldom comes up with suggestions of his own.

What confounds me most is that problems with kids are things I never wanted. But one can't foresee inheritance. Evan keeps illustrating that I am making more a fist of it than a thousand other girls might have done, yet that doesn't alleviate the problem. I am a woman, so should be better able to understand a budding woman's thinking, yet Leanne has no little hole through which I can enter her mind.

Here am I, a Mensa Graduate yet unable to circumvent this obstacle?

I wonder if this Romy can be somehow used?

For Leanne to bring her home from school to meet me was a milestone. One in her life and one in mine. At her age I had scores of friends. Romy, I reckon, has Eastern European parents. 'Somewhere in Europe' was all I can get from Leanne. I imagined they were likely early arrivals in the same immigration scheme that brought me. At least neither she nor Romy yet seem to have any interest in boys, any more than Paul and his mates continuing to find surfing more appealing than girls. Joining a horse-riding club is the girls' thing of the moment. Romy was brought here just for support in that. Evan and I were thrilled and quickly acceded when I told him, despite it's going to mean more time out, taking turns at driving them to the club and filling in time while waiting. Evan's luckier in that, he can ride with them, but no-one is ever going to get me on a horse.

"It will be alright if your father approves and can afford the expense," I told her. "But I can always help if it is just a matter of money. But I think it will be a wonderful thing for you girls to do this together. I shall try to convince your father."

Ah! The trials of motherhood. Am I at last finding some instinctive payback for my effort in this regard?

Thirty-three

Sister George was getting close to opening. With Maggie driving herself to rehearsals near every night, Paul and I began on his bedroom.

"I notice you starting to jibe back at Maggie's jokes, boy," I told him as we were up on scaffolds sizing the ceiling. "A good thing, I reckon, so long as you don't take it too far. Respect must rule, remember."

"I know that, Dad. I know she likes to needle people in a fun way. I just try to give her one back."

"She recognises it."

We are both pleased at him losing the touches of jealousy he illustrated on seeing Maggie and I were serious. Did she set out to break it down, I wonder? They are pretty much the same sort of person in many ways—a good sign all right.

"This ceiling is the most awkward part, boy. When it's done, I'll leave you to do the walls while I make a start next door, a temporary kitchen, so we can quit this one. While you were at school-camp during the holidays, Maggie and I worked out how we can do that without making the cooking too difficult."

The old third bedroom had become quite a mess when tearing down the back veranda. Unbeknown to council, I had then, on the existing footings, built a new timber-framed clap-board wall, yet unlined inside, and simply boarded-up the newly framed windows and new back door.

"Where will you get the water? And what about draining the sink?"

"I will run a temporary inlet from the old scullery, and the outlet will simply pour into the Big Hole. Just so long as the council doesn't get to know, that will suffice until cupboards are built and I get a plumber in for connection."

"Are you going to build the cupboards?"

"That is a tradesman's job, lad. I will draw up what we want and have a cabinet-maker build them. I can get Percy back for the electrical wiring and Bob for the plumbing. They can liaise with the council, for installation."

~ * ~

"Do you reckon you can cope alone with the kids for a few weeks, darling?"

"You thinking of leaving me?" I asked.

She smiled rather than raise the dreaded eyebrow.

"When *Sister George* is finished, I'd like to take a trip home to see my folks. It's been more than four years."

"Oh, indeed. Four years is a long time. I coped without family for eight years before you came on my scene, darling. I can manage now. You can get leave from work?"

"Yes, and that's another thing. Tensions are building there. Nothing I'm involved in but there's ill-feeling amongst the partners and floor-boys. A stock-exchange floor can sometimes be a mad place—akin to a riot on stage. Sometimes there are misunderstandings of signals, or words are lost in the mayhem. The atmosphere has lost its fellowship. Julie and I are thinking of quitting and starting a Secretarial agency. At least my time there has given me some insight into trading. I've made good money and learned much about running a business."

"Don't close a door too early, my love. I'd suggest take your leave of absence and wait until home before quitting. Getting away from things can give you a clearer view of your role there. Getting away from Julie for a while also gives you time to review that relationship too. A partnership is easily started, but friendships in business can falter. And running a business? Talk with your dad, then with me. Meanwhile you have a job still, while plotting with Julie."

"That sounds like being devious."

"Not at all. In the world of business, you need to be selfish as well as fair. Peter will understand that."

"At least in the secretarial world there are franchise options. I can decide exactly how much work I take on, the rest can be hived off to others. That gives me flexibility. And with no travelling to and from work every day, I have near two extra hours each day. I'm sure you can help me learn the financial side of small business."

"My charges could be pretty high?"

"I've allowed for that," she replied, pinching my thigh.

~ * ~

"What do we do with this old fuel stove, Dad? And the alcove?"

"What do you suggest, Son?"

"I reckon you can flog the stove off to an antique dealer, and the alcove would be great for a writing desk."

"Good thinking. I doubt the stove would bring much, but otherwise, it will fit in the Big Hole. I suggest you draw up what you want for the writing desk. Which side for the drawers? What sort of lighting? Which brings us to deciding where you want power points. They have to be wired before panelling over the tiles."

Malvern's *Odds'n Ends* was an ideal 'swap-shop' for people like us. It took our unwanted dining-room light fittings as a trade on a desk to fit in the alcove. It had two old wooden drawers with runners for foolscap sling-sleeves.

"We'll need sleeves, Dad."

We drove to the stationers and bought sling-sleeves.

"We'll need a chair, Dad."

We drove back to *Odds'n Ends* for a swivel chair.

"What about a desk lamp, Dad?"

"I'll build in a light in the roof of the alcove."

"My head will put the page in shadow."

I was beginning to think the lad might have discovered forward planning.

"The light should be on the left side, to avoid shadow over what you write."

We bought a lamp and were home in time for lunch, having forgotten the meringues Maggie wanted from the *patisserie*.

~ * ~

Driving back from seeing Maggie off to Europe, we were talking work on the house.

"You know, boy? Maggie's absence is an ideal opportunity for me to do that work in the new kitchen. I'd like it in at least a comfortable working area when she is home. We must get your room finished."

It was now quite stripped and ceiling sized, ready for papering.

Walls would be painted.

"Walls above tile height, that is, Son."

It had been agreed we cover the tiles with chipboard, wallpapering them.

"How about a shelf all around the room, separating bottom half from frieze?"

"Wow, Dad, a shelf wide enough for all the surf trophies I'll win next summer?"

I laughed with him. "Certainly not trophies for school-work, I'm sure?"

"He is a much brighter kid than his school reports indicate," Maggie had said to me.

"That can only mean he simply isn't trying hard enough," I'd answered.

Paul and I talked on this sort of thing as we stripped away the skirting boards and brushed Ajax over the dampened tiles. We needed to ensure all the grease was off before panelling over them. A smelly mould developing would mean it all had to be stripped and starting again.

"It's a good school, Dad, but I'm just not interested in business subjects."

"What do you have in mind?"

"Maybe something like we're doing here; building or something. Where'd you learn all this building stuff?"

"Watching my father. He was a businessman like me, but also a handyman. Many of these hand-tools were his. He died when I was a kid, then my step-father was a master-builder. So I have that in my background. And I've built two houses, the West Chatswood house you would hardly remember, then the Kenmore house in Brisbane when I transferred there. Those experiences taught me a lot."

"You were lucky, then, Dad."

"You realise it is impossible getting you into a change of school at this stage, Son. Sure, you make friends easily, so that part wouldn't be a problem, but finding an opening in a Technical High School is a problem. They have queues."

"I know that. I'm happy to string this out for a while. My mates now are great. I don't want to leave them. Or quit our surfing Sundays. And a Tech High wouldn't have a Cadet Corps so I'd probably have to play Rugby for winter sport."

We agreed to let school ride until finishing his third year— Intermediate stage. We were then back to the job in hand.

Thirty-four

It wasn't a pleasant feeling in the house without Maggie.

I never imagined I would miss her so much.

It was a long flight to England—long, lonely hours. The only comforting thought was that she was never at a loss opening up conversation with strangers—unusual in the British.

Likely her travels helped develop that 'sharing' attitude?

She'd been happy with the outcome of the *Killing of Sister George*. It was a great success, not getting the raves *Boys* earned, yet nor was it the same sort of show. It didn't set out to highlight all sides of gay life, only the bitchy. Yet reviews were positive and all were happy. I whispered to Mags that I wasn't surprised it being a play from which she didn't make even one bosom buddy!

"Except for Milt! He really did do an excellent job with some very tough girls."

So her obligations to *Rhombus* had been fulfilled and she was 'off home'. I promised to give her car a regular run and organised my time around getting on with work on the new kitchen.

Paul's room was soon finished to his great satisfaction. The bottom half of the walls and the ceiling were papered in his chosen design, an abstract pattern in sea-blue and white. The large frieze was painted a sandy shade, three coats covering all stains. The vertical joints of the lower panels were timber mouldings hiding the additional light wiring. The writing desk built into the old stove alcove was a feature and the carpet was mottled, a darker shade of the friezes.

What had been a condition, however, was that the door from it into the old scullery was fitted with a deadlock that couldn't be opened from the scullery side.

"It seemed pointless, Mags," I was to tell her when home, "having a burglar alarm yet leaving a teenager in charge of ensuring a door is always locked."

The task now was another messy start. Part of what would be the new kitchen was a 'dead' corner—a section of the old veranda blocked off when building the hospital staff quarters. Undisturbed over years, it had become a haven for spiders and all sorts of vermin. Its timbers were rotten. I had known a window was at back of it all, for it could be seen from outside.

I now scraped, gouged and shovelled all the mess into the Big Hole. Rather than the big old fashioned kitchen, ours would be compact with a large two-door fridge-freezer, the gas cooker Maggie had chosen, a double-bowl sink under the new windows and our shallow pantry would have sliding doors.

Best laid plans, however, again proved they needed revision.

One night, the kids watched TV while I again ripped up old linoleum with half rotten iron tacks rusted into it; again a shovel job. I was having to put considerable muscle behind my strokes to break the rusted tacks.

Bang! Something solid balked the shovel-nose, sending a painful jolt up my arms.

What the hell?

Something solid was hidden under the linoleum. Having scraped away much of the surface material, I discovered two rusted iron rings; grips for opening a pair of doors in the floor, doors with hinges as rusted as the rings.

I called the kids. Leanne reckoned it might be treasure, while Paul reckoned it more likely hid a skeleton.

No amount of pulling could budge the ring-pulls and the rusted hinges defied yielding. With the aid of my iron jemmy and a crowbar, Paul and I eventually got the iron-ring handles to move but the hinges held.

Leanne backed off to a far wall, shoulders hunched, closed fists under her chin.

"I'm going to have to patch the floor here anyway," I told the kids. "Nothing will be lost by simply smashing our way through here."

My twenty-pound iron hammer for knocking down brick walls, eventually broke the timbers. We cleared it away to discover a flight of five concrete steps leading into a small, shallow cellar.

The 'hole' measured but four feet by two-and-a-half. It was empty except for a rusted spike-file, remnants of paper slips rusted to it.

Most crumbled when touched.

"Leanne, pet. Bring me the egg-slice?"

I slid it under the file as carefully as the rough concrete floor allowed, laying it on a bench. *Oh how sad that it is all starting to crumble!*

Faded writing was barely discernable.

My mind was seeing it a sort of time capsule.

With scissors, I cut around where rust had eaten into the paper, bonding it to the metal. All three of us held our breath.

"These spike files," I told the kids, "people used for filing papers they wanted saved, akin to today's butterfly clips. My grandmother had several."

Only a few odd words were legible. It was part of a shopping invoice.

The date was *20 Aug 21.*

"That will be nineteen twenty-one, kids, even older than me," I joked.

The number was illegible but the product was *potatoes.*

After it came *1 cord wood*.

The only other legible writing was *1 lb butte...*

"The *lb* is 'pound'. That was nearly half a kilogram," I told them.

Neither of my kids had known British Imperial Measurements. They had been taught only metrics from kindergarten. I shone a torch all around the tiny cellar, hoping for other gems, yet strangely, not even a cobweb was evident.

"They called this a *chill room* for things like butter and milk. I wonder why it was here and not in what had been their kitchen, or larder?

"Leanne, you're nearest the door. Will you get my dictionary? On the living-room mantel-piece."

Most things were on a bench or in a carton, or on the mantel-piece in the living-room, awaiting their turn to find a home. I looked up the word: *cord*.

It was defined as *a measurement of cut firewood (usually one hundred twenty-eight cubic feet)*.

I did a quick mental calculation...

"I would reckon one hundred twenty-eight cubic feet would be about one point five metres times one point five metres times one point five metres. Wow, that would be a hefty pick-up load."

I was distressingly disappointed that prices had been on a part of the page already gone. I slid all the scraps into a jar and screwed the lid tightly.

"This is for Mags to see."

I took photos of the cellar and its broken doors, then sat to redesign the kitchen.

"I want that cellar for my wines," I told them. "I will build wine-racks to fit and make a new cover. I planned cork-tiles for the kitchen, kids, so I want this out of any traffic area."

My new plan put the ceiling-high pantry directly over the little 'cellar', leaving it part of the pantry floor. The kids went back to their TV and left me pondering over the rest of the kitchen layout.

Thirty-five

Driving upcountry in autumn, always proved a delight.

The Murray River Valley was a wine-growing area, formal lines of vines stretching as far as eyes could see—an inspiring sight. The area was home to not only vineyards but pine forests.

I was calling on a fertiliser packing plant in an attempt to win back business lost prior to my transfer. I had met the buyer during my survey and a few times since. We had been offered a chance to quote on the new contract and I was delivering it, using the opportunity to pump him for recommendations on local wines.

"I want to take home several heavy reds for myself, and Moselles for my wife. I will be led by you." We discussed business and he offered me another chance.

It wasn't a contract, but at least an order for a new product. I accepted the lesser quantity at the same price and came away a happy man, with at least a foot in the door.

All it needs now is to give him good service and quality, and to follow up.

I was now following his directions to two winemakers, both in dales ablaze with reds and golden yellows, leaves beginning to fall.

The countryside was spectacularly beautiful when confronted with endless kilometres of it.

I shall next time, bring my camera! And Maggie! Make a weekend of it, take in some wine-tasting.

Idle driving time was also opportunity for planning more Restoration.

Mags will yet be absent some weeks, enjoying England's summer while I'm starting to shiver.

With so much of the new kitchen needing tradesmen to satisfy council, plumbers piping fresh water in and waste-water out, gas-pipes for cooking, electricians wiring power-points and cupboards made and installed, had my mind buzzing.

Having all the business matter on tape, my mind could switch to our bedroom.

With wardrobes done, mirrors in place, the rest remains a shambles that I want tidied before Mags is home. Dare I even consider forsaking the Brussels carpet in this room?

A northerner hating the cold southern winters, especially for my feet first thing in the morning, was my only gripe with Melbourne.

Maybe I should just be buying woolly slippers and keeping the carpet and its timber surrounds?

We had agreed on papering walls to the ceiling, including the false wall atop the wardrobes, and painting the ceiling grey, except for the embossed circular centrepiece. We had already bought the paper, a "That's it!" occasion. Maggie's eyes were captured by it when choosing curtain fabric. I had measured up that very day and went back on the Sunday to buy it.

It was a deep grey background overlayed with huge rouge-red roses and bottle-green leaves. The roses were so large that the effect of it was somehow both dramatic and soothing, dark in its way, yet in a room with large bay-windows and a wall entirely of mirrors inviting in lots of natural light.

I would spend my home time until Maggie's return, scraping old paint from the woodwork and maybe even painting the ceiling.

~ * ~

Back from my rambles, Dawn handed me a message from Grant.

"He asked me to be sure it was the first message given."

I phoned.

"Are you free to come see me early tomorrow morning?"

"Eight o'clock?"

He hardly hesitated. "Okay." He hung up straight away.

I was habitually an early riser, my alarm permanently set for five forty-five a.m.

At six, in all seasons, I was diving into the local council pool. Just two blocks from our house, the indoor thirty-metre pool was the bizarrely named *Harold Holt Memorial Swimming Pool.* Holt was the Australian Prime Minister who dived into the surf for his morning swim, never to be seen again. His widow, Dame Zara, was to appear in Maggie's and my lives in the very near future.

Every weekday morning unless travelling, I stroked my twenty laps before jogging home for breakfast. By eight I was in the office. I liked to get my day organised by eight thirty. I then walked through the factory, chatting with my people. I tried including everyone, even if just a "Good Morning" or a wave or wink.

Every soul at DRC Bags called me 'Evan', floor-sweepers and apprentices included. I was their boss and they knew what I expected of them. They also knew I liked an informal atmosphere, so much so that my door was always open. Only time it closed was if in consultation with a client or employee on a personal matter. If any should close it on leaving, Dawn was quickly on her feet to open it.

I arrived at Grant's office to find him just locking his car.

"Evan, we're moving you."

My heart hit the floor.

What? Sydney again? My family's life ruptured again? Stanford Lodge?

"To where?"

"Port Melbourne."

Ah. At least Melbourne. But the Trudale plant?

Trudale had been one of Melbourne's first printers. It had flourished and was one of the companies DRC bought in the nineteen sixties. In Sydney it had bought two of the largest packaging operations, one being my old home-from-home. In Melbourne they bought Trudales by the Bay in Port Melbourne, a giant in label printing. The other was Carton Industries, a giant in carton production and with licenses for reproducing many traditional paintings. It owned the failing Bag division I now ran.

"Trudales?"

He nodded.

I was aware of the considerable enlarging been going on at the Trudale plant.

Grant unrolled a large print of the site. I gasped. For a printing plant, it was massive, just a block from Melbourne's huge Port Phillip Bay. The site now took up an entire block and a half, only a laneway dividing the two. It fronted the broad Bay Street, Port Melbourne's major thoroughfare and all three side-streets and its rear street.

"These several houses, we left. They simply asked too much money. As you see, we are building around them."

"The bank?" I asked.

The National Australia Bank had a branch plumb in the middle of our extended buildings. I'd known it part of DRC property but leased to the bank, a historical gem in the Georgian style, not big, yet quite a jewel in an industrial area.

"The bank stays, Evan, at least until its lease expires. We will be building overhead bridges across the laneway."

"To operate as a single company?"

He will have expected me to first want to know how this might change my role.

He smiled.

"Absolutely. All present company names will go, in favour of simply *DRC Packaging*. All General Managers will have senior roles adapted from old. You, Evan, will lose some responsibilities, as will Trent Harris from Fitzroy, yet have others in respect of expansion. You will retain your Marketing responsibilities in Bags, yet lose manufacture. Your Clayton property will be sold, as will Trent's at Fitzroy.

"Obviously the plan is to reduce costs. Manufacturing, Purchasing and Accounting departments from the three current companies will merge. Many roles must immediately change yet all personnel will be retained until mergers, in their turn, take place. The weaker personnel will be let go as the new routines settle down.

"The further plan we have for you, Evan, cannot begin until next year. Meanwhile I want you to join our planning bee in laying out your manufacturing floor.

"Right now, however, mate, start planning how your equipment can be moved with the least disruption to customer service. Get in forward orders so you can go into permanent double shift to build up stock. You will know what is involved. Let's start with the goal of moving everything over a hectic week. Use that, anyway, as the basis of your planning. All three companies have this assignment, although moving at different times. We are looking at making all moves during November. Can you have a plan for me in ten days?"

The bastard. He will know he has but dropped veiled hints at what I will be doing, yet doesn't attempt detail. But the mere fact he hasn't, means he is not going to tell, even if asked.

Thirty-six

Maggie phoned right on eight p.m.

"I leave Thursday afternoon, sweetheart. Arrival your time is nine a.m. Friday. Please don't take time off to come and meet me. I'll take a cab."

"Negative, my love. We will come to the airport. The kids will enjoy it and I certainly am anxious to see you. I have missed you dreadfully. I could not be happy with you arriving home to an empty house. I'll make a booking at the *Steak House* for Friday night for all four, so there is no worry about dinner. Or will you want a day to get over jet lag?"

"I will likely have a sleep during the day. Do I have a bed?"

I laughed. "Our room is finished except for painting woodwork, papering walls and gilding flowers in the ceiling."

It was her turn to laugh.

"I'm dying to see it all. Mum and Dad want to come see it."

"Good news. Ask them to bring wine from duty-free. We now have a wine-cellar."

"A what?"

"You will see it on Friday."

"The mind boggles, but okay. Is there hard liquor I can bring duty-free?"

"A *J&B*. I will have *Veuve Clicquot* on ice. Have a good journey, my darling. I feel all a-tingle."

"Maybe I'll have jet-lag?"

"I'll accept a promise."

She blew me a kiss and hung up.

"Friday morning, kids, we all have to be ready to leave at eight o'clock."

Their excitements were exuberant. I was thrilled at Leanne's being particularly so.

And when emerging from the customs hall, Maggie looked a dream.

"She's obviously been clothes-shopping too, kids," I remarked.

Despite having just arrived off one of the longest flights in the world, she really did look a dream. I already felt all a-tingle.

When greetings were over, Paul took her trolley and I took the duty-free bags.

"I bought cosmetics also," she admitted. "Mum and Dad insisted on driving me to Heathrow despite trains bring one right into the terminal," she told us on the drive home.

"We shed several tears, yet the parting was made the easier in knowing they will visit not this coming summer, but next. They insist on summer so they can quit their winter for several weeks. So we will have them for Christmas. I told them we couldn't have accommodation ready for them this summer, that I wasn't prepared to turf either kid out of their room. But by the following summer, our TV room could be made over for them."

"Extremely generous thinking, my love. And the rest of your family?"

"Oh, Evan, I was so disappointed. Since living here, I've always considered England as 'back home', yet now, I don't feel that at all. I was certainly happy boarding the aircraft yesterday, to be thinking of this as home. I don't want to sound unkind, because I love them all, yet Audrey's little boy is a brat and it just riles me that she has so little control over him. And her husband is never going to do much for her. And Martin? My brother is a gormless ass with a dreary wife. I simply found little interest in their boring little lives."

I could see her reaching for a tissue. I kept some in my door pocket and quickly pulled a wad for her. I let that hand then fall to her knee for a little squeeze.

She turned to the kids.

"I just feel so happy being back home with you all," she told them.

Then she sighed. "And oh, what a nice thought about dinner at *Steak House*. Yes, I certainly don't feel like planning tonight's dinner."

Malvern Steak House was unique in Australia. It was a block from the house and indeed homey. Beefsteak was the only dish on its menu, served with fresh salad or baked vegetables. Steaks could be ordered Tartare, Bloody-Blue, Very Rare, Rare, Rare-Medium and Medium.

"Wrong restaurant for you, I'm afraid," they would tell those who liked well-done steak."

If ordering Tartare, ingredients were wheeled up to your table and you nominated your choices. I always took capers galore. In my book, French Capers made steak tartare a feast for a king.

~ * ~

"Oh, my!" Maggie almost gasped on seeing the new kitchen.

It yet lacked much of the painting, the cork floor-tiles, the planned breakfast nook, yet showed all the promise of an easy and pleasant kitchen to work in.

Leanne slid back the pantry door to reveal the 'wine-cellar'. I had affixed new hinges and wooden covers, using the original heavy iron rings, professionally cleaned with acids, for handles.

She was quite amazed. "As would have been the dear Old Ladies. I doubt they could ever have known it was under their feet."

"Having got the tradespeople to complete, so far, this part of the house, I left the rest undone so I could get the messy part of our bedroom finished, darling."

She gave me a big hug.

"The bed is already turned down if you want to sleep off some jet-lag."

"Thank you, darling. But can we just sit and have a glass of wine?"

"At eleven a.m.?"

"My stomach thinks it's dinner time."

Thirty-seven

When the kitchen was done, we knew we were getting close to thinking about the outdoors.

"If you like, love, we can get a man in and do the weeding and preparing the rest of the beds. You call the programme."

She pinched me on the bottom. We left it at that and got back to finishing our bedroom. I remained dubious that the chosen wallpaper when seen *en-masse* might simply look too 'heavy'.

She proved right, of course. We were as thrilled with our bedroom as any other.

I painted our bathroom ceiling and friezes, tiled the wall where the old doorway had been and finished the woodworking repairs around the en-suite doorway. We chose a water-resistant carpet in a purple shade, to match the ceiling.

We did get a man in to do the heavy digging for Maggie's rose gardens and she concentrated on buying and planting the rose bushes.

I had her choose the papering and painting for the old linen-room. It was to be her study once beginning her own business. It already had considerable shelving, much of which was left in place.

I added a moulded wooden 'rail' around the walls at the eight feet mark, creating a frieze for the upper, painting this and the ceiling, white. The large expanse of white increased daylight in the smallish room.

For the lower half, she chose some of the living-room paper saved by not doing the ceilings.

To cover where old linoleum had been, now despatched to the Big Hole, I bought, for her birthday, a Turkish Carpet, and blacked the floorboards around its perimeter. Through the room's doorway, this met the 'black border' around the long hallway's Brussels carpet.

For the hallway itself, we decided to do the same as her office. It had archways at each end, to also limit natural daylight.

"I'm sure the Old Ladies would see the wisdom in that," she claimed.

~ * ~

Mags and Julie struck out on their own, working from homes; secretarial work and manifest copying. A roneo machine was installed in Julie's home and Maggie installed two electric typewriters, one a wide carriage. They lived but a twenty minute drive apart, so communications were easy.

We purchased a desk, desk chair and 'visitor' chair and the stationery she would need, business cards, letterheads, note-paper, invoices and receipt books. She chose the cushion for her chair. I suggested replacing the stained glass in her window, to add more light, yet she insisted it remain.

"Both for the Old Ladies' satisfaction, and for mine," she insisted.

She did, however, approve fluorescent lighting, and bought prints of old England to grace the walls.

Paul also had a natural sense of painting and design and helped Mag's hand-draw small banners for posting in shop windows up and down Glenferrie Road and Trak Village, promoting her service. Julie did the same in her district. One of Mag's first enquiries was from Dame Zara Bate OBE, widow of Prime Minister Harold Holt and now married to Jeff Bate. She was a leading light in the Melbourne

Glitterati community and on the board of a number of business enterprises. She led a busy social life as well as business life.

"She is the founder of *Magg,* did you know?" Maggie asked me on returning from her interview.

"What the devil is '*Magg*'?"

"Trak Village's leading glamour shop for the elite, my dear. Many Toorak matrons clothe themselves from *Magg.*"

"What is her home like?"

"Not as palatial as the St. Georges Road mansion, yet elegant enough for hosting large events. Even the swimming pool has a large entertaining area alongside."

"And the lady herself? Her reputation is certainly colourful; she's reportedly tarred with many a different brush."

"She has a wicked sense of humour, even with someone she's just met and looking for a job. She certainly doesn't put on airs, in fact she is quite down to earth. Most unlike the way a *Dame of the British Empire* would act in England."

"Will she be giving you work?"

"Of course. She seemed delighted at my CV and references. She knows my old boss well. 'Not an easy man to satisfy,' she insisted. So yes, she has given me four letters and a small stock of both her personal and business letterheads. She seemed impressed with my shorthand speed and I am to take the correspondence back to her tomorrow afternoon. It is all test stuff, so I shall, of course, give it royal attention."

I flung my arms around her in congratulations.

"We should open some champagne!"

"No. Let's wait until we see her reactions. Right now, I want to phone Jules and give her the news."

~ * ~

Maggie went whole hog painting our bedroom ceiling centrepiece. It was heavily embossed with flowers. I had to move our heavy bed away from the centre of the room to build a platform. I again hired two more tall stepladders and planks to build a solid scaffold.

"I just feel so elated at getting all Dame Zara's business," she gloated, "that I want to celebrate by doing something adventurous, like defeating my fear of scaffolds."

We had our celebration over dinner that evening, Champagne for all four.

"She wants me two full days a week at quite a generous rate. She told me Peter Stirling had given me a glowing personal recommendation. 'If you could satisfy a man in his position in respect of security, Maggie' she told me, 'I feel confident you can do the same for me'."

So we made it clear to the kids that they should never be discussing any of Maggie's business they overhear, with anyone else.

"Even best mates!"

"Especially best mates!"

Maggie had Paul draft out three different areas of the moulding so she could practise the colour mix. She had Julie roneo several copies, then practised different colour schemes until we all felt she had it right.

"I need it to be something I can enjoy when lying in bed meditating."

"When have you ever lain in bed meditating?"

"Let's just say it's something I want to look forward to?"

I let my eyes roll across the very ceiling she was working on.

And we were to become parents again.

Maggie wanted a cat. She chose a kitten at the local pet-shop and named her Piddles. She earned the name, even as we drove it home.

Piddles soon realised her place in our household, even making friends with Tiffany. During the winter they would lie in front of the fire in the TV room or Dining Room, each nudging and prodding its way to be nearest the grate. They soon leaned to compromise with Tiffany stretched out, Piddles sound asleep on top of Tiffy's belly, or crooked in a Tiffy headlock, all great subjects for camera-clicking.

Tiffany also provided enjoyment at mealtimes. She knew she wasn't allowed in a room when we were eating, so would crouch in the doorway, ever inching when we were not looking, just that little bit further into the room. We had only to clap hands at her and she knew why; she would scuttle backwards into the hall, only to start the antic all over again.

~ * ~

Next on our Restoration list was the formal sitting-room-come lounge. We already had the wallpaper and I already knew the procedure—strip and sand woodwork, scrub carpet, paint woodwork, hang wallpaper, paint ceiling white, gold tips to flower petals, paper door panels, clean and lacquer the black floor surrounds.

All left then would be wall hangings and buying furniture. We had already seen along Glenferrie Road, what we wanted.

The biggest fireplace in the house had a mantel about my shoulder height, heavily carved wood panelling below it. It had years of grime ground into it. I asked the guy at a gallery selling only paintings, sculpture and carved wooden panels, about getting it clean. He sent a man with various spirits and wire brushes to properly clean it. He then stained it back to its mahogany colour, adding a heat-resistant lacquer. I never knew such a thing existed, yet some was now part of our household. The fellow was surprisingly interested in the carpet.

"I reckon you have one of the few houses with such carpet, in all Australia," he informed us.

Leanne came home one day, Romy with her, to tell us her parents were trying to sell a piano.

"They call it Italian Walnut whatever that is," they informed us. "It's very old."

We went to see it and straightaway wanted it—an upright *Steinberg*.

"Our piano was what I missed most when moving to London," Maggie told us. "I used to practise all my songs when in the choir."

I had learned piano as a kid in Brisbane, but when my father died, we moved back to Sydney minus the piano. Naturally, I began losing the art. The thought of having one in the house again, had me quite excited. We bought it despite lacking two brass candle sconces.

"I remember it having them," Romy told us, yet maybe my parents didn't like them. They just disappeared."

We added those to our list of things to look for when in antique shops, then had the piano delivered home.

Our lounge-room had bay-windows in two walls, both onto the wide veranda that ran along the front and down the east side. One of the features I liked most about the house was that the main roof, in all its contours, covered even the verandas, a reason its posts were not only so plentiful but robust. Once quit of remaining storage, we were surprised at how big was the room. Its bay windows, unlike the dining-room, had no window-seat; the bays were floor-deep and the trusty Brussels carpet again followed their contours, leaving the regulation black floorboards surrounding it.

With Maggie fitting as much time into the work as her business allowed, all the restoration was done by end of winter, many hours of it made the more pleasant by having a coal fire burning in the grate as we worked. We had meanwhile measured up for furniture, sited the piano and ordered our lounge-suite made. It was just two wing-back chairs and matching sofa in a traditional damask, studded and skirted. It was in blue, same shade as the wallpaper. We loaned the piano stool to the manufacturer, that he could cover it also. All three lounge pieces were in the centre-of the room, none against walls.

Our old traymobile bar that could be trundled when needed across the vestibule into the dining-room, had found its intended home. I stripped it and lacquered it in a colour to live happily not too far from the piano.

Stanford Lodge's interior restoration was getting near to completion.

It was nearing November and the critical week for moving all heavy equipment from DRC Bags to Port Melbourne.

"And the start of summer to boot," I announced with glee.

However, I knew there would be considerable time before, during and after that week, that my work hours would be extended. Moving an entire manufacturing plant from an outlying suburb to central within a week, then getting all operational again in its new site, would be a frantic time.

"And I'm still trying to appease the disappointment of many operatives, Mags, who, over the years, moved their homes to Clayton, even built there to avoid long drives. Now their ten minutes becomes an hour of heavy traffic. All remain unhappy. Fortunately, none of the essential people have quit, although most of the unskilled, have."

Thirty-eight

December, 1974

We awoke Christmas morning to news of disaster.

Overnight, Cyclone Tracy had devastated Darwin.

Australia's most northerly city had been totally rebuilt after Japanese bombers in raid after raid during World War II, levelled it. Its entire population had been evacuated south. Now it had happened again, not by enemy bombers, but by nature.

Eighty percent of its houses, along with presents carefully stacked under Christmas trees during the night by Santa, had literally gone with the wind. The entire population was again being evacuated.

Darwin had no train service in those days so busses, aeroplanes and ships were rushed to Darwin to bring people south. Emergency accommodation was established in City Show-Ground pavilions across the nation. Pleas were out over radio and television for food, clothing and bedding for multi-thousands of people left with only their pyjamas. Also needed were large packing cartons. Addresses for collection were being broadcast in every Australian city.

I spent the next hour of Christmas morning on the phone to my departmental managers asking all to contact subordinates right down to floor-sweepers, to come to the factory and pick up cartons for themselves and neighbours to pack with goodies, then get them to the collection centres. I was off to open the plant, closed for our annual shut-down, to fork-lift packing cartons to our despatch dock. Whilst there I had the kids fill our own car with every carton they could squeeze in.

I helped our delivery driver fill our trucks to capacity.

"Make sure you leave the side-boards up, so our name can be seen when making delivery."

When most were loaded and gone, Mfg. Manager, Doug, stayed on to service stragglers.

I took my loaded car home so Maggie, Paul, Leanne and I could spend Christmas afternoon leaving cartons in every home in our street and surrounding streets, until the car was empty.

Televised newscasts for several weeks were still showing the devastation of Darwin. The city had been named after Charles Darwin when he visited. He was keen to inspect wildlife of the continent longest isolated from creature migration.

~ * ~

Boxing Day in Melbourne proved a markedly contrasting excitement.

Melbourne Cricket Ground, largest in the world and affectionately known as the MCG was a riot of hysterics every boxing day. Ninety thousand people packed it to watch the opening day of a cricket test-match. Some thirty countries around the world would send teams abroad on regular occasions to play cricket. Every fourth year the frenzy was electric, the protagonists being Australia and England, the world's traditional cricket foes.

Maggie's tee-shirt had a roaring British Lion spread across her breast and the Union Jack graced her back. Mine had a Foster's Beer ad on the front, and "Belt the Poms for Six" on the back. I wore my large brimmed bushman's hat with a dozen corks dangling from its brim edges, with fishing gut. This was the Aussie outback's means of keeping bush-flies off one's face when outdoors.

Bay Eleven was an excellent spot for studying through binoculars, a batsman's face while waiting for the ball. His concentration suddenly changing was the sign that the ball was in flight. Binoculars were then dropped so we could quickly see the wider result of his sweep, or prop, or slice, or miss. With the crowd in full voice, the noise was unendingly deafening.

Like everyone else we had come prepared with our esky packed with ice, beer and white wine. Sandwiches and fruits were in backpacks shoved under our seats. Beer was available in bars under the stands, of course, yet who wanted to miss the excitement?

Another advantage of Bay Eleven was being both not too near, yet not too far from Bay Thirteen, renowned for the most one-eyed of Aussie supporters who enjoyed their beers. They kept up chants and cat-calls all day, every day of all five days of the test match.

Maggie and I kept up our own little niggles, of course. I was subject on many occasions, of her one raised contentious eyebrow. Day one of Australia versus England test matches could, in some respects, call for considerable self-control.

Thirty-nine

During the festive period, other than exchanging dinners with Julie and Olaf that were becoming ritual, we concentrated on finishing the indoor Restoration.

The linen-press in the Octagon now not only hid the unsightly switchboard but its concertina-folding wooden doors with wallpapered panels, accentuated the Octagon decor. We had the old chandelier professionally cleaned and returned it to its centrepiece—a proud feature.

Only the TV room had yet to be done and it was straight-forward. It had no bay window, rather a pair of glass doors, again lead-lighted stained glass matching the rest of the house. They opened on to its own little veranda from which the original owners would have watched the tennis. That was the piece of land now a neighbouring property. The windowed doors now looked out on Maggie's glorious expanse of hydrangeas. The higher fence level was wire-lined and draped with blooming wisteria.

Today it was solely a TV room, its walls and ceiling painted in what Maggie called "a diarrheic shade of shit". Actually, it was a pleasant neutral shade that satisfied the entire family. Its only furniture, apart from the TV was beanbags and several low and easily portable drink or food tables. One entire wall was lined with bookshelves.

We had cameras clicking all over the house, indoor shots of what we considered a delightful transformation.

"One entire half of completing our promise to the Old Ladies," Maggie termed the celebration.

Restoration could now be turned outdoors.

~ * ~

During summer, I was again officiating in the surf-beach driving pool and Maggie shared driving the girls to their riding-club, with Romy's parents.

Both, however, were interrupted for the annual school camp weeks.

Paul's was again in the Grampian Mountains and Leanne's camp, an irregular one of a private nature, to a vague sort of camp from their school only. Leanne and Romy were going as a pair, of course.

"How many girls?" we asked.

"Oh, ten or twelve, I think."

"You think?"

"Well, maybe more."

"And where is it?"

"Down Gippsland way, somewhere."

"For four days?"

"Yes."

"How do you get there and back?"

"By bus. We have to find our own way to school, and parents are to pick us up on return, at five p.m."

"How many teachers are going?"

"I don't know."

"Do you know any of the teachers going?"

"Yes, our maths master."

"I thought your maths master was a man."

"He is."

"Going on a girls only camping trip?"

"I guess so."

Maggie phoned Romy's parents. She came back to me shrugging shoulders.

"Yes, this happens every year, it seems. Romy went last year and reported all orderly. No problems arose."

"I wonder what 'problems' were covered, Mags?"

Maggie and I took time out to visit Romy's parents.

Yes, they had made the same sort of enquiries last year. It seemed the male teacher was along to supervise erecting tents and toilets and seeing to fireplaces and cooking gear. Everything seemed above board.

Mags took Leanne aside for a deep conversation on the dangers that could arise.

"She illustrated a ready approach, Evan. She promised that she and Romy would never separate, that even going to the toilet, one would wait outside for the other."

She pleaded to go and we agreed to accept her word, buoyed with the knowledge that Romy would be on the same promise to her parents.

~ * ~

Our list of work in the *Stanford Lodge*'s outdoors was near as long as the list just finished. I was 'in charge' of building, Maggie of gardening, even to hiring and instructing men for the heavy bits.

"At least, Evan darling, with the inside finished, one very happy lady is Evelyn."

Evelyn's chores had kept changing as the Restoration progressed. She was no longer left with washing breakfast dishes and cleaning the odd restored room. The dishwasher took care of dishes and the washing machine and dryer took care of laundry. Evelyn would spend three or four hours each day, cleaning and ironing all but Maggie's clothes.

"I've ever done my own, so will continue so," Maggie insisted.

"I'll only be sorry when you finish filling the Big Hole," Evelyn exclaimed. "It has been so handy!"

We were, however, getting near that stage. Much of the old soil, lacking fertiliser over the years, would soon complete the job as Maggie's 'muscle-men' as she called them, kept chucking in barrow-fulls of old soil as my cheque-book bought new.

My first priority was stripping, sanding and painting the score of veranda posts and intricately carved fretwork supporting the roof. Federation posts were round and Maggie was keen to have climbing roses winding up them. The fence between us and neighbours, it was pointed out early that on the western side, the 'dead' side of our house, comprised my nemesis' as I called the holly tree that we had kept cropped. The tunnel was now a feature, a great aid in getting to the side aisle painting the outsides of windows.

When the piano was moved into its final home, Maggie called in a tuner.

"The poor fellow was blind," she told me that night.

"He found his own way to our front door with his cane, although it might have been Tiffy's barking he was following, but I had to lead him to the piano. I had already cleared its top and he had me help him take off the front panel and lay it on the floor. Only when finished would he accept refreshment. I talked him into sitting at the dining-room table with me over a glass of wine. He had been blinded in the war."

Mags had tears in her eyes.

"He wanted to phone a taxi to drive him to an appointment in Prahran. I drove him there."

~ * ~

Mags and I had already agreed that we would not yet, at any rate, renew the decking on the verandas. It was repaired in patches yet fell within our objective of retaining as much of the house the Old Ladies had lived in, as possible. None was yet dangerous.

"Something for them to feel comfortable with," was her way of putting it.

I happily crossed that off my list, yet the day we looked forward to finishing, would linger a while yet.

Leanne and Romy, home safely from their camping excursion, arrived at the house with the missing piano sconces. Her father had found them when cleaning out his workshop. We had them professionally polished and I was able to buy the six small brass screws needed for returning them to their old home.

They got plenty of use, for we lit them whenever the piano was being used at night, for which, with the inside finished, we now had guiltless leisure hours.

One Saturday morning, about a month after school started, Paul asked if he could have a "word in my ear in private."

Maggie was in the front garden, Leanne was at Romy's, so Paul and I perched on the wall of the Big Hole out back.

"I want to quit school, Dad."

I could tell by his demeanour that he anticipated a tough ride. He had just finished his Intermediate, year three at High School, having two more years to his Senior—the time to either proceed to university, or begin a working career.

"You know my attitude. This is your opportunity to specialise in subjects towards your chosen career. What influenced you to give away the thought of a career?"

He shifted from this foot to that.

"Gees, Dad. Why do you always twist things to make me feel guilty?"

"Guilty of what?"

He thought again for several long seconds. "All the guys at school are quitting. They..."

"I cannot believe, for a minute, that all the guys are quitting."

"Well all my friends. Well some of them are reckoning that we should have a time in our lives when we can have a break. That..."

"A break to go surfing? Living on a beach? Doing enough odd jobs to earn the cost of canned bully-beef every day of your lives?"

"Gees, Dad. You make it hard. What I mean is..."

"What you mean is yes, that you would break into houses to steal money to buy bully-beef?"

"No. You've got it all wrong."

"All right, I'll just sit here and listen. Spell out your alternative to remaining in school."

He seemed to feel a little relief at that.

"I'm seventeen, Dad. I don't have anything planned as a career. I don't want to be in business like you. And I don't have a feel for trade-work like plumbing and things. I want to work outdoors. I reckon at Phillip Island I can get a job in the Penguin Parade. And I reckon with a bit of help down there I can learn to make surfboards. Many blokes want special things on their boards, shape of fins, placement of runners and things like that. I want to do things with my hands like you, but do it for money. And we wouldn't live on just bully beef. With a job each, four of us, maybe five, can get a house on a beach, pretty cheap, and learn to cook."

He stopped.

"It's 'pretty cheaply', not 'pretty cheap'," I corrected.

He sighed and shuffled his feet again.

"Do you want a beer while we talk? I could do with one."

"Oh, yes please, Dad."

"You get them. I'm too unsettled to walk straight."

He brought out not only two opened stubbies, but the beach umbrella.

He's expecting to spend a long time over this.

He screwed the umbrella into the ground and opened it. He sat beside me, other side of the pole.

We talked for an hour. He kept coming back to not only his particular friends but many others who talked of quitting. He said some had already done so. I told him I would go to the school and talk with the head.

Bloody hell. His school is among the highly rated. There's more behind this!

He didn't seem phased about that. Just shrugged his shoulders.

I asked if these were his friends in the regular Sunday surf group. Most were.

When I persisted, he told me which ones. And seemed perturbed.

"That I might have in mind phoning their fathers, worries you?"

He nodded. "Only because some mightn't have talked this over with their dads yet."

"Ah. So this is an organised project. I'm beginning to get a clearer picture."

Once abed, I talked it through with Mags. She knew that I knew her answer would be that it was my call, yet was keen to discuss it. I'd learned over my years with her, to trust her implicitly—both her devotion and her ability to sum up people.

"It doesn't surprise me, darling. This must happen to many fathers. I did it with mine! I knew my parents wanted me to marry and give them grandkids. That was the career they had in mind for me. They even had guys in mind—listed in priority! When I said I wanted to leave home to live in London, they were horrified. But they knew my determination. It was like Paul's, so they didn't put up much of a fight. Yet I knew they were dreadfully disappointed."

"But you had finished school, Mags. And they still had your younger sister."

She thought on that. "Yes, and Audrey certainly was the marrying kind. And yes, I realise Paul is your only son, and of course you want to see him prosper. I also agree he is a brainy kid. He has a great aptitude for measuring people. And situations."

"I guess all that is fair comment, yet I have no particular course for him in mind. I've tried to teach him to think or look on things from all sides, then make his own decision. I've no desire to see him a doctor or anything else in particular. I really wish something of his own volition emerges. Yet he is dipping out too soon. I sincerely feel he should do these next two years before taking this step."

Did you say that to him?"

"No. We've left it that I talk with both his school and the other fathers. Leon Parsons is Paul's closest friend and Stan Parsons and I have a pretty good rapport. I will sound him out."

Next morning I called the school and made an appointment with the Head. I was in for a shock.

"Yes," he told me. "We meet this situation every year with Year Four lads. There's little we can do about it. They either have a career in mind, or they just want out."

On asking what approach they take with these boys, I got another shock.

"We don't try to influence them. Experience has taught us that the vast majority of those we deter from quitting, approach the rest of their schooling with a grudge and make poor grades. It is amazing how many cases we learn of, where these quitters make good in this or that direction. Nothing requiring formal qualification, of course."

This I could understand. Some of the brightest guys in my plant never finished school. Many went back to night school even after marriage, in order to graduate. I had taught guys like that in my marketing classes. One, orphaned when young and didn't finish High School, had since built not only a business, but his own home in Sydney's exclusive Palm Beach.

I phoned Stan Parsons and the other fathers to report on my visit to the school. All realised that we were facing defeat.

"The boys are otherwise, Evan, going to do just that—face the rest of schooling with a grudge, and fail exams."

When I told Mags the reaction I'd got at the school, she was horrified.

"What is this world turning into? That psychiatrist believed children's rights more important than parental advice? That's what influenced me not to let Leanne come too much under his influence. So what are you going to do about Paul?"

I breathed deeply, the sense of defeatism exasperating me.

"I'll make it clear that quitting school is against my wishes, wishes for him having a joyous life. If he goes, he must accept that he doesn't come back except as an ever-welcome visitor. A frequent one. That I would always be here to talk with or help with worries. That we continue facing life as a family."

"There is a saying, Paul," I told him face-to-face, "that when a child leaves home, parents should burn its bedroom."

He looked querulous.

"It is a way of saying, 'In choosing to leave the family home, you relinquish that room for Maggie and I to convert into anything we wish."

Paul's eyes widened in surprise. "You mean I can never come home?"

I put my arm around him. "Not at all. We want to see you here as often as you can visit, but you might have to doss in a sleeping bag. Can we visit you?"

"Of course. I know I will miss you all and will make you welcome."

Tears were plentiful as he packed his things, but pack them he did.

There are some things he reckoned he mightn't have room for.

"Can I leave these here?"

They were several of his schoolbooks which could easily fit on our bookshelves.

"Anything bulky, Son, we've oodles of space above our wardrobes."

"Will the cockroaches get to things there?"

"Quite likely."

It seems his school didn't teach him much about cockroaches. Or is his memory confusing him about the time he lived in Queensland?

"Do you have cockroach bait?"

"I doubt it, Son. If you want to buy some before you leave, leave it with me. I'll pass it on to Evelyn. You have to learn to do things for yourself now, you know."

"Oh, come on, Dad, you don't have to keep pressing it home."

"Pressing it where?"

"Oh, be reasonable. I know I'm going to find it tough for a while."

I had an icy lump in my throat, when we wrapped arms about each other. The house would never feel the same. My heart was going to be empty without him.

Stan had offered to drive three of the boys to Phillip Island where they would sleep in Paul's tent while house-hunting. Two further lads would follow after Easter.

I gave Paul five-hundred dollars and urged him not to waste it.

"It's for food and board-wax, only," I told him.

It hurt horribly when he didn't even look me in the eye as he left. A great emptiness somehow enveloped me, tore me into little bits. I felt my Adams' Apple rising to choke off air.

Mag's could see it. She poured me a Cognac and herself a vermouth.

"Little bastard," I said to her, "why couldn't he have done this before I swore off cigarettes?"

She cuddled me as I knew she would. She could feel me fighting back the tears.

Forty

After finishing the back terrace, Oregon pine trellis for grapevines and all, I had decided to leave the crazy-stone facing on the brick wall for another day, also the barbecue on the east end of the terrace where Maggies' rhododendron shrubs were thickening. They promised a delightful start to organising the back yard.

On arriving home one evening, Maggie brought my habitual glass of wine and exchanged our ever welcome kiss.

"Kay is coming to visit."

I liked Kay. She was a dreadfully self-centred girl martyring herself to a guy who really didn't, by the sound of him, deserve her. Kay lived in Canberra. She was tall and skinny, ever complaining about her weight and who had a great appetite for whisky-sours.

Is that what I liked most about her?

She was part of the Prime Minister's press corps, a permanent situation. Wherever he visited, she followed. She had come from Canberra to our wedding and now, I supposed, the Prime Minister was visiting Melbourne. She would be part of his entourage. She had come to see us when at St. George's Court, but had not yet visited *Stanford Lodge.*

"She has a night off from duties tomorrow night and I took the risk of assuming you would be free. So I've tomorrow to get something in for her finicky stomach and some lemons for whisky sours."

"Clever thinking, my dear. Will she be sleeping over?"

Last time Kay had come, we discovered her *penchant* for whisky-sours. Maggie did not drink whisky, yet Kay and I absolutely stoned ourselves. It had been a night to remember.

Maggie did her shopping, filling my order of a dozen large and juicy lemons, a half-kilo of sugar and another bottle of Scotch.

Kay burst in. "You live somewhere a taxi-driver actually knows about, darlings!"

She was really a theatre-party girl misdirected somewhere, but she and Maggie were first ones to seek shoulders if feeling misunderstood. She loved the house and could "absolutely smell the aromas pouring out of your happiness in marriage, darlings."

It was her contribution to being polite.

"Would you like a whisky-sour, Kay? I've started some. You may like to taste?"

"Can I help with dinner, Maggie," she asked out of politeness, hoping for a rebuff.

"Absolutely not, Kay, dear. I know what you are like in kitchens."

"Yes, dear. I'm still allergic to them."

I poured her a whisky-sour.

"A touch more sugar, do you think, darling?"

A touch more sugar and another taste.

"I think it's more lemon juice needed, Kay."

Another squeeze or three of lemon and another taste...

"A drachm more Scotch, do you think?"

Maggie called us to dinner and we drank wine.

Kay and I went back to whisky-sours while Maggie made the finishing touches to dessert and recalled us to the table.

After everything was stacked in the dish-washer, Kay flopped into a bean-bag.

"Can I sleep here, darlings?"

~ * ~

A heavy hailstorm dislodged a chimney-pot from one of our chimneys. It rolled down the tiles to smash into an irreparable heap in the eaves-guttering.

"Why couldn't it have been from a chimney on an outside wall? Our bedroom? Leanne's room? Paul's room now guest-room?"

Dame Fortune's frivolous nature made it the chimney stack most central in the complicated contours of the roof. It was the dining-room's fireplace backing on to the Octagon, the longest crawl by a repairer over roof-tiles having already weathered near a century, let alone to then affix the replacement.

And where was I to get a replacement? It's not the sort of thing even the Odds'n Ends store will have on a shelf. And chimney-pots must match. An odd chimney lacking one would attract critical eyes like a magnet.

I would have one made. That meant the ceramics man had to come with an extension ladder long enough to reach the height of the chimney from our bedroom, through the tunnel in the holly tree, to measure up.

"And if your weight brings the chimney down," I threatened him, "I'll murder you."

He laughed, yet understood. He sent his lean son aloft.

"Can he do the replacement too?" I begged. "All those tiles he has to cross, then stand on? It could be a disaster."

"I know where Marseilles tiles can be bought. They are always saved from demolitions. I'm going to check for pots anyway, yet don't feel confident about those. Even if I have to make one up, I will do a second so you can keep one on stand-by."

Maggie's concern, however, was not how fragile were the tiles, but where the ladder need be sited.

"Right amidst my foxgloves?" she said with the nicest smile to the poor fellow.

Then in her terribly, terribly royal accent, "If you crush my foxgloves, my good man, it is I who shall murder you."

She then invited him in for coffee.

~ * ~

A month later, I arrived home to find a message on the answer-phone.

"Evan darling, I'm stuck at Dame Zara's. Her typewriter is playing up. Can you please bring the 'Empire' from my desk? I may have to eat here. You will find food in the fridge for you and Leanne."

I took the 'Empire', to be greeted by housekeeper, Rose. I had met Rose when Maggie and I were invited there for a pre-show party to some event of which Dame Zara was Patron.

"Hello, Mr. R. I cannot call Maggie for she is taking dictation; Dame Zara is in the pool. Just carry it to the study for me? Thank you so much."

I'd been told about this pool thing. Dame Zara was the shape of a Mr. five by five, stumpy and round, yet insisted on swimming naked, either a cigarette or glass of wine in hand while Maggie took dictation.

"Sometimes both," Maggie had said.

I understood people liking to swim naked, it was certainly the most relaxed way if among the right sort of people. Yet her on a lilo? My mind boggled.

Maggie later added to the story. "You should see her bedroom, my love. It has the full treatment, draped tulle up the wall from behind the pile of satin covered pillows. A large naked cherub is its centrepiece. Many times I have to sit on the bed while Dame Zara perches on pillows, a sheet almost covering her breasts, dictating."

In private, she would tell me other snippets.

"How she ever came to marry that creep," she one time said about Jeff Bate, "I shall never know. He is the greatest gauche creature in existence."

Australia's laws on 'missing people" had a seven-year definitive. If still 'missing, existence unknown' by then, they were legally considered dead. Dame Zara had then married socialite Jeffrey Bate.

"A sponger!" many cried. He was a rich man illustrating a severe lack of protocol.

"He chucks his empty beer cans and champagne bottles into the swimming pool," Maggie continued. In so many ways he is an embarrassment to her."

Both Maggie's and my business sense, however, told us that surely, Personal Secretary to one of Melbourne's most known socialites, must be good business. So we kept this sort of comment from the kid's and other friends' ears, and Maggie continued getting a great kick out of the incongruity of it all.

Forty-one

By May, most merger headaches at the Port Melbourne site were easing. I now drove to work on city edge via Lakeside Drive that every year was closed for the F-one racing carnival. It was indeed a 'serpentine'.

Grant Gorman one day stuck his head around my office door and asked me to follow him into the boardroom.

"I want you to continue your marketing roll with Bags, but to now take on two further projects. First is a marketing exercise, the second a one-off project that can be achieved within six months. Can you clear your desk of daily detail for a month?"

"A month from when?"

He smiled. "The annual Printing Fair in Düsseldorf is next month. It has a major slant on Packaging. God has approved you giving it a few days."

Sir John Cameron, CEO, DRC International had visited Australia on several occasions, meeting Maggie on two. He had congratulated her on seeming to have bested the difficult challenge of fitting in with the Australian lifestyle while retaining such British 'poise'.

"I am just so pleased he recognised it," she had told me in her mocking but haughty tone.

Grant Gorman had more. "You will spend some time with Alec Grover, your counterpart at DRC Bags Bristol, and seeing over the Fishponds carton and label plant whilst there. Also go talk with the fellow running the Mint Pack department. Go see the plant at Yate that makes packaging for the new Microwave Cookers. Microwave ovens will hit the Australian market before year end. Pre-cooked foods can be heated straight from the freezer, container and all. This could be big stuff for us and I need you to familiarise yourself with it.

"You will return via Toronto, talk with our marketing guy on Cookie Bags. Biscuits are mainly packed that way in the Americas. With Australians the biggest biscuit eaters in the world, you can imagine what that could do for us.

"When you get home, along with your marketing duties, restore the National Australia Bank building for this plant's offices. We want the kudos it will earn us if you give it the same treatment you are giving your house. Sir John has given the nod and approved the expense. The bank will be quitting end of June. Can you be ready to leave for Europe by June fifth?"

I almost fell to the floor, mentally exhausted, my mind boggled by the expected near future.

Maggie was delighted. Leanne jumped up and down and asked if we were going to open a *Veuve Clicquot* on the strength of it.

"I must tell Romy," was her second reaction, and rushed for the phone.

It was well recognised in Australia, that being halfway across the world from Britain, it was just as easy to do the entire round trip than travelling half way and back again. All in all, I would be flying quite around the world longitudinally and almost laterally.

"Grant has also," I told Mags, "given the nod for me to add a side-trip to Wisconsin, an easy air-hop from Toronto. An American company is right now manufacturing a new machine for us. It actually lines the paper bag with a heat-sealing and moisture-proof cellulose, either printing in line or from pre-printed reels. I want to talk with them on sending a man to oversee installation here, and instruct our operators."

I had two weeks to get passport and visas, make bookings and prepare things at the office for my three to four week absence. A Qantas officer would visit me. He would be already armed with the particular hotels DRC demanded in some areas.

Maggie phoned her parents to tell them I would arrive at Heathrow on Friday sixth.

A DRC policy had long-distance travellers always arriving on a Friday. This offered opportunity to wear-off jet-lag before starting exhausting hours of business.

"We also, Mags, get a three day lay-over at our last port. Grant recommends San Francisco. It's not a holiday, however. I arrive in Melbourne on a Friday and Grant wants my report on the Tuesday. So I must have my microtape reports ready for Dawn at the office, Monday morning."

Another DRC policy on travel was that never could wives travel with a husband on business. He must have his sole concentration on the job in hand.

"Are you likely to get other trips abroad?"

"Don't know, Mags."

"Where else do they have plants?"

"Maybe a score in England, the Stationery group having no less than five paper mills in Somerset alone. I've no idea how many printing plants the group has. Trent told me the carton plant in Glasgow makes little other than retail cartons for Scotch Whisky around the world. In Australia, two plants in Sydney and now one in Melbourne instead of three. I know of Cape Town, Johannesburg, Salisbury, Nairobi, Toronto, Kuala Lumpur and Auckland. When buying us, they claimed twenty-four thousand employees in twelve countries."

"Big all right." She gave me a great congratulatory hug. "I phoned Mum and Dad. They want you to stay with them over your arrival weekend. They will meet you at Heathrow.

O-oh. Meeting in-laws? That could prove the most trying of all appointments!

~ * ~

I took a day off before departure.

I wanted to ensure Mags had a more regular set of steps from her new back door on to the terrace and then, at least the naked brickwork of steps to ground level.

The Qantas rep who came to my office had been briefed by Grant. He gave me my air tickets and the few nominated hotels.

"I am to make recommendations for the others," he told me.

On my first Monday, I must take the nine thirty a.m. train, London to Bristol, where I would be met. I was booked there, three days, then fly to Germany. I chose to take my then two days off, travelling by train, Duisburg to Amsterdam, to see some countryside. From there I flew to Toronto, then Milwaukee, San Francisco and home.

Maggie thumbing through my tickets gave me her one-eyebrow look.

"Bloody First-Class flights everywhere? And bloody five-star hotels everywhere? *Inn-on-the-Park* must surely be one of the most expensive in London. On Park Lane no less—opened by the Queen!"

"Well she is not on my appointment list, dear."

I was holding one of my eyebrows down with a finger, so I could raise the other.

"Only the best for the best, my love. I shall bring you one of their beer mats."

"Hmph," she scoffed. "They probably have Waterford Crystal mats for Waterford Crystal glassware!"

Leanne wanted to see me off, so played hooky. Maggie drove us in her car.

Particularly exciting for me was that Boeing's 747 Jumbo was the world's brand new and biggest airliner. Qantas had the longest flights in the world to reach either Europe or America and their upstairs lounges had won international awards. On my twenty hour flight via Sydney, Perth and Bombay to London we used our downstairs seats only for meals, take-off and landing. The upstairs lounge was, in those days, not for passenger seating. The Qantas lounge had a baby-grand piano, a fully stocked bar, chess tables, bridge tables and crib tables. Cushioned lounges for those wishing to just relax and chat or read, abounded.

During our stop-over in Bombay, I bought a colourful chiffon shirt for Leanne.

Immigration and custom procedures in those days were quick, and on exiting into the Arrivals Hall, found Maggie's parents holding a card with their name. We recognised each other, however, from photographs.

~ * ~

They insisted on me calling them Annie and Gerald.

Driving up the M1, Gerald explained how Luton was home to Vauxhall Motors.

"It surely is a coincidence about our careers, Evan, you a Package Manufacturer, me a Package Designer. I am in constant contact with our package manufacturers."

They now lived alone, their house a typical semi-detached in an entire streetscape of similar houses, so common in England. On arrival, I presented them with the duty-free perfume and Scotch, Maggie had recommended.

"First off, you should call Margaret to tell her you arrived safely," suggested Annie.

Mags answered on the kitchen extension. "I am just doing dinner, darling."

We chatted for not too long, they each spoke to her briefly, then I was shown through the house and told to "please feel at home here."

Despite semi-detached, it was a spacious house with ample light. Gerald's hobby was electronic 'gadgets.' I was both amused at, and admired his skills when noticing an open window sash, move of its own volition.

"They all do," he answered. All our windows, whilst large panes, open laterally like louvres. I have them sensitive to both moisture and heat. If rain starts, they remain on tilt while the rain is light, or will close if the rain is heavy."

In the kitchen was a dial adjusting all moveable windows in the house, to temperatures. I was quite impressed at his clever hobby.

After lunch, Audrey and her husband arrived with little Max and brother Martin brought his wife. The afternoon was spent getting to know each other. While I was handing around photos of our house, little Max on the pedal trike brought to amuse him, found considerable satisfaction in, at high speed, driving it into my shins. He did it again and I rubbed my shin again. No-one made any attempt to stop him. When I saw him making a third approach, I stuck my foot out. The bike ran into it and he fell off, rushing to his mother, crying.

I smiled heartily, making no attempt to hide it. Gerald got up, took the bike out into the garden and closed the door on it.

Annie announced she would make tea and left for the kitchen.

That night, we all drove in separate cars to a local 'caff' for an easy dinner, after which all retired to respective homes. I slept in the spare room.

"Last guest in that bed was Margaret," Annie informed.

I did enjoy my week-end with them; actually thrilled that little Max lived elsewhere. Monday morning was early breakfast. Gerald was off to work and I had to leave early to catch my nine thirty train in London. Annie drove me to the station and gave me directions for changing in the tube, for Paddington.

She gave me kisses for Maggie and wished me a successful tour.

Forty-two

As the train pulled into Bristol, I thought, *Here we go!*

A liveried chauffer met me. He held a small DRC plaque.

"Mr. Robson, sir?"

Toting my bag, he headed for the exit, me following.

The car park held rows of vehicles, yet our car stood right in the exit doorway, making it difficult for the crush of people to get past. I was quite surprised.

Polished into a startling glare was an antique Daimler. He opened the back door to reveal leg room so large that I walked in. There would have been ample space for my luggage and still room for dancing. He stowed the luggage somewhere at the back before taking his seat. He slid open the separating window.

"We go to your hotel, sir. I shall call for you at two p.m. for DRC Bags, sir."

He closed the window and drove me to *The Dragonara Hotel* (later *Bristol Hilton*). I was informed that my room and restaurant were on the DRC account, but drinks to my room or at the bar would be at my own expense. I had been given, by Grant, in traveller's cheques, what I considered a generous allowance for 'Out of Pocket' expenses.

My stay in Bristol was crammed with appointments. I also wanted one of my evenings to myself. One of my Sydney reps, Stuart Russell, had emigrated from Bristol. His girlfriend missed him so much that she flew to Sydney to shack up with him. Maggie fell into easy rapport with Gabby. They had attended our pre-wedding bash. When Stuart heard I was coming to Bristol, he phoned me in Melbourne to inform me that Gabby had returned 'home'.

"Her mother was ill and needed her," he said. "I am not the most popular guy in her Mummy's book, but I'd love to think you can visit Gabby and give her lots of kisses from me. She lives just outside Bristol."

He gave me her telephone number.

"Try to find time to go see her home, Evan, you will love it."

When I told Maggie of Stuart's call, she told me Gabby had confided that she, nor Stuart believed her Mummy ill.

"She simply wants Gabby away from Stuart."

I had liked both, yet certainly didn't want to be drawn into that sort of problem. Yet he had pleaded so vehemently that I at least wanted to ask Gabby to dine with me. I saw it a friendly duty.

I unpacked, hung my clothes to lose their crush, then went to lunch.

~ * ~

On the dot of two o'clock, my driver was waiting.

"We are off to DRC Bags, sir."

I asked his name.

"Jervis, sir."

"Thank you, Jervis. Will you be my driver for my time here?"

"Except for your visit to Sir John, tomorrow, sir. Mr. Grover will drive you there, but I shall pick you up from there. You have two appointments in the afternoon."

DRC had world rights to a machine that manufactured at lightening speed, the little brown glassine pouches printed in gold for After-Dinner Mints. DRC supplied them to Rowntree Confectionery world-wide, all manufactured off five machines in Bristol. In Melbourne I had one, making them for Red Tulip Chocolates. One of tomorrow's appointments was to seek advice from our Bristol manager.

The Daimler was, of course, parked right at the hotel doorway.

As we appeared, a man emerged from the back seat, hand outstretched.

"Alec Grover, Evan, your counterpart here in Bristol."

We small-talked all the way to his plant. I remarked on the Daimler.

"The company has five, all the same vintage. It is a kudos thing. Some of us wonder how long they will persist with the cost. Taxis would be far cheaper."

We spent the entire afternoon inspecting his works and liaising with his senior people. I recorded things I should feed into my Melbourne operation.

At the end of an exhaustive afternoon, Alec and I, with three of his fellows retired to what Mags would surely call a typical English pub. It was packed. During an hour there, then at a nearby restaurant, I received more valuable information than during the entire afternoon. As beer flowed, however, tongues loosened and Alec's three guys began discussing Head Office, some comments not too complimentary. Alec was quick to divert the subject.

Little different from many an occasion back home, I thought.

Next morning, clad in my *Zegna* 'creation' seeing I was calling on God, Jervis was again on time. It was back to Bags for further intensive study until time to leave for Head Office.

~ * ~

Mags...

Melbourne, 8:00 p.m.

Maggie answered the phone. It was Milt, Director of *Boys*.

"Hello, Milton. What's the name of this one."

He laughed. *"Irma La Deuce."*

"As the musical comedy, or as the film?"

"Musical Comedy, as written."

"Well, great, but surely there is nothing rhomboid about Irma?"

He laughed again. "No, but it's time we did such a spunky comedy. I've already signed Jimmy Hannon as Nestor, and I want you for Irma. You're a stage pro, you sing, and you have a great sense of nuance. *You are Irma!*"

Maggie's face screwed up.

Just as well he cannot see this, she thought.

"I simply cannot, Milt. I certainly appreciate the honour, but I cannot."

She explained about her business now, much of it rush work overnight.

"Also, I have two full days a week with Dame Zara. Can you imagine her just changing her social and business life to fit in with my rehearsals?"

"That does sound a massive barrier. But you are just so perfect for the part."

"Milt, there are lots of bit players in that play. I'd love to be part of the fun. Are you using many of the *Rhombus* troupe?"

"All, if I can. As you say, it's a big cast. And has many mass dance numbers. What about Evan?"

"Evan is in Europe. His job has him very busy too. I know that when he gets back in a couple of weeks, he has a busy programme waiting."

"I need you both, Maggie. Please think again on playing Irma?"

"I've already thought again, Milt, honey, but with my job now, I simply cannot commit to many nights out. I cannot answer for Evan, but yes, I could take a bit part."

~ * ~

Bristol, England...

The visit to DRC House was to prove a further eye-opener on Britain's class distinction. My first sight of DRC House, however, was to be the day's first surprise. In those days, DRC House was Bristol's only claim to a skyscraper—fourteen stories.

"God's office is the entire top floor," Alec said. "Billiard room, bedroom, gymnasium and all."

Alec's surprise was when, once into the inner sanctum, Sir John came through a door, hand out towards me.

"Welcome to Bristol, Evan."

"Thank you, John…" It was then I could sense Alec, close beside me, nearly have a seizure. I stopped for a moment before continuing, "nice to see you on your home ground for a change."

He then shook Alec's hand. "You've been able to find compatible help, Alec?"

"Yes, quite, thank you, sir."

I can almost feel Alec shuddering with nervousness. And was that flick of a hand a hint of a salute being in mind?

"I'm sure we've both benefited, John," I added. "My tape recorder is running hot."

"Ah, yes, quite an art the way you use that. And Maggie is well?"

"Yes, John. I told her I would be with you for a few minutes. She sends regards."

I sensed Alec feeling further shocked.

"Well it's going to be more than a few minutes. I have sandwiches being made. We can chat over them. The damned jet has a cough and is grounded. I have an appointment at the Düsseldorf fair this evening and must dash to Heathrow."

I'd forgotten being told back in Sydney, that the company had its own jet.

A uniformed lady came to the door to inform him sandwiches were served in his lunch-room. They were accompanied by flutes of iced soda water.

He asked what hiccups prevailed in the Port Melbourne merger. I was able to report that from my desk, the manufacturing arm seemed up to schedule, but creases were still being ironed out in communication.

"Changes in command are taking time to settle down, John. A few of us continue falling over each-others' feet. Old habits don't quickly die. Nothing major, however. Grant's fingers seem on the pulse of things."

He smiled. "Such a major change meant disruption was expected."

A knock on the door. "Your car is here, sir."

'I must run," he said. "What is your programme now, in Bristol?"

"Two p.m. Fishponds, four-thirty at Mint, dinner with Gabby Harvey."

"Gabby Harvey? Horton Court?"

"I don't know Horton Court, John, but Maggie and I are close friends of Gabby and Stuart."

"Stuart Russell?"

"We were friends during Gabby's time in Sydney. I've brought kisses for her."

He grinned. "Give them to her, and add my compliments to her mother."

He nodded goodbye and rushed out.

~ * ~

Alec looked utterly stunned.

"You calling him 'John' just shattered me! No-one in Bristol but Senior Directors calls God, 'John'.

"Let me tell you a story, here, Alec. Don't be phased by it. Our Chairman of Directors is cute enough to realise that Australians are, socially, of a different class from English. Australians do not hold with class distinction."

Was that the hint of a smile on his otherwise aghast face?

"Yes. The entire western world realises we have little time for pomp and splendour. Many movements are afoot, calling for quitting our Royal connections. Eighty percent of Australians, before the influx of immigrants after the war, were descended from convicts. Australia was founded as an English prison and even today, British pomp is considered a joke. Phoms are okay, but their pomp is not. We call a spade a nigger, and every man equal. John is cute enough to realise that going along with it, is the way to earn respect in Australia. When he visits there, once or twice a year, he acts as one of us. He gets to meet only down to middle management, but insists staff at my level, call him 'John'. He becomes one of us at our level of respect. He is a clever Brit."

Alec was shaking his head, yet now smiling.

"But the Harvey thing? Horton Court?"

"You please help me here, Alec. I just don't know what he was talking about here. My wife and I are friends of Stuart Russell, ex DRC Bristol in some form. He arrived in Oz saying DRC would not give him a transfer, so he resigned. He simply wanted to get away to Australia. He came, cap in hand to me in Sydney, looking for a job when I was seeking a salesman. He knew packaging and he knew DRC. I gave him a trial and he turned into a bloody good operator. He and Gabby came to my wedding party."

"I met Stuart briefly, Evan. I cannot remember where I heard the rumour that he was in love with a Harvey daughter and was simply not accepted by her family."

Then I sat back in wonder.

Was his migrating to Australia, then, a ploy towards them having a life together there?

"In Australia, most people at work start a social life together and class is never a barrier. My English wife and Stuart's Gabby quickly became buddies. We realised she was of 'good stock'. But then, she got this phone call from her mother pleading frailty and she needed Gabby back home. Stuart simply asked me to look her up while here. I have kisses to give her."

Alec sat back.

"What you don't realise, Evan, is that the Harvey family of Horton, is real old money. They will not tolerate anyone below their social class, into the family. I know the old man died. I don't know Gabby, of course; she is above my class. But it seems obvious our God is part of the Harvey clique."

Alec now seems quite amused and I feel quite bemused.

Jervis was waiting with the Daimler to take me to Fishponds, and Alec and I made our goodbyes, promising to keep in touch.

Forty-three

I phoned Maggie who complained of having to keep the home fires burning for the Old Ladies, while I was enjoying Europe's delightfully warm summer.

"I had ice on my windscreen this morning," she complained. "And your car!"

"Did you have to go out?"

"If you don't mind me borrowing a quote, my dear, I'll say 'Not bloody likely'. I looked in the fridge to see if we needed anything for dinner and decided on omelettes. Leanne left for school, all rugged up. How are things with you?"

"Hectic, hectic. Sir John sends regards. I just left him."

"Have you seen Gabby?"

"I have another appointment here this afternoon and another tomorrow morning before training to London. I really feel like an early night tonight. I'm about to phone Gabby to see if she will drive down early to dine at my hotel."

"Didn't Stuart want you to see her house?"

"Yes, but I'll give it a miss. I need an early night."

She told me about *Irma La Douce*.

"A great compliment, my love. But yes, I agree we should seek bit parts. Have you heard from Paul?"

"He phoned. It is too cold for surfing, so he has two jobs. He phoned to say he got his job with the Penguin Parade and works nights at a supermarket. I told him we have 'burned his bedroom', that it was now our guestroom if he wants to visit."

"Good girl. I'm glad he is seeing it in that spirit. If he phones again, tell him I am pleased to hear about him getting the job. It is what he wanted."

"Exactly. Enjoy *Inn on the Park*. I shall think about you dining in such elegance while we might be having omelettes again."

"Yes, I love you too."

We blew each other kisses.

~ * ~

I phoned Gabby, asking her to dinner.

"Yes, I want to see you, Evan. But you come here. Stuart phoned and said I must show you the house."

I pleaded tired and asked her to drive to town. "I'm at the *Dragonara*."

"Eight o'clock?"

"Can you make it seven?"

"Of course. Did Stuart send me love?"

"A million kisses."

~ * ~

My visit to the Mint plant was quick but worthwhile. I had excellent answers to my problem packing off the end of such fast production. I had him order another of his mechanical 'offtake' unit, with spare parts, and ship them to me.

So simple, yet our best brains hadn't considered a moving belt!

Jarvis dropped me back at the hotel.

"Eight-thirty in the morning for the Yate plant, sir?"

"Yes, Jervis. Thank you for your help today."

He touched a forefinger to his cap and smiled.

I reckoned he seldom received words of thanks.

~ * ~

Gabby was but ten minutes late. We kissed.

"Stuart asked me to give you several for him, but it is hardly prudent here."

"Absolutely, darling. It might not be a big city, but gossipy eyes seem always in unexpected places. Is my darling well and happy?"

"I haven't seen him in months. Maggie and I have been in Melbourne four years now. I get to Sydney several times a year, yet seldom call at the plant. He phoned me on hearing via the company grapevine that I was to visit."

"I want to hear about Maggie, but let me say first, that I want you to come home with me now. Certainly I would like a plate of oysters, for they are always delightful here, but then let me show you our house. Stuart insisted. It is only a twenty minute drive at this hour."

Seeing her brought back what wonderful company she and Stuart had been. I was also anxious to hear her side of the separation problem so I could report the facts to Mags.

And Stuart will surely want to hear from me, everything of Gabby I can glean.

"All right. I will join you in the oysters. How do you like them?"

"Natural, with just a little salt."

"Same for me."

She had a glass of wine while I finished my *Dubonnet*.

"Sorry about the car," she said as we crossed to the car park. Mine is in service. I have this beat-up little beetle."

It was indeed a well-used old *Volksy*.

"What do you drive, Gabby?"

"Aston Martin, darling. The most gorgeous amber colour you've ever seen."

I hid my gulp. Maggie and I had realised she was of 'good stock'.

"Old Money too," Maggie had assured me, which Alec confirmed. "You can always tell," Maggie explained, "Old Money aristocracy simply never lets it show. New Money people always give at least hints. Very New Money people, flaunt it."

Gabby had never let a hint slip. Her 'Aston Martin' didn't sound like either flaunt or hint. It was said as simply an honest answer to a direct question.

We left the city and passed through the village of Chipping Sodbury.

"Many an ale Stuart and I enjoyed with friends in that pub," she declared.

I asked her about family. She had an only brother, Richard.

"He spends considerable time in London. Had he been home, I could have borrowed his car."

I took the plunge. "Does Richard also have an Aston Martin?"

She giggled. "Yes. But I keep telling him I don't like its colour."

The countryside began rising. The sun had well set and only a half-moon gave me any idea of what we were passing. We talked much on Maggie. I was chuffed hearing someone toss so many compliments her way. None surprised me, just suddenly made me wish she were with me right now.

Our road wound up and up. To our right, a high stone wall seemed to go on and on—when suddenly, a break appeared. We turned in.

My eyes went goggle-eyed. Out of the shadows as the car turned, its lights picked out the stone walls of indeed a grand house. At the foot of broad stone steps climbing to a pair of double-studded oaken doors of centuries past, stood an Aston Martin.

"Ah. It seems Richard is home after all."

"Oh no, darling. That's Mummy's."

~ * ~

She had a key for the modern lock and the great door swung open.

Inside was a softly lit but vast stone lobby with cathedral ceiling. A giant stone stairway curled up one wall.

"What do you think now, darling? Pleased you came?"

"This is home?"

She laughed. "Knew you'd love it. I'll show you the old part later."

"This is the new part?"

A figure moved at the top of the stairs and a soft voice called.

"Oh, I am pleased you are home, Gabrielle. I so worry about you in that old car."

A gracious lady was holding the balustrade.

Gracious? She shouldn't seem so in slippers and gown, yet gracious still.

"Mummy this is Evan. He and his wife were friends in Sydney."

I began up the stairway, but she held up a palm.

"Pleased to meet you, young man. But please excuse me now."

She turned and quit her stage more quickly than having stepped on it. She seemed gone in an instant. I looked at Gabby.

Her chin was withdrawn and her eyes shut. She then smiled and took my arm.

"That's one of the reactions I thought we might be graced with. But don't worry, she changes like the wind. Come, we'll sit in the library. We use only part of the house. It is a National Trust and we are 'Open to View' two days a week, including the library. We use it in between, as our common-room."

She led off to the right into a huge hall, 'library'...with no bookshelves. And little furniture. Two massive stone fireplaces, mantels at my head-height, graced one wall. Opposite were three pairs of glassed French doors looking out on manicured lawns, lit by soft outdoor lights.

Still inside, two large Labradors lazed in studded wing-backs.

"Off, darlings," Gabby called, clapping her hands. "We need these chairs."

Having first run to her for a welcoming nuzzle, they left the room.

"Pull that chair closer, Evan, so we can chat."

I looked up to see a heavily beamed ceiling some twenty feet high. The floor was polished hardwood with scatter-rugs here and there. There would have been seating for six or seven, and but a small coffee table and *cradenza*.

"We have a private kitchen and dining room in the modern back of the house, but the rest of downstairs and gardens are 'Open to View'. We have upstairs to ourselves."

We talked about her and Stuart.

"Mummy is starting to come around. Brother Richard has to illustrate a bipartisan attitude of course, yet supports my marrying Stuart. Mother keeps changing her mind, so I am sandwiched between love for Stuart...and family duty."

I didn't want to get involved, yet kept remembering the Sydney friendship. I admired Stuart greatly. He had proven an asset in my marketing responsibilities.

She pleaded with me to help convince him to return to England.

"Richard agrees that if Stuart were to come home, Mummy could be convinced to us marrying if we live here. The gatekeeper's cottage would be ideal for us. I could then remain tour-guide for the National Trust, which Mummy uses as a major excuse for me being here, and Stuart could find work in Bristol. Mummy would also then, have me at home as Companion."

I promised to talk with Stuart on it when next in Sydney.

"He is a DRC employee, of course, Gabs, no longer in my division, but I cannot afford being seen influencing a valued employee to quit. I need to wait until we can sneak out for a lunch or something. I would love to see you two together again. You obviously were so happy back then."

She broke down in tears, but as quickly wiped them away.

"Come. You wanted an early night and I promised Stuart to show you the house. You cannot see the gardens but they are indeed delightful. We have our own lake with Kingfishers galore, even some badgers. The house and Ambulatory..."

She went to the wall by the windows and turned up the garden lights. Part of a glorious old Ambulatory was visible through trees. It reminded me of paintings of King Arthur's time with cone-capped ladies perambulating.

"...are Tudor extensions to the old part. All that remains of the Norman Castle, we call our Norman Hall. Let's go to our kitchen and grab some snacks. We can gnaw them as we go."

Passing through a low door she went ahead. In the dark, she opened another door and switched on a light to a small stone anteroom, obviously now, a store-room.

"What you are about to see is all that is left of the old castle. The rest was torn down by the Tudors, to build this house."

She took a Tilly lamp from a wall shelf.

"The Norman Hall has no electricity. It remains authentically true to its history."

The lamp lit, she turned off the electric light and closed the door.

"The roof collapsed just over a hundred years ago but was rebuilt in the original style, according to National Trust pundits."

As we emerged through a stone archway, I was not only amazed but mesmerised.

The floor of the Norman Hall was stone, worn into hollows here and there by the passage of feet since the twelfth Century. I raised my eyes to see suits of armour standing, helmeted heads to steel boots aglitter in the Tilly lamp's glow. Shields, broadswords and antlered trophies adorned the stone walls. Coloured pennants hung from extending wall brackets in lacquered iron. A score of round tables waited to be set with linen and dining ware.

"We are getting ready for a weekend wedding reception. It is a popular venue for locals. Caterers do the entire thing."

She pointed up, holding the lantern high. I could not see the roof's apex. From the walls, massive oak beams swept upwards, disappearing into blackness.

I was quite transported, imagining how it all could be made into a stage set.

"Has it ever been used in a movie, Gabby?"

"Once." But they damaged so much of it, a court case arose. Despite many approaches to the National Trust, all are now refused."

I leaned down and touched the floor where men trod nearly a thousand years ago.

Gabby telephoned for a taxi to take me back to Bristol, and I came away in thrall.

Forty-four

Before crashing into bed, I phoned Grant advising my commitment to the mint-machine expenditure. He was quite excited about that.

After crashing, I dreamed of knights in shining armour extending lances to Maggie, for her to wrap her scarf around.

I breakfasted early enough to be ready for Jervis at eight.

Ah, my last Bristol appointment! My two days had seemed more like a month. My four days in England like six months.

This appointment too, proved mind-boggling. The microwave-proof material approved by British and Australian law for packaging and freezing precooked meals, a new concept in our modern world, had immense potential. I recorded many notes. Declining an invitation to lunch, I took an earlier train to London.

~ * ~

Having picked up my laundry from the hotel desk, packed and had a light lunch, I trained to London and taxied to the impressive *Inn on the Park*.

Exhausted, I slept out the rest of the afternoon to then dine sumptuously, wondering if Mags and Leanne had had omelettes again. I met a most interesting Frenchman at the adjoining table, and after dinner we sat in the lounge swapping small talk. Then slept soundly.

After an early breakfast I put on walking shoes and took to the streets. It being on Hyde Park Corner it was a long, long walk to Piccadilly Circus and by the time I reached it I'd been pushed and buffeted by thousands of pedestrians obviously expecting the world to soon end. They seemed desperate about defeating time.

The curving architecture of Regent Street, however, captured me.

I now realise what earned Christopher Wren his saintly reputation!

I valiantly hugged shop windows. I was determined to walk all the way to Oxford Street. Every Regent Street shop window hinted 'style'. I was feeling high enough to insist on buying a dress for my Mags. Her image when donning her *Balenciaga* and *Givenchy* after Leanne and I pleaded for a showing, had been stunning. I wanted something to show her off in a frock she could wear today in public. Looking for designer names, however, was impractical. I wasn't in that league, yet knew I must click on something in one of these windows. I would know it when I saw it.

It jumped out at me. I normally didn't like green, yet this was an olive green, very subtle. It had a choker neckline, so was low at the back. Looped across the breasts from shoulder to shoulder was the mere hint of frills. It came with a tight waist, nothing like anything else Maggie wore, yet it looked just right. Maggie wasn't a nymph in build, yet, to my mind, all in proportion.

Confident this was just right for her, I fronted up at the counter.

"No," I had no idea of her size number.

"No," I didn't carry a photograph."

"Can you see any of our sales staff with her size and build?"

We went looking until I pointed when finding one. She was asked to pose for me, turn, raise an arm, do all sorts of not too embarrassing poses, until I agreed.

I bought it. I'd find space in my bag along with Leanne's shirt from India.

I feel great! Yet I'm damned sure I won't find microtapes in Regent Street.

In Oxford Street however, one could buy anything. Yes, even girls on street corners but they weren't on my list. I there got my microtapes, then found Carnaby Street. It didn't jump out at me, but I found a tee-shirt to fit all sizes. It announced: *'True Blue Aussie blokes live for Beer and Surf-Boarding'!*

Forty-five

The Düsseldorf Fair exhibits were mind-boggling advances in printing and packaging equipment and had me almost missing my appointment. CEO of the Wisconsin company making the exciting new film/paper bags and I, had an appointment at the DRC stand.

"I head for Spain tonight, then the rest of my European clients," Gene told me. "I cannot be in Wisconsin on Friday of next week. But I wanted to meet you."

He told me who would be meeting me on arrival there.

I survived the fair, although couldn't get a minute to myself other than when filling my recorder with thoughts and actions once home. So many things seemed so vital in saving money in the long term, that I was already filling the extra tapes. I was exhausted when my two days and nights were up.

My train journey offered stunning scenery. Holland's countryside itself seemed one continuous flower garden.

At Amsterdam I flipped a coin on hotels listed at the station, choosing a typical Dutch house, tall and narrow with a steep staircase, basic but adequate. The city proved one of great inspiration to a new traveller. Its waterway system of 'roads' and its psychedelic museums and floral displays all proved teasing magnets. Street-side ads even invited one to not only movies of explicit sex but live sex-shows on stage—an entire night's performance. I wanted Maggie with me, however, when doing that.

I noted it.

~ * ~

Flying KLM to Toronto, I was met by my DRC counterpart. We clicked. After checking me into Toronto's *Inn on the Park,* he took me through his plant and next day visited his major client for cookie bags to see the packing operation.

On my third day I flew to Milwaukee and its *Marriott West.*

Tomorrow I have another first in a lifetime experience—driving on the wrong side of the road! I'm to drive near a hundred miles north, then back again, without even a minute's practice!

I taxied to Avis and asked for a small car. "Two doors will be fine," I told them.

I bought a district map and turned in time to see my car pulling up at the office door, to nearly die! Each of its two doors looked four feet wide!

The Chevrolet *Caprice* Hardtop Coupe became the longest car I had driven, with all other challenges to instantly cope with.

What didn't help, was that Avis Milwaukee's exit gate was on to a freeway ramp.

Within seconds I was trying to hug the slow right lane when used to it being on my left. My left door mirror showed vehicles rushing past when I should have been kerbside. I was trying to cope with both the 'slow' lane being right rather than left, my rear-view mirror being left rather than right, traffic whizzing past on the wrong side as I tried reading both my map to see where I could exit and overhead direction signs so I could pull up to get my bearings.

I was hopelessly lost.

I however survived those dreadful helpless minutes that seemed like hours, to begin enjoying glorious countryside. I found the little village of Holstein and the rest of my day went like a dream. I achieved my purpose and was feeling so confident with the car that

I drove home via Sheboygan and south down the Lake Michigan shoreline. I was able to drive straight into the *Marriott* where I sat over a *Dubonnet* to top up my notes.

Next morning I dropped the car off at the airport and flew to San Francisco.

Wow, was I ever feeling brain beaten?

~ * ~

Grant had recommended *The Sir Francis Drake* on Sutter for my wind-down. It was old yet delightfully comfortable and with, obviously, a British tinge. Even the doorman was dressed as a *Beefeater*.

At the airport, I was feeling so confident that I chose the same model car at Avis. I found my own way to the hotel and managed considerable sightseeing around the scenic city for three entire days. I used nights for assembling my report.

I also had a healthy surplus of travellers cheques for OOPs, DRC jargon for 'Out-of-Pocket Expenses'. I had the hotel direct me to *Tiffanys* on Post Street where I bought my Mags a diamond ring. I felt really chuffed.

Qantas flew me home via Honolulu. I left on Wednesday, flew overnight, arriving on Friday.

Whatever happened to Thursday?

Forty-six

Not only was Maggie at Melbourne airport, but one of my reps. He had driven her there in my car.

"I just wanted Maggie present," Ken explained as he drove to Malvern, "so I mightn't get chewed up so much."

Sitting in the back with Maggie, I tensed and waited.

"I crashed my car," Ken said.

"Again?"

"Again. The insurance company declared it a write-off. I've been using yours."

"Were you sober?"

"Quite. You know how often we all drive home after a few beers at the pub, but this was broad daylight, and I was clean sober. I tried shooting a yellow light. A red-neck cop was watching, hoping someone like me would come along. He charged me with running a light."

"Did they suspended your licence?"

"Not yet. There's to be a court hearing."

"Anyone injured?"

"Only the red-neck feigning a bumped head."

"Okay, I'm glad you're not injured. We'll talk about it Monday. Take a taxi from my place and pick up a rent car."

I let him see I was not happy, yet had a salty taste in my mouth. This was his second such 'accident' and second company car write-off.

Arriving home was a delight—first sight of the house after coming through the front wall was indeed welcoming. Wisps of smoke from the TV room chimney told me Maggie had a fire burning. It immediately put me back into a good mood.

We had the house to ourselves and I was given a loving welcome.

She made tea and we lounged in beanbags while I came down from my high. She knew what long flights do to one, a sort of tiredness, yet one that won't let you sleep. We knew the best remedy was to simply rest and let the jet-lag drain itself dry. I'd discovered during the last few weeks how a stomach, having missed its normal feeding routine over so many hours, needed time to readjust.

"A rough trip having to ride first-class all the way, darling?"

"If I were on my feet, I'd be slapping your bottom over that, darling."

"I accept the promise, darling."

I got up, but not to mete out punishment. I went into our bedroom, dived into my bag and fumbled until finding the little red box with *Tiffany* gold-blocked on its lid. I would leave the dress for later.

I gave it to her, then resumed my seat. "It's because I love you so much!"

Her mouth gaped on seeing the *Tiffany*.

"Oh," she exclaimed on opening it."

"I deliberately asked for a large ring size, sweet. You can have it sized to fit."

She gasped on seeing the diamond—not large enough to seem ostentatious, nor small enough to be an embarrassment. She jumped up and threw herself into my bean-bag, flinging arms about me. Her mild perfume reminded me of so many intimate moments and I just wanted to love her again.

"Throw a few more cubes into the ice-bucket and come to bed?"

"Oh yes." She slid the ring on to her third finger right hand, then closed the fist and turned it to her face. She then picked up the little felt-covered box.

"I'd really love to stitch some rubber band or something on this so I could wear it too," she added with a laugh.

I rose and went to turn down the bed, hearing the clink of ice being added to the bucket. I quickly stripped and leapt into the shower.

Our love-making under the duvet was urgent and wild.

"Oh, how I missed you," we told each other.

I licked her all over and gloried in the smell of her. After climaxing, we lay panting, staring up at Maggie's gifted handiwork on the ceiling.

~ * ~

I climbed out of bed to open the *Veuve Clicquot,* collecting flutes from the traymobile on the way back.

"What are you going to do about Ken and his car?"

"I'll talk to Grant, check on company policy with it being his second offence. He deserves the bloody sack, yet is a bloody good salesman...and we could lose out by sacking him. He is popular with his clients and that is a major advantage. It's just that he can be so damned irresponsible at times."

"Grant might advise, but is the sort to still tell you it's your decision."

"Yes, but it depends on policy. I'll worry about it later. Let's not waste that fire burning out there. Come, get dressed and we'll return to its glow."

I briefly talked through my journey and how much I'd learned, and she gave me a run-down on local things. I explained in detail, however, my visit to *Horton Court.*

"That poor girl. She and Stuart are just so much in love. How sad a situation."

"I shall engineer a trip to Sydney shortly, and take Stuart to lunch."

She nodded, smiling.

"What is happening on the *Irma* scene, Mags?"

"Into rehearsals. I am in a law-court scene and Milt is saving a part in it for you. I get to sing a number and we both get roles in a couple of dance and mob scenes."

"We are in the law-court scene together?"

She had a wicked smile on her face.

"What's so amusing?" *I sense I am to be somehow a victim here!*

Her smile broadened. "I am the prosecuting attorney in the Emile Zola-Dreyfus affair. You are defence lawyer. I win, of course. Costuming is easy. We both wear black cloaks and mortarboards."

"When do we rehearse?"

"The schedule is on the breakfast table."

"Later."

"Did you need sleep?"

"Not really. The set-down at Honolulu was two hours and I slept most of that, then also on the leg from Fiji."

"If you want to crash, just say so. However, Dawn is coming at two p.m. for your tapes. We plan on doing half each."

"Oh, good news. I had to cross fingers and hope you could give it time. I hadn't realised how many tapes I would need to fill. I had to buy extra in London."

Then my brain clicked...

"Speaking of London, I bought you a present. No fancy box. They packed it in one but I swapped it for a paper bag; square-bottomed of course."

I fetched her dress.

Her eyes opened wide at the Regent Street address. And wider on opening it.

"Oh, darling, what a gorgeous colour. But size?"

I told her the story and she laughed, then rushed into the bedroom.

While she was donning it, I topped up our flutes and collected a third for Dawn.

Mags returned, wearing it.

"The length is perfect. It's a bit loose across my back, but that can be fixed. The sleeves need taking in a tad and I will have to lose a kilogram or two around the midriff. I'm trying to hold my breath at the moment."

"Does that mean you can wear it?"

"Yes, darling, so long as I don't breathe. I'll just have to diet."

"And exercise?"

"Since getting the car I've put on weight around the middle. Maybe I'll have to take walking Tiffy off Leanne for a while."

I showed her Leanne's floppy shirt and Paul's tee-shirt.

"Both excellent for them," she said.

~ * ~

I phoned Grant to let him know I was home.

"All's well at Port Melbourne?"

"No calamities, but I'd like to see more cash flowing."

"Anything new, I meant."

He laughed. "Yes, there's a big hole in the cash balance of course, until the Fitzroy property sale comes through."

"That was surely budgeted?"

"Yes. But if I ever seemed satisfied, you'd all reckon I was getting soft."

I let a silence pass.

"When do I see your report?"

"Will you be in your office Wednesday morning?"

"Eight o'clock again?"

"More like nine. Is that okay?"

"Make it Thursday, nine o'clock?"

"Will do. Thanks."

~ * ~

It seemed no time before that great travel experience seemed like months ago rather than weeks. And what a contrast it was when I got to thinking about my other Restoration, the Bank building. It took considerable measuring to work out exactly where we must break holes in walls of different buildings so this hole met that hole. A three-metre long bridge had to be built for upstairs traffic. Downstairs, a covered walkway would suffice. I envisaged the three-metre no-man's-land either side of my walkway, planted with shrubs and trees.

"A word for your ear only," Grant whispered in my office one day.

"Bear in mind when restoring the bank, that there can be additional kudos if restoration could earn even a notation from the National Trust, even if not citation?"

He delivered it as a question rather than direction.

"I shall keep it in mind, Grant. One consideration jumping immediately to mind is fireplaces. If wanting to submit inspection for National Trust recognition, those bricked up fireplaces must be restored. They wouldn't consider an obviously bricked over fireplace a 'restoration'."

He shrugged his shoulders. "Then do it."

I nodded. I now had my guideline on limits.

"Downstairs, Evan, must house the entire accounts staff. Andrew and I will work on how we use the five upstairs rooms, but in your planning, realise that all will be Senior Management."

It was comforting to know I had license to use initiative. The door was always open if striking problems. I also knew I could not ignore my responsibilities in the marketplace on bags. I was still wholly responsible for its sales and marketing, and now had the Cookie Bag market to develop.

I persisted with my morning walk, however, through the sales office where now all reps had licence to promote bags, and through the bag manufacturing area where all my old staff and I still shared performance standards for customers.

Part of my project was to design the sales offices to be built above the canteen. That way, senior offices in the bank and sales offices, had direct communication via the bridge, a corridor between the buildings, wide enough for a photo-copy machine and cupboards for paperwork.

The bank wasn't a huge building, but solid. Its plastered brick walls were fifteen inches thick. It was L-shaped. Upstairs were but three rooms facing Bay Street, each huge, a smaller room each side of an extremely large room. In the L shaped wing was a hallway with two more offices and a gents toilet.

The 'small' offices looking out on Bay Street from windows reaching to the floor, were each fourteen feet by twenty-four feet (four point three metres by seven point three metres) and the large office thirty feet by twenty-four feet (nine metres by seven point three metres). Office doorways opening into a gallery nine feet (two point seven metres) wide, its many windows looking over the back garden. I would also have the garden professionally landscaped for staff recreation.

Ceilings were the same height as the Home for Old Ladies. The three main upstairs ceilings had not only large embossed centrepieces but all rooms had fireplaces.

Downstairs comprised a large entrance lobby, stairway and what had been the large area for the public to do their banking. The stairway was glorious, very much old style with low risers and deep treads, leading up to the wide gallery. I envisaged it carpeted. Shiny brass rods would keep the carpet in position on each tread.

Freddie Barlow, he whose paintings graced our dining-room walls at home, I called on for thoughts on decoration—light fittings, colour schemes for ceilings, walls and carpets.

"Whilst practical as office space, Fred, I want to retain every possible essence of the Georgian era."

The building had been well looked after. All modern strip-lighting was torn down and ceilings repaired. Under architect supervision, floor timbers were torn up, brick stumps replaced where necessary and new laid. Plumbing installations were inspected by council and found sound. We had our own electrical engineers on site to carry out work I needed there, several additional power-points, for instance, in every room.

For the large open space the bank had downstairs for public use, I liaised with our Accounts Manager as to office layout. He also had the two offices in the L wing at his disposal.

So that was my project.

What should I use as inspiration for this? There are no Old Ladies here!

Forty-seven

Irma la Douce rehearsals were loads of fun. Both loving dancing, we fitted easily into show rhythms. Musical comedies made all sorts of allowances in dance routines so the fun was for all ages.

Maggie particularly enjoyed the occasions we rehearsed our courtroom scene. What she hadn't told me was that she had to slap me across the face with a real fish. I could now see why she had those devilish grins on her face.

"I think we should rerun that scene often," she would goad Milt.

When arriving home from work one evening, she had my glass of wine waiting.

"We are having a visitor for dinner tomorrow, darling. Can we barbeque?"

"Who, and yes."

"Leslie from Sydney. My 'daddy' in *Man Mattie*."

"Great. How is the old bugger?"

"He says 'fine'."

Les and his then new wife, about his third when he was about sixty and with as many wrinkles as an eighty-year old, had come to our pre-wedding bash. She was Spanish and to maintain their bohemian lifestyle, brought as our wedding gift, a giant-size can of anchovies preserved in salt. It lasted many a month.

"Is he working?"

"Well tomorrow at least. He's in Melbourne to make a toothpaste commercial."

"Why barbeque?"

"When asking what he liked these days, he said: 'Sirloin, big, thick and bloody blue. I will bring wine'."

"What time is he coming?"

"He said about six so he has me to himself for an hour before you get home."

I laughed. "Yeah, I guess that adds. I'll try and be early, but if I'm not home by seven, will you put a match to the fire? I'll set it tonight so it will be ready."

I was a great believer in cooking over eucalypt fires. It didn't matter what other timber we had, a few small splits of gum-tree imparted great flavour to red meat.

It was September and the days were already lengthening.

People joked about Melbourne weather.

"Only city in the country that has all four seasons...every day."

One heard that over and over. Certainly unpredictable showers cropped up during days starting with promise of beach weather, but it didn't have cyclones to devastate areas like the tropical north. It also had vivid autumn colours most of the country lacked. Sure it sometimes had day after day over forty centigrade (one hundred and four Fahrenheit) in high summer, yet it was not a humid heat. I could thoroughly enjoy a dry hot day. For Mags, however, we kept one of our bathtubs filled with cold water, for regular dunks.

I hated Melbourne's cold winters, despite finding some consolation in log fires. In the Home for Old Ladies we would usually have at least one burning. On weekends we would light it Friday night and keep it burning through Sunday night. When relaxing, we could read or play *Bezique,* or enjoy the piano.

Next evening when locking the car, I remembered Les was coming, so ignoring the steps up to the front door, I continued down the broad side path. When level with the little veranda off the TV room, I could see the glow of the back terrace lights. Turning around the thick clusters of Mag's rhododendron trees, now big enough to hide instant view of the terrace, I could smell barbeque smoke.

"Here's the man of the house," I heard from Mags.

Les was turning, as I suddenly had full sight of the terrace, putting down his glass. He then just stood in a sort of stoop, reaching out a hand.

Bloody hell, I thought. *He's absolutely pissed!*

He put a foot forward and almost tripped.

His smile seemed more like a drunken leer.

Bloody hell, I thought again. *What a damned hide to turn up in this state.*

I looked at Mags and she had a half grin on her face.

I turned back to face Les. As he came forward, eyes fogged over as if blind, he staggered against me. I had to steady myself to support his weight. His arms wrapped around my shoulders and he began laughing.

Looking straight at Mags, I could see her face now, changing from her half grin to a full grin. Les stepped back, eyes suddenly as clear as fine crystal. He took my hand with both his, his body now shaking with laughter.

The crafty bugger is stone-bloody-sober!

And so he was.

"Great to see you, mate." he said. "My God you're looking prosperous."

It hit me then that it was likely the first time he'd seen me in suit and tie.

"And you, you old bugger, had me convinced you were pissed."

I went in to change and Maggie followed. We kissed.

"He's not been here long. But, Evan, I was absolutely amazed the way he so suddenly changed. He is quite sober, of course, yet the instant I said "here's Evan", I was mesmerised at how his face changed. He'd been staring me right in the eyes and I watched his simply glaze over. I've never seen anything so eerie. His entire body went into a listlessness—you saw that. Within the instant, both body and face adopted the drunken state that greeted you. It was all an act he enacted in seconds."

We laughed. She went back to the old trouper while I changed into slacks.

Well that's the professional actor for you. He had me utterly thrown.

~ * ~

September was Australia's springtime and we were surveying the gardens.

"It is all such a tribute to you, Mags. I'm sure the Old Ladies are impressed."

Both had been working hard at business and gardening and decided on a Sunday off. With Leanne and Romy in back, picnic hampers in the boot, we made an early start for Ballarat—a town renowned for its Australian wattle trees being first into bloom each year. An elevated gold-town founded in the eighteen fifties gold rush, it now featured a reproduction Old Town incorporating a still operating gold mine.

It was also known for spring blossoms in general and we picnicked all day in halcyon surroundings, serenaded by the drones of a million cicadas.

At work come Monday I was telling Freddie Barlow of our Ballarat experience. He had seen two of his paintings in our dining-room and I wanted to know if a gallery anywhere, might have a wattle-blossom by Barlow. He hadn't one.

We invited him and wife home again now the indoor Restoration was finished.

They were highly impressed, even by Maggie's ceiling centrepieces.

"Seeing you haven't a wattle, Fred, what do you recommend here?"

It was the big empty space over our living-room mantel.

He recommended the well-known "Shearing Shed" by Tom Roberts. The original hung in Australia's National Gallery. DRC had the licence for reproducing it in print. I obtained one, having it framed by the gallery that retailed Fred's paintings.

It did indeed complement our Lounge. And Maggie's gilded centrepiece.

~ * ~

Irma la Douce lived up to its promise. Several work colleagues and partners came to our opening night at Melbourne University and pronounced it great fun.

Five more times Maggie hit me across the cheek with a fish.

It was indeed a fun show and after every performance was the traditional cast party and we took our turn.

During it we toasted the Old Ladies of *Stanford Lodge* who we reckoned would have loved the show. One cast member said he'd recently bought the latest edition of the Melbourne Street directory and the lodge was still marked 'Hosp.'

~ * ~

When December rang in summer, Paul phoned, inviting us to visit the island for his club's annual carnival. He told us he and Leon had changed houses.

Maggie's parents were due for Christmas, after which Leanne was due on her summer camp again.

"Again with Mr. Raines?"

"Yes, I guess, so."

Romy would join us on our trip to Phillip Island. We tried booking motel rooms for an overnight, but the island was booked out.

"Not to worry," Paul assured us. He had four guys from other clubs with motel bookings, surrender their two rooms to us. They would doss on Paul's floor in sleeping bags. Paul loved his work with the Penguin Parade, a major tourist feature.

"Most times we have four or five tour coaches from Melbourne every night," he told us. "And busloads of school kids three days a week. I do my share of lecturing."

We did not try seeing the penguins on this occasion.

"Both nights will be packed," Paul insisted. "People will be jostling for the limit of four-hundred tickets. Even at that, many will need binoculars to see the penguins."

We had seen the parade, indeed a spectacle to remember. It covered a large area of beach and there could be a thousand penguins gather on shore, waiting for quiet. Sometimes, then, on the boardwalks built for observing, they would scuttle underneath to reach the rookeries. People noise could deter them.

"The parents will never feed strange chicks," Paul told us. If a parent is taken by a seal out at sea, its chicks simply die of starvation. We try to seek them out to feed them by hand, but most simply die in their burrows."

Saturday afternoon, he took us along some 'hiking' paths. On one high point commanding a sensational view, he swept an arm across it.

"This is my office, Dad!"

At his house, a typical 'piggery' of untidiness although well-stocked with food and beer, we got two surprises.

"That's my car, Dad," he said pointing to a weather-beaten Holden (Chevy) Statesman. Five surfboards graced its roof-racks, ready for tomorrow's carnival.

"Where'd you get the money for that?"

"I've got three jobs, Dad. The Penguin Parade, I design and make surfboards, which pays more than my Park Ranger salary, and if the weather's really lousy, I work in the island's tee-shirt factory, hand-painting silk screens."

"You can afford all your surf-suits and cold weather gear?"

Then I got the other surprise. In their living room was a wall near full of trophies.

"How many are yours?"

"That lot." He pointed to a collection of twenty to thirty cups.

"I now get my wet-suits and gear from *Rip-Curl* for free. They sponsor me."

I felt pangs of guilt surge through me. I hadn't known any of that.

Next day he showed us what he could do. The surf was 'up' and he had taken us early to a site where we could sit on our rugs to get a good view of the carnival events. He was in several. We sat amongst his colleagues' parents. We all had binoculars. One of Paul's 'runs' through a veritable tube of rolling surf, won him another cup for his wall.

I drove home feeling very proud as well as guilty.

He had proven himself happy with what to me, was a strange life.

During our time there, we were introduced to Sharon, the little lass he was to, some years ahead, marry.

I had always enjoyed my beach and surfing experiences yet always considered it a break from work. My son had taught me it could also, in its way of satisfactions, be turned into a career. It was to persist into middle age!

~ * ~

Despite Melbourne's century heat in summers and frosty winters, I simply swept away all requests for installing air-conditioning and underfloor heating in the bank.

"You must be satisfied with fans and radiators," I told everyone involved.

I knew that restoration of a historic gem didn't stretch to holes in walls or ceilings with metal grates. I relented only as far as agreeing on ceiling fans in the large gallery downstairs and left them to take it higher if they wished. Higher meant Grant.

"But do it before the new flooring is laid," I insisted. None did.

Freddie did a great job choosing light fittings. 'Modern' chandeliers proved more practical than period when eye-strain had to be considered, and for the front offices, all matched. Appropriate lights and shades were as carefully chosen for all others.

Three weeks before Christmas nineteen seventy-five, a phone call from Maggie's father was sad news in two respects. Annie had contracted a virus and the doctors advised against extended travel. It wasn't life-threatening, but rest was essential.

We took the opportunity to take now, a tour we had promised ourselves for the following Christmas. And yes, accommodation was available.

We boarded, for three weeks afloat, *SS Orsova*, largest Pacific and Orient liner of the day. We did it in style, sporting ourselves a stateroom on the boat-deck.

Ah, three weeks cruising Melanesia and Polynesia!

We expected Paradise and found it. From Sydney Harbour, a day was spent on the Great Barrier Reef, then on to Noumea, Vanuatu, both Lautoka and Suva in Fiji, both Vava'u and Nuku'alofa in Tonga and to Pago Pago. We made friendships that would last for years and arrived home totally relaxed.

In the Home for Old Ladies for the next few months I spent 'leisure' hours painting outside—the tedious cutting in around lead-lighted panes, not only the several bay-windows, but all the straight casements, most with a separate horizontal sash at the top for drawing in fresh-air. It was nearly three month's work.

In back of the house we had allowed much of the garden go its wild way, with patches of raspberry and blackberry vines. A different vine, however, was carefully cultivated over the terrace trellis. Several white grapevines were methodically threaded up, through and around trellis timbers to quickly give us not only grapes but shade, for we used our open-fire barbeque a lot during Melbourne's hot summers when it seldom rained.

When Leanne moved out to a flat with Romy, we 'burned' her bedroom too. It became our guest-room, releasing Paul's old room, initially the Old Ladies' kitchen, as hobby room. If either wanted to shut ourself away from other disturbances, we now had options galore. We even began making our own wine. The hobby-room had a work bench on which stood many a demijohn popping away. Our wines were not all from grape. We experimented with various fruits, apples from our own tree, passionfruit and raspberries from our own vines, cantaloupe, even figs from our own two trees. If we should leave the door open at night, even from the far end of the house, we were serenaded by 'pop-pops' every several seconds as the wine matured. It was like they were rehearsing some melody.

Winemaking remained a hobby over several years.

Forty-eight

When world weather turned into the Northern hemisphere's late spring, Maggie announced she would pay another visit 'home'. She was concerned for her mother, despite reports had her recovered enough to visit us next Christmas.

"I've never visited the Americas," Mags told me, "so I'm making the round trip. I go via the US and return through the Middle East. Is it all right with you if I go, say, end of the month? I'll be away three or four weeks?"

She was simply checking if my social-business diary included a 'wife' function.

I checked it. "Free, darling. Where will you visit in the US?"

Being Maggie, she had it well planned.

"You were so chuffed about San Francisco that I would like to see it. It is also jumping off point for a coach tour to Yosemite, then down the Big Sur to Los Angeles and Disneyland. From there I fly to New York to take in a Broadway show, then on to England. In London, I will go see *Cats*. I fly across the Pacific with Qantas and fly home with Brit Air."

"I envy you, sweetheart. Will you ask Kay or someone to go with you? I Guess Julie and you both cannot be away at once?"

"No, Jules will be flat out—especially with Dame Zara. And no way I will travel with Kay. She is my dearest friend, but putting up with her minute-by-minute over weeks, would be purgatory. But, now alone, how will you fare? "

"Good heavens, girl. I have a barbecue and am within two minute's drive of a dozen or more of Melbourne's best restaurants."

"Jules and Olaf will have you there on occasions. I'd like to think you will cut back on the Restoration work. Relax more. Join a chess club."

I playfully pinched her bottom, which she never resisted. I held every confidence in her managing the journey on her own, okay.

Ten days before departure I found the dinner table set with candles and wine.

"Why, darling, what is this all about?"

"I've been thinking. It's a long while to leave you. Also you've been working hard and should take a break. Have you anything on your plate that you cannot take ten days out? Come with me on the coach tour? Yosemite and Disneyland?"

Bloody hell. She knows I just can't run away on the spur of the moment. Sure, I'd love the break, but...

My mind drifted off into what I could see of that period.

"Give me a day to talk with colleagues and see what appointments I can swap around, or one of my guys to sub for me. A few owe me favours."

I talked with Joan, my new secretary, made a dozen telephone calls, got Grant's nod, then phoned home.

"See if you can fit me on your programme including Disneyland. Then I can fly west for home while you fly east for New York."

That night, she had mixed news.

"Yes, they can fit you in on the SFO-Yosemite-Disneyland coach tour."

"Good stuff, dear." I gave her a kiss.

"But...I cannot get you on my Qantas flight. Best the agent can do is you leave three hours before me with United. You get into SFO four hours after me."

Maggie would fly Melbourne-Honolulu-SFO. I must fly Melbourne-Sydney-Auckland-Fiji-Honolulu-Los Angeles, then take a domestic flight.

"Bloody hell. A man will need a holiday just to get over that."

"You can have it, dear, in San Francisco and Yosemite, then all the way down to Disneyland. But that is the best the agent can do."

I kissed her again.

We put Tiffy and Piddles into kennels and arranged with Leanne that she would look in at the house on occasions. We warned neighbours and the local police. The latter were wired anyway, into our burglar alarm. I was well within my five-year visa for the US so had no paperwork. I gave Joan my itinerary and phone numbers at the hotels we were booked into.

"Did you really want to go back to work on a Thursday, darling?" Mags asked on her last night at home.

"Why?"

"The travel-agent phoned. What we are spending, entitles one of us to two free nights at a Hilton Hotel anywhere. I booked you into the Honolulu Hilton for two nights on your return trip. It doesn't include food, only accommodation. If you want to stay longer, they can extend your stay at a discount rate. I thought you might like to take your holiday there."

I kissed her again. "So I'll pack my Speedos."

I arranged with the agent to add a third night in Hawaii, because neither did I want to go back to work on a Sunday. Also, a day later, I could catch a midnight flight that flew me home with just a single stop in Fiji.

~ * ~

My flight wasn't quite a nightmare. It did make me feel, however, somewhat like a grasshopper. My wait in LA was more than two hours—a 'so near but yet so far' situation. On arrival, Maggie had a bottle of Napa Valley wine waiting. San Francisco was memorable on this occasion, for I finally fulfilled a desire I missed on my last, to drive Lombard Street, the 'crookedest' street in the world. And I did.

Yosemite was magic, the scenery spectacular. We were quite amused when right atop, at the antics of wild chipmunks. They proved a sideshow all their own.

I had never been on a coach trip, having always carefully avoided them in favour of trains. However this company was worth congratulating. It used top class hotels down the Big Sur, not quite all the way because a section of the highway had collapsed and we had to take the inland road. A highlight lunch was at Santa Barbara's *Biltmore Hotel*. At Disneyland we were in the *Hyatt* and enjoyed two days of great fun in that wonderland.

On departure day, I was first away west, Maggie thirty minutes later east. We had been lucky enough on the coach to chum up with an elderly couple from Flushing Meadows. They not only picked Maggie up from her flight at New York, but for the next two days took her sightseeing and shopping.

Ensconced in my *Honolulu Hilton* room, I was surprised when my phone rang.

Bloody Hell. It must be Joan. What can be wrong at the office?

It was Maggie.

"Oh, darling, I am so sorry you are there. I was hoping you would be out so I could leave a message."

"Eh? You are sorry you caught me in?"

"Yes. I wanted you to have to ring back. I just wanted to tell you my number here is Pennsylvania six five thousand!"

Yes, she had been booked into the *Hotel Statler*.

She told me how Cy and Lyla had met her and been such a help.

"Tonight, Evan, darling, I have my ticket for *Forty-Second Street*."

She sounded all agog at her journey, so I was thrilled about that.

"Hope you enjoy London and *Cats*, darling. And my love to Annie and Gerald."

I hired a car and spent a day driving around Oahu, taking photos of spectacular mountain scenery and the huge surfs on the west coast, for Paul. Driving back through the centre was so reminiscent of Queensland—bright red soil and endless acres of pineapples. For the rest I spent surfing. Back door of the *Hilton* opened on to Waikiki Beach. Just the thrill of simply being there, was great.

I flew out at midnight and slept much of my journey.

Forty-nine

My plans to get back to painting our outer windows was put on the backburner.

"Mr. Gorman wants you to call him," Joan told me first thing back in the office.

What does Grant want now? Something gone terribly wrong?

I hadn't yet even got to my regular walk around the plant.

"Hello Grant. You asked me to call?"

"I guess you have a busy first day, so I'll come to your office. Will you be there in an hour?"

"Dare I say 'No'?"

He laughed. "See you shortly."

He was on time. "Mind if I shut your door?"

Bloody hell! He knew my dislike of that.

A shiver ran through me. This is indeed something personal.

He tossed his suit-coat on a chair and sprawled in one of my 'visitor' chairs.

Neither of us smoked these days.

"Four days ago, Andrew Trudale resigned. He is opening his own print-works."

My boss? General Manager of DRC Australia's now biggest operation?

I was stunned.

"How long has he been working on this? Such a thing doesn't happen overnight, Grant. Did you have any idea?"

He shook his head. "I had no idea. He's been cleverly quiet about it. He told me he wanted to work until the end of the month, helping to hand over."

"I had no idea either, Grant. I saw not one iota of difference in his manner or anything else. Have you asked Joan this question?"

Andrew and I had shared secretary Joan—one of the merger's cost-savings.

"She had twigged that he had other interests. That he would go out not knowing what time he might return, nor leave a contact number. But she realised it wasn't her position to tell anyone. She simply thought he had personal problems."

"It's only a week to the end of the month, Grant, I..."

"He's already gone, Evan. I told him on the spot I didn't want him anywhere on DRC turf until invited. I asked him to list his personal property in his office and I would have it sent to his home. I took his car keys and he had to leave by taxi."

I could read the fire in Grant's eyes.

We tossed over the ramifications it would mean for us, but they were brief. He held up a hand.

"I've talked with Sir John and he is in full agreement that you should move into Andrew's chair."

How many times have I ever been flummoxed? And Mags not even here to talk it through with?

"It stands to reason. You've met all challenges thrown at you, and we don't see anyone else measuring up. You know my attitude to bringing in outsiders."

I sure did. The Geoff Brahms brought in from England as Production Manager of the combined plants, couldn't cope with the Australian karma. He insisted on being called Mr. Brahms or sir, nor could he walk on to the factory floor without his suit-coat on and hair combed. Morale suffered and Grant paid out his superannuation and had him 'resign'. I had then told Grant of my experience with Alec Grover and God.

Grant insisted I should immediately move next door.

"Have Joan, Mr General Manager, move everything from your desk. She has already emptied Andrew's. You now share your office with the Board Room. Joan was, incidentally, thrilled when I told her I am promoting you."

"What of the other managers?"

"None know, though likely guess. I want you to go to your senior managers now, personally telling them of your appointment. Come to my office tomorrow morning. We need to talk on the recommendations you will by then have, on separation of duties."

"Thanks, mate," I told him, my mind still in a whirl.

"The change comes with a whacking great increase in salary, Mags," I told her on the phone. "And my car is now a *Fairmont Ghia*, renewed every eighteen months."

I realised I could give no more hours to the *Stanford Lodge Restoration*.

"Every minute of my thinking, Mags," I told her when home, "needs devoting to work for quite some time. I've a hell of a lot to learn about other areas of the plant before able to properly administer them. And we've yet to know what clients Andrew Trudale might be inveigling away from us, which will require me stepping in. Remaining Restoration is not much, but I must call in tradesmen to do it."

"I'm sure the Old Ladies will understand, darling."

I realized I could most likely count on the Old Ladies understanding.

~ * ~

What surprised us most about the house as time went on, was that like magic, the Brussels carpet never seemed to further age.

Maybe it was a little more worn in the hall just inside the front door, yet still serviceable. Maggie felt the colour of it there, the deep blue and black was a little duller, yet the fabric sound enough.

"And to think we nearly tore it up and tossed it out."

We began realising that with all the traffic it had had since the days of the Old Ladies, it had changed little. It had been down nearly seventy years, so likely had another ten to twenty left in it.

We thoroughly enjoyed our house. We continued burning fires all winter weekends. I would mostly win at Bezique, but Maggie invariably killed me at Scrabble. Or she would play the piano. I couldn't get her to sing, however.

"It's the fags over years, darling. Smoking has played havoc with my lungs. I thought that with us both giving it up, it might come back, but 'No'."

We several times in those years brought sheep-skin rugs from the 'library' as our TV room seemed to be developing into, with a duvet, to sleep the entire night in front of the fire. I considered it a luxury. Why we didn't simply build a fire in our bedroom fireplace, we never thought to ask each other.

When Annie and Gerald visited, they loved the house and gardens. Weekends we would drive out into the eucalypt forests, sometimes taking both cars so they could share a front seat. Over ensuing years, sister Valerie decided to sell her beach-house on Queensland's Gold Coast. Her son was buying a house and she wanted to 'invest' in his interest. I bought it as an investment. Maggie and I would often then, once or twice a year if I could take the time from work, drive up for a short holiday.

We enjoyed trips away, but always felt a thrill on arriving home.

When my three month long-service leave came up, Maggie and I took an extended holiday to Europe and Britain, spending several days at *Horton Court* with Gabby, Stuart and little Toby. Mummy had relented when Stuart returned. They married and settled into the gatekeeper's lodge.

'Mummy', on this occasion, maybe now knowing I was on a Christian name basis with Sir John, was more civil to me.

Leanne, just shy of turning twenty, arrived home one Sunday with her fiancé, showing us her modest diamond engagement ring. Mags and I were both cast into a cruel, shocked disappointment. We hadn't even guessed such an event was in her mind—hadn't even been aware she had a boy-friend! And he was hardly a boy—he was ten years older—but not new to us.

We well remembered having met the fellow at a school Parents' Day. It was the maths master who went on camping trips with the girls! A fellow we both, at the time, took a distinct dislike to.

"There is something sneaky about him," had been Maggie's summation.

"He is the sort of fellow I would certainly not employ. He simply oozes distrust," had been mine.

We didn't have to tell Leanne or Ronald Raines how we felt; it surely showed.

I sat them down and Maggie went to make tea.

I poured myself a Cognac, without offering either of them a drink.

"Why have you been so secretive about this, Leanne? Surely we deserve having been taken into your confidence?"

"I wanted it to be a surprise."

"Well it certainly is," said Maggie, arriving with a tea tray yet lacking the teapot.

She obviously isn't wanting to miss any of this conversation, I mused.

I stared at Raines and he offered not a word, simply looked at Leanne who, I reckoned, was wishing he would help her off the hook.

I chucked a dare at him by asking a leading question.

"Leanne, I wish to talk with you privately on this. Can you, Ronald, leave her here and depart? I shall then drive Leanne wherever she wants to go."

She grabbed his hand, as if for support.

"I think you should do as your father asks," he told her. "But not now. We should talk first."

He looked at me. "What about you driving to Clayton Station car-park tomorrow evening, Mr. Robson? That's where Leanne leaves her car when off to work."

Leanne looked aghast, but I didn't care. Maggie gave me the slightest of nods.

"All right. What time?"

Leanne, by now, betrayed tears.

"Six-ten?"

"I'll be there." I stood and did not offer a hand.

"You have a kiss for me, Leanne?"

She reached up and gave my lips a peck, then Maggie's.

Maggie and I, both shattered at being kept in such ignorance, talked on it long through the night.

"It is so utterly deceitful of her," I insisted.

"Surely she realised we would have objections," we agreed.

Fifty

I parked in a conspicuous position and wasn't aware of Leanne approaching.

First notice was her opening the passenger's door. She carried only a handbag and offered no greeting. I put a hand on her knee.

"I realise that yesterday, you must have expected the reception you got from Maggie and me?"

She nodded.

"Did you expect it because you knew we didn't deserve being treated this way?"

"I knew you didn't like him. I remember things you said after meeting him at school."

"Well at least you realised that. But wouldn't it have been the honourable thing to talk through such a change in your life, with us? We are family, you know. Or we had thought it so. Does your brother know?"

She shook her head.

"Do you want to talk it through, now I do know?"

"You won't believe anything I tell you."

"What makes you think that? There are always two sides to an argument."

"I just love him."

"Have you met his parents?"

"Yes."

"They live in Melbourne?"

"Yes."

"Leanne, you are but nineteen. You've never had another boy-friend—well not to Maggie's and my knowledge anyway. You cannot yet know what love is. You've heard me say how at twenty-two, I married too early. I only realised it much later in life, when widowed. I by now have experience in the world, my pet. I don't want you to make a mistake when so young."

"Look," she declared. I looked. Never had I seen such fire in her eyes.

She turned and opened her door then looked back at me, her quietness suddenly gone. She now shouted...

"I know what I'm doing! Just get out of my fucking life and stay out of it!"

I had never felt so hurt and abused. Never had I struck her, nor had I heard her ever swear, yet for the first time in my life, I think, I instinctively struck out. I slapped her across the face.

She jumped out, screaming, "He hit me! He hit me!"

I felt absolutely washed out, as if every gramme of energy had been sucked from me.

She ran across the car park to a small green sedan. Ronald Raines sat behind the wheel. I watched him lean over to open the passenger door. She jumped in and they sped away.

Too stunned to even think of driving home, it seemed an age before finding energy enough to press the starter.

~ * ~

Mag's seemed as stunned as me. Having phoned Romy's parents, knowing the girls hadn't a phone in their flat, we were told Leanne hadn't lived with Romy for near a month. She now had a room in Robert's parents' home.

Further stunned, we had to accept that things had gone too far to think we could make our daughter rethink.

"Especially, Mags," I told her, "when she has proven so deceitful. I believe the best thing we can do, darling, is sell this house and start a new home. I would rather we had the memories of this as a happy home, one giving us so many satisfactions. Staying here could spoil all that."

She thought long and hard.

"Yes, it will never be the same. I certainly need new things happening in my life, to cast off dwelling on this disappointment."

She broke down in sobs then. It racked me to see her this way.

She simply doesn't deserve to be this unhappy.

I took her in my arms and cuddled her.

We talked on the alternatives, coming up with the thought of buying a smaller house, old but requiring only decoration rather than restoration.

"Not to be overlooked also, Mags, is that with the selling market currently high, we can likely buy smaller, for cash—a commercial reason for sure, yet a weighty advantage!"

~ * ~

The auction was held on *Stanford Lodge*'s front lawn among Maggie's brilliant displays of roses in near every colour of the rainbow. The auctioneer stationed himself on the veranda as if on a stage, bay windows his background.

When knocked down after spirited bidding, the middle aged couple who were successful, were invited into the dining-room to complete the paper work and have coffee.

They told us their two teenage children would love it as much as did they.

"What is it that most prompted you to want it for your home," Maggie asked.

"Oh," said she in an accent from America's deep-south. "For me it was that unique old carpet. It just adds the homey touch to everything else."

"Oh, that's easy," said he. "The English Gardens! Especially that magnificent holly tree. It dominates so proudly, like a giant statue."

Epilogue

Receiving a formal invitation from Lynn and Norman Stroud to our own daughter's wedding, somehow put the final seal on our relationship with Leanne. We didn't answer. We finally had the answer to pondering on where our support had ever stood in Leanne's mind.

"Her last words to me," I reminded Mags, "were…'get out of my fucking life and stay out of it!' I shall ever remember the hate in her eyes as she said that."

We heard years later that immediately after their marriage, Robert took up a teaching post at Geelong Grammar School, some eighty kilometres from Melbourne, to live in a staff cottage.

Paul too, chose to sever relationships with her.

"We are not happy about that, boy," we told him. "It is surely a situation where a door should be left open."

"She shoved me out of her life, same as she did you," he told us.

We let him know we still thought he should leave the door "at least ajar".

He married his Sharon who was to bear him three sons, all taking to surf-boarding. He and Leon bought out a small tee-shirt factory, Leon working the machine, Paul created the designs, cutting the silk-screens and printing. Paul was also still designing and making surfboards to order. They did so well that they bought a second tee-shirt machine. Paul bought the building block next to the house he and Sharon purchased and, having planted high hedges, built a factory next door. He bought out Leon's share and added a third tee-shirt machine, plus a 'baseball-cap' machine. He was, by them, employing five staff.

Maggie and I bought a smaller house just two streets away from *Stanford Lodge*, some fifty years younger and in better repair for us to begin with. Not only did we soon have it as 'homey' as had been the Lodge, but over several following years I built during night-times and week-ends, a brick-veneer extension down a flight of but five indoor stairs, a huge study. It had a wall of sliding glass opening onto our garden and was large enough for two writing desks and a roll-away desk for the amazing invention of a desk-top computer and Dot-Matrix printer! Mags turned out to be a computer whiz and me an utter dunce.

We often thought back, however, to the happy years of *The Home for Old Ladies.*

The new owners did, shortly after moving in, break down enough of the street wall and its glorious hedges, to push through a double-park garage.

But we were sure they would have kept the carpet and holly tree.

Meet *Kev Richardson*

A retired journalist, Kev continues writing. His several novels on the founding of white Australia and its convict history are by now legendary. He spent many years touring the world writing travel articles for airline magazines, his many experiences now the bases of his *Brogan* series of action/adventures, and more recently his *Beresford Branson* series. Kev has the distinction of having all his eighteen novels published to date in North America, awarded 5 stars or 5+, 5++ and even his **My Red Cross** (February 2013), a 10 star (first 10 star in the history of *Conger Book Reviews, USA*) All his books are available in both eBook and Paperback. He is twice married yet now enjoying single life, relaxing in the Himalayan foothills of exotic Thailand. Another title is in the publishing pipeline and three more in work in progress.

Other Works From The Pen Of
Kev Richardson

Letitia Munro (October 2008) - A true tale of Australia's first white settlement. In witless ignorance, convicts transform the world's biggest prison into a land of free enterprise and pride.

To Plough Van Diemen's Land (June 2009) - Children of convicts spawn a new ethos. Titia's descendants, learn by surviving hard knocks and bad luck. Some fail, yet many convert empty pockets into acres of sheep. Social taboos become interwoven in the nation's spawning culture.

The Terrible Truths (December 2009) - Third in the *Letitia Munro* trilogy finds children and grandchildren swept up in the traumas of having to hide the truths of their heritage as society values change. Australia emerges as a veritable beehive of mines as minerals of every description begin showering riches on the land.

Brogan (May 2007) - Life on Australia's desert edge. Brogan, born in the drifting sands of the far outback, exemplifies the blood-and-guts characteristics by which Aussies are recognised, even today.

Brogan's Bust (November 2007) - Flying a courier service in the Amazonian jungles where graft and corruption make mockery of the law, Brogan finds backstabbing amongst cartel middlemen turns a hiccup into a stumble that generates into a fall to begin a slide that snowballs into an avalanche.

Brogan's Bella (March 2008) - Isabella and Brogan are victims in a deadly hijack. A carefree journey becomes a nightmare of death and terror. A year of incarceration and intimidation finds them facing the cutting of their very throats for even knowing the truths behind the hijack.

Brogan Abroad (February 2010) - A modern Brogan is embroiled in three simultaneous adventures. He plans none yet finds each destines him to having his throat slit in some dark alley. *Yet what can a man do,* he laments, *when to accomplish one I must fail at another?*

Misadventure (March 2011) - Brogan is off on a spine-tingling adventure in South America. He and his Becky hadn't counted on FARC taking hostages, military coups and drug-smuggling. This tale will really keep you turning pages.

Gerard Rawes (November 2010) - Gerard's life is transformed from rags to riches. In England's eighteenth century, the emerging industrial revolution catapults him out of his world of serfdom into London's elite.

An Epic Life (August 2010) - True tale of reaching across the world to fulfil dreams—a major achievement in the nineteenth century. Two couples whisk their very lives into a froth-and-bubble existence to create, on the far side of the world, a dynasty.

A Welcome War (May 2010) - ***Finalist in the EPIC Awards 2011!*** WW2 was the most welcome and alluring war of all time. A ten-year-old lad becomes influenced more by military strategy, political power, and bathos than by parents or mentors. "It beats schoolwork, hands down!"

Pacific Paradox (March 2012) - A British son is banished to the South Pacific to learn responsibility. Suffering hunger and kidnap, he is working in Guadalcanal when Japan invades.

My Red Cross (February 2013) - ***First 10 Star Award from Conger Book Reviews!*** Red Cross agent in France during German occupation faces intimidation, fear, love, hate and pleas for help. He is trying to be Father Christmas, Jesus Christ and everybody's parent, yet has little to give but hope.

Faith and Frenzy (March 2013) - Religion is shattered as families opt to support this or that faith in England's Civil Wars. Peace and Order are themselves ripped into frenzied shreds as faith in God is torn asunder.

A German Stirring (January 2014) - ***Aslo awarded 10 stars out of five!*** Deprivation in occupied Germany immediately after WW2 seems greater than that in most occupied countries during the war. Are the Allied victors guilty as charged, of major malpractices?

Letter to Our Readers

Enjoy this book?

You can make a difference.

As an independent publisher, Wings ePress, Inc. does not have the financial clout of the large New York publishers. We can't afford large magazine spreads or subway posters to tell people about our quality books.

But we do have something much more effective and powerful than ads. We have a large base of loyal readers.

Honest reviews help bring the attention of new readers to our books.

If you enjoyed this book, we would appreciate it if you would spend a few minutes posting a review on the site where you purchased this book or on the Wings ePress, Inc. webpages at: https://wingsepress.com/

Thank You

Visit Our Website

For The Full Inventory
Of Quality Books:

Wings ePress.Inc
https://wingsepress.com/

Quality trade paperbacks and downloads
in multiple formats,
in genres ranging from light romantic comedy
to general fiction and horror.
Wings has something for every reader's taste.
Visit the website, then bookmark it.
We add new titles each month!

Wings ePress Inc.

3000 N. Rock Road

Newton, KS 67114